TERMINATION NOTICE

Andy Phillips

CHAPTER ONE

Music to Die For

The killer was a woman. Her wide hips, smoothly curved crotch, and busty figure left no room for doubt.

Her silky, crimson-red outfit was tight and impractical, with no folds or trapped air pockets. She was a ninja - the fictionalized, non-sneaky kind. Sharp-edged throwing stars dangled from her belt. Dagger hilts glinted in sheaths strapped to her knee-length leather boots. The hood was Japanese in design, with a single elongated slit across the wearer's dark blue eyes and nose. Staring straight ahead with both hands gripping a katana, she looked ready for battle.

A street lamp flickered on and off, irregular flashes illuminating the advertising board. The extra light revealed tears and bumps in the poster, making the ninja look even less realistic.

The artwork was photographic, with a slim, athletic model playing the role of the female warrior. There was nothing on the pitch-black background except a superimposed title: *Crimson Shadow*. The font was bright red and Asian-themed, with letters sharpened to points like knife blades. And under that in small print: *The Epic Adventure from Taurus Studios - Available December 2015.*

The advert was in far better condition than the decrepit warehouse behind it. Constructed with crumbly bricks, eroded mortar, and dirt-blackened windows, the slope-roofed, three-story building was poorly maintained. The freight vehicle access gate was shut tight, its locking rings secured with grime-smeared bolts. Beside that was a hinged metal door with a five-button mechanical combination lock.

The security device was cleaner than its surroundings, one of the few indications the warehouse was in use. Other clues were an ever-so-slightly-lit, third-floor window and — more noticeably — thumping music. Loud enough to be heard across the secluded street, the overall tone and composition were Far Eastern. Frequent bursts in volume and sudden, dramatic changes in tempo added a modern twist.

A wailing siren got progressively louder. Then a white, glossy-bodied ambulance whizzed by, flashing emergency lights turning oily puddles pale red. The vehicle traveled at high speed. With no late night traffic to navigate, it was gone in seconds, and the whining noise faded soon afterwards. No pedestrians walked the pavement. There were very few parked cars, and the other warehouses — with dark, boarded-up windows — seemed abandoned and foreboding.

A shadowy figure stepped out from behind a bus shelter. Gloom-shrouded eyes — just about visible through small, oval-shaped holes in a leathery balaclava — moved from right to left, scanning the warehouse opposite. There were no clues to the person's identity. A cloth veil stitched over the mouth slit allowed them to breathe without exposing their lips or skin. The watcher was dressed entirely in black leather: a loose-fitting jacket with sleeves rolled down inside matching gloves, and leggings tucked into flat-soled boots.

After scanning the lower levels, the mystery observer checked the warehouse roof. Both eyes stopped moving and simultaneously focused on a skylight at the far right end. Its frame was a few inches ajar, the exposed locking hinge potentially accessible from above. The masked figure looked one way, then the other, checking the street. Nobody else was around.

The watcher broke cover and dashed swiftly across the road, zigzagging between shadows. For a few brief moments, light reflected off shiny leather, but the stealthy, half-crouched approach suggested a well-trained individual with predatory instincts. The figure in black moved to a darker patch between two streetlights, took a deep breath through the veil, and scaled the warehouse wall.

Fingertips and toe caps slotted into gaps in the mortar. The cat-burglar-like climber, using the cracks as handholds, reached the advertising board in under a minute. The masked figure was intermittently visible in the flickering amber light, body spread flat beside the female ninja. After a quick look at the poster girl's face, they continued up to the warehouse roof. The person moved fast, with acrobatic skills worthy of a world-class gymnast.

Showing no evidence of tiredness, the silhouetted intruder crept toward the open skylight. Loud music helped conceal the light footsteps. The figure squatted in a nearby dark spot — as if by natural habit — and reached into an exterior jacket pocket. Their partially obscured, gloved hand bulged behind the outer lining, clutching an unseen object. Its outline was thin, palm-sized, and rectangular.

* * *

The musician squinted with concentration as he adjusted a slider, one of the dozens on his desktop control panel. He turned a numbered knob a few notches anticlockwise and nodded along to the music's rhythm.

Oriental inspiration had been ditched in favor of Western Rock. The pumping, never-quiet score hinted at thrilling action and high-stakes drama. It was the sort of piece that might accompany a climatic battle scene from a blockbuster movie.

The greasy-bearded composer looked about thirty and could pass for a biker. Long, blond hair obscured the rear of his neck. His clothing choice was appropriate, too: a leather jacket with *"Proud to be Indie"* printed on the back, well-worn dark brown jeans, and dusty cowboy boots. The musician's bulky earphones also covered a good portion of his spotty cheeks, and his mirrored, metallic-blue shades reflected chains of indicator lights.

His headset had rubber buffs designed to contain noise, but they did little to dampen the booming music. The screechy composition was audible across the room: a spacious, concrete-walled area with pallets and leftover shipping crates stacked under dirty windows.

The converted loft was furnished with a steel-framed, wonky-sprung bed, and extended into an open-plan kitchen. Appliances were limited to the bare minimum: a fridge, microwave, and electric stove. The plastic dining table and chairs had cracked legs. Empty green bottles and cardboard pizza boxes were dumped in overfilled waste bags. Flies buzzed around the garbage, and there were many of them.

A newish mobile phone — on the control panel beside an opened beer bottle — lit up. Its speaker played a retro computer game theme from the 1980s. Text displayed on the LCD screen was from the same era. Rough-edged, low-resolution lettering in a vibrant shade of green. Despite the blocky characters, the message was still legible: *Unknown Caller.*

The musician lifted one earphone and pressed the phone's answer button. "Hello," he said, without the slightest hint of enthusiasm.

"The only limit... is ambition."

The man's voice had a noticeable stutter. Even with the composer's music playing over it, the accent was unmistakably American. There was a distinct, abrupt change in tone and loudness half-way through the sentence, as if he had stopped talking and started over. The first three words were spoken boisterously, the second two a lot more subdued.

The musician turned down the music and leaned closer to his mobile. "Come again? Is this some kind—"

"At Taurus studios..." the caller interrupted him, "we expect... loyalty."

As before, the message was disjointed. Snippets of dialogue with jarring gaps in between.

"Pryce?" the occupant said. His lips widened into a cheesy grin. "It's you, isn't it? Calling to say screw you? Well, the feeling's mutual. How you doin', boss? Oh, that's right. You ain't my boss no more."

The musician turned the volume all the way to maximum. The throbs were so pounding a candy wrapper on the desk vibrated and slid off.

"Hear that!? You're listening to the work of a genius. This is what you missed out on. But I'm not feelin' bitter. It's the future, and you're history."

The composer ended the call with a fierce button jab, replaced his earmuff, and nodded to the rhythm. He moved sliders, flipped switches, and rotated dials.

He didn't so much as glance at the cellphone, and gave no apparent afterthought to his argument with the mysterious, jittery-speaking man. When the phone rang again, the composer let it go unanswered. He picked up the beer bottle without looking, leaned back in his chair, and took a long swig.

The loft's bathroom was at the musician's rear, in a separate, concreted-off area. A moldy toilet seat, sink, and cracked shower divider were visible through a riveted steel door that had been left half-open. Halogen lamps were installed high on the warehouse ceiling. With the distance and almost-vertical angle — and no lights switched on inside — the illuminated floor segment only extended a few feet beyond the threshold.

The ambient light brightened — a slight, subtle change only hawk-eyed observers would notice. The leather-clad figure dropped silently through the open skylight, their knees bent to absorb the impact of the fall.

Almost immediately after landing, the masked intruder shuffled sideways into the shadow cast by the door. Barely visible in the darkness, the person remained still, their mouthpiece veil fluttering in response to slow, steady breaths.

Without looking down, the figure reached into their left jacket pocket and removed a long, flexible cable. The quarter-inch thick plastic insulation was as black as the figure's outfit. Its loose dangling strip ended in a hard-cased, gold-pinned connector designed to fit an electrical device such as a television or computer. There was a similar fitting at the other end, but the intruder's glove mostly hid it.

The masked figure stepped into the warehouse proper and closed in on the musician from behind. Fisted gloves gripped the two connectors, stretching the cable taut.

Now brightly lit, there was nowhere for the black-clad

assassin to hide. Out in the open, the intruder remained calm and methodical. They approached the occupant with caution, treading gently on the concrete. Background music and rubber soles helped to mask their footsteps. The musician took another swig of beer, unaware of the stalker's presence.

The assailant lifted the cable above the composer's head, forced it into a U-bend, and brought it sharply down. Black plastic blurred past, briefly reflected in the musician's shades. The assassin snapped the makeshift garotte tight around the startled man's neck and pulled the ends so hard the connectors came within a finger's width of touching.

Taken by surprise, the musician opened his lips wide, coughing a mouthful of frothy beer over his control panel. Sparks flew from a short-circuited indicator light. Synthesized music continued to play, drowning out the man's strangled gasps.

The composer gripped his bottle tight and swung his arm violently back. Glass smashed upon contact with the intruder's head, striking a blow just below the right eye. Beer trickled down the balaclava, but there was no sign of any damage, and the killer's grip on the cable remained strong.

The musician stared with defiance at the shattered bottleneck — jagged-edged and still useful as a weapon. Before he got in a second swing, the intruder kicked the chair out from underneath him.

The assassin had no trouble maintaining their stranglehold while the stumbling drunk floundered to regain his footing. In retaliation, the victim stabbed backward with the sharp glass. The killer twisted aside, and the composer missed his target, elbow knocking his mobile phone off the desk.

Swayed off balance, the musician could do nothing to

prevent the intruder from forcing him face-down on the ground. The strangler stepped on the hand that held the broken bottle, crushing glass and finger bones with a single, well-placed stomp.

Choked gasps turned to shrill whimpers. Arm shaking, the composer reached for the mobile phone and dialed the emergency number. The murderer watched, but did nothing to stop him. Instead, the masked figure kneeled over the weakened victim's back and tightened their deathly grip on the computer cable.

A female operator answered the musician's call for help.

"911. What's your emergency?"

Her voice was calm and professional, seemingly unfazed by the loud, ongoing struggle in the warehouse. The musician — trapped under the mystery assailant and growing weaker by the second — could only gurgle and scrape the floor. With his uninjured hand, he reached for the broken beer bottle and collected a long, sharp-edged piece of brown glass.

"I can't hear you," the operator said, raising her voice. "You need to turn the music down."

Cut thumb dripping blood, the musician rubbed the shard against the computer cable, hoping to sever it. But his sawing motion was tame, and he only succeeded in smearing his neck with bloody fingerprints.

"Are you there? Are you able to respond? Sir?"

Her questions went unanswered. The glass fragment dropped from the composer's limp fingers. He stopped moving, eyes staring vacantly down at the floor. The strangler gripped both cable connectors with one hand, keeping the loop closed.

"Are you still there? Sir, I need you —"

The intruder picked up the cellphone and ended the call,

silencing the operator in mid-sentence. Letting the plastic go slack, the killer wiped it on the dead man's jacket until it gleamed and all visible traces of blood had been removed.

A featureless, dome-headed shadow passed over the musician's body as the assailant moved away. They tossed the mobile phone on the red-trailed concrete, then the cleaned-up murder weapon.

Without a composer to direct the music, it came to a deafening crescendo, and then stopped. All was quiet except for a wailing police siren in the distance.

CHAPTER TWO

Icy Blonde

A brilliant white camera flash lit up the musician's body. Then gloom returned to the crime scene.

It was broad daylight outside, but the dirty windows only allowed a few faint sunbeams to shine in. Particles of dust floated through the pale rays, making them appear smoky. Lights on the electronic control panel — far more red than green now — appeared bright in the shady warehouse.

Yellow and black crime scene tape crossed the entrance doorway, and the scorched metal frame showed recent signs of welding. Conditions weren't optimal for the forensics team, and two strong-armed workmen were busy setting up portable floodlights to provide some much-needed illumination.

The woman examining the body was a moderately attractive redhead in her early thirties. Other technicians shifted to avoid her as she paced around the dead man and studied the crime scene with attentive eyes.

Her plain black work shoes were wrapped in blue plastic to match her surgical gloves. A laminated name badge clipped to her white lab coat identified her as *Dr. Teresa Vickers*. Like the antique, film-loaded camera hanging from her neck, much about the woman appeared old-fashioned. She had two fountain pens in her breast pocket, well-worn gray trousers below her coattail, and mosaic-patterned marble earrings set in undecorated silver.

"The victim's been dead for some time," Vickers said, her voice clear despite speaking through a facemask.

The doctor kneeled down and used tweezers to take a dried blood sample from the composer's broken finger. She worked quickly but precisely to deposit the flake in a plastic evidence bag, which she then sealed to keep out the dust. Her steady hands and calm professionalism suggested a lot of previous experience.

A man by the control panel — a detective with a brass, number-etched shield clipped on his belt — wafted the air under his nose. He gulped, lips tight as he held his breath.

The policeman's neatly trimmed, dark brown mustache was a shade lighter than his balding hair. His cheap burgundy suit and spot-patterned tie had collected a lot of feathery fluff. The shirt he wore was plain white, bulging around the stomach area. At least ten years older than anyone on the forensics team, he looked far more uncomfortable.

The detective stepped back and turned away to breathe. "I gathered that," was his sarcastic reply to Vickers' analysis. He coughed before continuing. "Could you be a little more precise, Doc? You are supposed to be our forensic expert."

"Just giving you a chance to get settled, Ron."

Vickers paused a moment, then dipped her tweezers in a pool of liquefied flesh under the musician's flattened cheek.

"As you'd probably noticed, the decomposition's

started. The body is already bloated, so I'd estimate the time of death as three to four days ago."

"Not a bad guess."

Ron looked a touch less pale than earlier, but a wry smile suggested he hadn't finished with the banter.

"That fits with when our records said he called 911."

Vickers gave him a hard, cold-eyed stare. Her lower face was hidden behind the mask, but it was unlikely she found it amusing.

Ron placed both hands in his trouser pockets and stood upright. The smarmy expression was gone. In the joker's place was a morbid, businesslike policeman.

"So Mister Handsome here didn't have any close friends? Three days, and nobody cared enough to report the guy missing."

"The puzzles I leave to you." Vickers moved away and pulled down her face mask. "You are supposed to be a detective."

She and Ron shared a grin. Then their faces hardened as a tall, physically fit woman walked into the studio. The late arrival took out a black leather wallet and flashed her police shield at a uniformed cop by the door. She paid little attention to him after that and proceeded directly to the body.

The workmen - now finished setting up the equipment - made way for the humorless, icy-eyed blonde. The woman never deviated from her straight path once. Bathed in industrial-strength floodlights, her formal trouser suit and flat-bottom shoes remained as black as night. A tall female, she didn't require high heels to bolster her presence.

Nobody spoke as the detective took out a pair of clear surgical gloves. "ID?" she asked, pulling the elastic material up to her wrists.

"Justin Norris," Ron said. "Music producer. Or a wannabe rock star. Depends on your taste. I wouldn't recommend listening to his stuff. Not unless you plan on torturing yourself."

He smiled, somewhat hesitantly. The female cop remained flat-lipped and ignored him to concentrate on the body. She showed none of Ron's squeamishness, or any adverse reaction as she walked by the signposted evidence: mobile phone, computer cable, broken beer bottle. The woman spent half a minute pacing around the corpse, then turned to Vickers.

"You verified the C.O.D.?"

Her tone was direct and ungentle. Vickers said nothing, looking somewhat puzzled. Her eyes moved past the detective to her partner, who responded with a warm-faced shrug.

"I know you have a strictly by the book, no assumptions approach, Duvall." Ron spoke slowly, as if testing the proverbial waters. "But strangulation by computer cable seems a safe bet. I'm sure you spotted the marks on his neck, the deep red depression. And we found no sockets here that the cable fits. But if you'd prefer a professional opinion..."

He looked at Vickers. Back in Duvall's unflinching gaze, the forensics woman followed Ron's lead.

"Everything is consistent with asphyxiation. There's some evidence of a struggle, but not much considering how long it would have taken. The only blood we've found belongs to the victim. Which suggests he was overpowered."

"So, the killer's a strong guy?" Ron asked.

"Above average." Vickers looked over the broken glass, and the many bottles piled with the trash. "But Norris was a heavy drinker. Likely had been drinking the night of the murder. So…"

Duvall maintained her unsmiling, statue-like pose. "So?"

"I haven't done a full autopsy, so this is only a hunch. But we might not be looking for a two hundred pound Sumo wrestler. Doubt whether I'd be strong enough to do that, but either of you could have."

Duvall's eyes hardened even more at the suggestion. She kept Vickers in her sights, maintaining a silent, accusing glare that almost demanded an apology.

"For example," she added quickly.

"When you come up with a more plausible suspect, let me know."

Duvall turned back to her partner. Released from her gaze, Vickers exhaled a relieved sigh and relocated to a quiet, out-of-the-way corner.

Ron directed her to the control panel. Forensics had moved the deceased's personal items and the murder weapon to the top while they'd been talking.

"The emergency call was made from this phone. Norris wasn't the original owner. Must have bought it secondhand, which is why we didn't trace the address sooner. Some cheerful well-wisher left a message. Listen to this."

Ron tapped some buttons, using arrow keys to highlight *Voice Messages* in a retro font menu. He navigated to the most recently received call and pressed the play key. There was a pause, followed by a heavy breath. A three second delay, and then another.

Duvall gave Ron an unimpressed glance. He raised a calming hand before she could speak and extended his flat palm at the cellphone.

"The only limit… is ambition," the male caller said. "At Taurus studios… we expect the best."

Duvall flinched back, and her icy, no-nonsense stare disappeared for a moment. Her lower lip dropped ever so slightly. Focused on the phone, Ron didn't notice her unease.

"You didn't… meet… my expectations."

"End of message," a computerized female voice said.

Ron switched off the cellphone and swung round to face his partner. She recovered just in time to greet him with her usual iciness.

"Real creepy, eh? Mysterious, threatening, not on best terms with our stiff. Could be the killer, or at least a good bet. Don't you think?"

"Maybe," Duvall said. "You know my opinion about jumping to conclusions. Find anything else?"

"As it so happens…" Ron turned to shout at a spectacled forensics technician. "You got that note?"

The man brought over a single sheet of paper sealed in a plastic bag. Ron took the evidence and spread it face-up on Norris' desk. He shifted aside to let Duvall see over his shoulder.

A company logo was printed in the upper right corner of the page: a cartoonist's impression of a red bull's head. The creature looked angry and dangerous, with smoking nostrils and gleaming, solid-gold horns. Stenciled underneath that was *TAURUS STUDIOS* in bold black, with hoofprints in place of the three letter Us.

The paper was creased across the center third, as if someone had folded it in two. Duvall moved her gloved hand slowly down the printed text, scanning each line.

We value team players at Taurus, people who put colleagues' well being above their own personal gain. You failed to meet our standards, Mr. Norris. Consider your employment terminated.

"Seems somebody wasn't too happy with his job performance," Ron said. "We found that stuffed in his pocket. That note's cleaner than anything else in this dump, so we're assuming the killer left it." He nodded at the title. "Taurus studios. Rings a bell. Sure I've heard that name mentioned somewhere recently."

Duvall moved her fingers back to the top and browsed the entire letter again.

Ron raised his eyebrows in curiosity. "Already checked the company out. Some big computer game firm. I called to book an appointment with the president, a guy named Adrian Pryce. Apparently, he's famous, but I never heard of him. Didn't tell him what it was about. Figured it would be best to surprise him with the bad news."

Ron looked up at his partner — who hadn't moved or taken her eyes off the bagged letter.

"You coming?"

"Yes," Duvall said frostily. "Let's see what Mister Pryce has to say about this."

CHAPTER THREE

The Bull's Head

Underneath the morning sun, central Philadelphia was a repetitive landscape of glass, steel, and concrete. The tall corporate skyscrapers positively sparkled, silver-tinted apexes catching the light. Less grand buildings were literally left in their shadow.

Seen from overhead, rush hour traffic appeared dense but organized, with neat lines of cars, trucks and minivans queued at every intersection. A vehicle horn broke the silence, followed by another. And then a chorus of dozens. Despite the noise, nobody gave way to their fellow motorists. Pedestrians — the little people meandering about on pavements and cross-walks — wore thick thermal coats and scarves, wrapped up for a cold winter day's commute.

One relatively nondescript car — a dull, forest-green sedan with a wide dent in its roof — sped across a four-way junction. It navigated the marked yellow square moments before a garbage truck roared behind. Ron was the incredulous passenger, struggling to hold on to a polystyrene cup. Creamed coffee spilled through the lid's mouth hole and formed a puddle inside the outer rim.

"Mind slowing it down? You're giving women drivers a bad name."

Duvall's grip on the steering wheel was tight, her intense eyes focused on the traffic ahead. She remained silent, her hovering foot poised to push the accelerator pedal should an opportunity to overtake present itself.

Ron sipped the spilled coffee and quickly followed up with another mouthful. "Something about this case bothering you?"

"A dead guy," Duvall said. "Brutally strangled to death in his own apartment. That doesn't bother you?"

"We're homicide cops. We do this stuff every damn day. Get woken up in the middle of the night, travel halfway across town to find someone smelly and deceased, receive all the gory details from Vickers. Nothing new about this one."

Ron took another sip and studied his partner through narrowed eyes.

"Apart from the unusual choice of murder weapon," he said, "and that letter. What's got you on edge? You have some history with Taurus Studios? An old case or something?"

"I'm not on edge." Duvall relaxed her grip on the wheel as if to prove her point. "I just hate wasting time in rush hour."

She sounded the horn, but only elicited louder beeps in response. The traffic lights turned green, and she followed the vehicle ahead through the intersection. There was barely a ten-foot gap between the cars.

"I'd suggest using the siren. If you weren't so particular about your rules. For emergency use only. Though I might class this situation as one. Lucy Duvall getting frustrated. So there is a human being under that wall of ice. Who would have guessed?"

"Up ahead," Lucy said. "Taurus Studios."

Ron followed her gaze. A black-windowed office building dominated the view through the sedan's front windscreen, rising thirty stories high. The enormous, cuboid edifice resembled some ancient monolith, with glass sheets joined seamlessly to form a continuous surface. Before the main entrance doors was a roundabout-enclosed garden, and — at the center of that — a sculpture of a bull's head carved from dark red clay. It was the same shape as the logo from the letterhead, with gold-painted horns to match.

"Almost missed the signpost," Ron jested. "Do you think they could make it a little more obvious?"

Duvall circled the roundabout, drove into the parking lot to the right, and stopped the sedan in the nearest vacant bay. Her expression remained stern through the whole maneuver, and she said nothing as she yanked the hand brake.

* * *

The Taurus Studios lobby was enormous, measuring a hundred yards from wall to wall, and at least half that to the railed, first-floor balcony. A dark marble reception desk faced the sliding entrance doors. There were dozens of chrome benches behind it, and plenty of space left over.

Twin, black-glass-stepped staircases went all the way to the top, alternating direction every other level. For those that didn't fancy the long climb, there were four elevators: disc-shaped platforms that moved up and down tracks in sealed, transparent tubes. Tinted windows dimmed the natural sunlight, while inverted pyramid-shaded bulbs underneath the balcony made up the deficit. Futuristic decor was the overriding theme on display.

Geeky high-school-age teenagers — boys and girls wearing sweaty shirts, jeans and branded trainers — gathered around an enormous television screen to watch a street racing game demo. The graphics were next generation, and the depiction of New York City — and its famous landmarks — so stunningly detailed it could be real-life footage.

Lucy headed straight for the reception, paying little attention to the teens or the glossy banners hung from the balcony. Some were cleaner versions of the *Crimson Shadow* poster that had been on the warehouse. Others featured the busty lady ninja posed in different stances. A rear shot emphasized her red-clothed thighs and buttocks, and a side view of the masked woman showed her katana in mid-swipe. The largest was a shadowy depiction of the warrior perched on a rooftop ledge, readying a throwing star.

Ron nodded at one particularly exploitative poster as he walked past: a frontal image of the woman's body, with the sword held so its blade crossed her curvaceous breasts.

"Tits and action. Who says it doesn't sell?"

His gaze shifted to the receptionist behind the desk. She was a shapely brunette in her early twenties, wearing the *Crimson Shadow* outfit minus the mask, weapons, and gloves. Her glossy lipstick, nail polish, and eye makeup were all blood-red, and her raven-black hair glistening. She had the same height, build, and busty figure as — and probably was — the model for the photographs.

As the two detectives approached, the sultry lady leaned forward across the desk and rested her thigh on the rounded inside edge.

"Can I help you?" she asked in a soft, almost seductive voice.

Lucy opened her mouth to speak, but the receptionist hadn't finished.

"We're not releasing *Crimson Shadow* until late December, but I'm available to give you a sneak preview…" She stretched further, moving her breasts to within inches of Ron's suit. "…if you're interested."

His eyes shifted downward. The employee responded with an acknowledging smile that vanished when Lucy held out her opened wallet and police shield.

"We're not," she said. "Detective Duvall. This is my partner, Detective Wallace. We didn't come here to sample your products, so if you've finished flirting, show us to the boss."

The receptionist retreated to an upright position and brushed her hair back to reveal a wireless communicator around her ear. She reached for a flat touch-screen panel on her desk. It displayed a simple image of a telephone keypad.

"Which boss?" the woman asked, sounding a lot less sexy.

"Which do you think?"

Ron gave the receptionist a tension-easing smile.

"As you can see, my partner's not one for being messed around. So let's cut out the middle management. Why don't you take us on a ride on those fancy elevators over there, all the way to the top?"

* * *

The president's office — as Ron had correctly assumed — was on the uppermost level. Its four panoramic, single-paned windows weren't tinted like those downstairs. The morning sky was clear of clouds, and only two skyscrapers were taller than the Taurus Studios tower.

Taking up the full width and breadth of the floor, the cubical chamber was even emptier than the lobby. The L-shaped, chrome-and-black-glass computer desk, swivel chairs, and pyramid-topped lamp pillars took up little space. That left plenty of walking room around the display pedestals that showcased Taurus-designed games and electronic gadgetry.

The man himself was about Lucy's age and unquestionably handsome, his stubble-free chin creamy with aftershave. His straight-combed hair was light brown, trimmed around his middle neck and ears. He was dressed for business, wearing a maroon shirt, silvery silk tie, and a black trouser suit. His gold cufflinks were too well crafted to be imitations. The man's eyes moved constantly as he scanned the twin monitor screens in front of him.

"The head of Taurus," Ron said, nodding toward the trademark bull symbol embossed on the floor. "Very appropriate."

The receptionist trailed him into the room. "Sorry, Mister Pryce, but they insisted on seeing you without an appointment."

"We're the police," said Lucy, entering last. "We don't need an appointment."

Adrian Pryce eased himself from the chair and stepped around his desk. He opened a black painted cabinet to reveal a stoppered crystal decanter and tray of drinking glasses.

"Lucy Duvall." He filled a glass with still, clean water. "I must admit when my personal assistant mentioned your name, I thought it couldn't be possibly be the same girl. She was too rebellious to be a cop."

Ron gave his partner an inquisitive glance. She ignored

him, shifting further into the room while keeping her attention fixed on the president. Adrian filled the second glass, replaced the decanter stopper, and brought the drinks across.

"So what happened?" he asked, holding out the two glasses.

Ron accepted the drink with a fake smile, but Lucy declined his hospitality by folding her arms. She took up an observation position by the window, with her back to the sunlight.

"This isn't a college reunion, Mister Pryce."

She said his name with brutally strict formality. But the suspect didn't seem too concerned.

"So enough small talk. We're here about Justin Norris. Do you know him?"

Adrian remained composed as he drank from the glass he'd offered Lucy. The assistant gave the president a nervous glance.

"Hold my calls, Sophie. Go back downstairs and continue your preparations for the expo. There's no need to call security. I'll handle this."

Sophie left promptly, her low-heeled boots clacking on the marble tiles. The black double doors slid shut with a click.

Adrian sat on his desktop and sipped his water. "Yeah, I knew Justin. He used to be our lead composer."

He answered Ron's quizzical-eyed response with a glance over at Lucy, who showed no reaction.

"Do either of you play games?"

"We don't have a lot of time for games, Mister Pryce."

"Too busy solving crimes," Ron said, pacing around the office.

"This isn't the eighties anymore."

Adrian put down his empty drinking glass. He gestured to a display that showcased floppy disks, and a second with an oversized video game box from the 1990s.

"Beeps and buzzes worked well for *Pacman* and *Space Invaders*, but modern audiences have much greater expectations. And when they shot up, so did production values. These days it takes a lot more time — and money — to design a game."

Ron walked around the desk. He tilted the primary monitor back, inspected the cable that linked it to the computer's hard drive, and loosened the connecting pin's locking screws.

"Customers want quality graphics." Adrian was seemingly oblivious to what the detective was doing behind him. "Quality sound. And Justin was our sound man."

Ron gently pried out the insecure connector and lifted the cable above the monitor screen to show Lucy. The pins, shielded by a hard plastic case, glinted gold in the sunlight.

"Was?" she probed, keeping her stony gaze on Adrian. "So he's no longer working for your company?"

"I fired him six weeks ago. Over a personal matter. Not something we need to go into. So what's that ungrateful jerk accused me of this time? Intellectual property theft? Non-payment of royalties? Enforcing our dress code?"

"First degree murder," Ron said.

Adrian turned sharply and saw the detective holding the cable. He twirled the connector in his hand, lifting it so the plastic wire stretched straight.

The suspect's earlier calmness dissipated. He lifted himself off the desk and stood there with his mouth wide open.

"Lucy, I..."

He looked to her for support, face creased with anguish.

She gave him no reassurance at all.

"We found Norris' body this morning." Her blunt statement was devoid of sensitivity. "In the warehouse he was using for a recording studio. Strangled to death. With a computer cable just like that one."

She moved closer to Adrian, advancing with purpose as she looked him straight in the eye.

"So, that personal matter you touched on. We do need to go into it."

CHAPTER FOUR

Under Observation

The Downtown police precinct, identifiable from a chiseled marble sign above the ornate wooden doors, was based in an early twentieth century building. Dirty exterior stonework was crumbling, and the United States flag flew above a quaint clock tower. The patrol vehicles parked in the bays out front were considerably more modern, with bodywork waxed to a shine and emergency lights so clean they sparkled.

A few scarf-wrapped pedestrians slogged past, armpits tucked tight to their woolly coats. None paid attention to the unmarked car that pulled up to the precinct. It was a battered relic, a poor cousin to the sleek police fleet. Lucy exited the driver's side and hurried up the steps. Her uncapped head was exposed to the elements, cheeks slightly redder than usual, and breath visible in the winter air. Adrian — left in the custody of her partner — was shaking. Whether that was because of cold or panic, only he knew.

"Sorry for taking you outside your comfort zone, Mister Pryce. We've had a lot of budget cuts recently, so our interview rooms are more basic than your fancy president's office. You won't want to spend too much time in them."

"I didn't kill Norris!" Adrian protested. "You have to believe me. I—"

"Save it for later. I'd rather talk over a warm cup of coffee. And jot down a few notes. Who knows? You might even say something incriminating."

Adrian walked faster. He caught up to Lucy by the entrance. "Am I a suspect?"

She said nothing and went through the precinct doors without a backward glance.

"Don't take it personally." Ron closed to within breathing distance. "My partner's very focused on doing her job. A real cold bitch to work with. But one thing I like about her… She's got no time for bullshit."

The hard-faced detective gave Adrian a smile that bordered on sinister, and ushered him into the building.

* * *

The police holding area was functional to the extreme. Table and chairs were all stainless steel, so tarnished they appeared dull gray despite the light from fluorescent strips above. A polished mirror filled the upper two-thirds of one whitewashed wall, the side facing the interview seat. Adrian's anguished reflection was crystal clear, forehead and hair wrung with sweat. His clammy hands were clasped together, fingers twitching as he studied the photos spread before him.

Glossy images of the warehouse crime scene showed Norris' body from varied angles. Red strangulation marks were visible around his neck. A second photo was of the discarded computer cable and phone, and a third the typed letter from Taurus Studios.

Ron sat opposite Adrian, conducting the interrogation while Lucy watched in silence from a standing position by the mirror.

"So, if I understand correctly, Norris did the music for your next big game. What was it called?" The questioner referred to his notebook. "*Crimson Shadow*. Gives me violent vibes, that does. Anyway, back to Norris. Despite the generous paycheck, he made a few poor decisions, borrowed money from dodgy characters. He was struggling to pay off his debts. Hey, none of us are perfect, right? So he came to you — his close friend — and asked for a little extra cash."

"I wouldn't call fifty grand a little extra," Adrian said, bitterness creeping into his reply.

"For a company worth over a billion, fifty thou wouldn't break the bank, would it?"

"I run a business, not a charity. If I'd given him the money, Norris would have come to me a month later asking for more."

Ron leaned back, causing his chair rest to squeak. "Don't worry about it. You won't need to pay him anything now."

Adrian looked away from his interrogator, eyes shifting to Lucy. Her death stare was Medusa-like, her lips almost perfectly horizontal. Ron slid the photo of the letter across, turning it so it was the right way up from Adrian's viewpoint.

"Colleagues' well being above personal gain. Team players. Do you meet these standards? Maybe you should have terminated yourself."

"I told you." Adrian bowed his head, talking toward the table. "I didn't write that. It doesn't take a genius to cut and paste my company logo onto a letterhead."

"But you are a genius. So it wouldn't be too hard to do.

And that letter sounds like something a boss would put together."

"What about the cable we found at your office?" Lucy asked, circling round the outer wall. "It matches the murder weapon. Can you explain that?"

"Standard equipment for connecting an external drive to a monitor. There are hundreds, probably thousands, of cables in this city just like that one."

"And the message on Norris' phone? The last call he received before he was killed. Don't pretend that wasn't your voice. It obviously was. Make us request an analysis, and we'll book you for wasting time."

"Anyone who's used the Internet could have recorded my voice off a company video. I'm a public figure. Successful. It makes people envious. Can't you see I'm being set up!?"

"Calm down." Lucy softened her tone a little. "We need to ask these questions. We're only trying to help. Let us do that."

Adrian glared back at her, reciprocating none of the warmth. "By pinning a murder on me? Is that what this is about? Do I need to call my lawyer?"

"Depends," Ron said. "Have you done something illegal, Mister Pryce?"

The suspect chose not to answer. He looked between the two detectives at the mirror behind them.

* * *

On the reverse side, the mirror was an observation window. The see-through glass had a slight blackish tint, giving the dull interrogation room an even grayer appearance. Events and conversations were recorded by a surveillance camera, and replayed in real-time via a flat-panel, high-definition television and speakers.

The monitor showed Adrian in close up, sweaty patches visible on his cheeks. A slightly blurred, out-of-focus crop of mannish hair obscured the right side of the image. Though Ron was mostly off screen, his voice came through clearly.

"With Norris dead, what happens to the money? Do his family get the royalty payments?"

"No," Adrian replied, his response delayed. "The artist's contract becomes void upon death. There's a no inheritance clause included."

"So, the company profits. Nice little loophole you snook in. Bet you omitted to mention that detail when you hired him."

Ron paused, giving the suspect time to contemplate. A dense puff of smoke floated toward the two-way mirror, thinning as the particles dissipated.

The man in the observation room had a rough-edged, but clean-shaven face. Deep wrinkles and a spotty bald head hinted he was well past his prime, most likely in his early fifties. His expression was totally serious, and his black suit and tie were closer to funeral attire than work clothes. He gripped a lit cigarette tight between thick fingers, squashing the white filter end as he watched the interview.

"Money," Ron said. "The oldest motive in the book. Maybe you should call that lawyer of yours."

"That's enough, Wallace," Lucy butted in.

"Excuse me?"

He turned to look at her, shock clear on his face. The man in black pressed a button next to the television screen. An intercom system whined as static feedback came through.

"It's okay," the observer said, though his direct tone suggested it was more of an instruction. "Let Duvall finish the interview."

Ron stood up without a moment's hesitation. "If you're hoping to sweet talk her," he advised Adrian, "I wouldn't bother. She doesn't have a reputation for being soft."

He ended with a sharp-eyed glance at Lucy, then exited through the door, letting it slam shut behind him. A few seconds later, Ron walked into the observation room. The suited man didn't turn to look, electing to take another puff from his cigarette. The detective stood in the back corner, far away from the spreading smoke.

"I didn't kill him," Adrian said. "How many times do I have to say it?"

Lucy remained by the wall, apparently unconvinced. "Where were you three days ago? Between midnight and two AM?"

Her question was met with silence and a disgusted sideways glance.

"Alone with the ice queen," Ron said. "Don't envy the creep."

The black suited man took one last puff and stubbed his cigarette out in a dirty metal tray. Charred paper and dark gray ash scattered as he squashed the butt down hard. There was no way Adrian could see the observer's mean-eyed expression from the mirror side, but he squirmed in his seat, regardless.

"Where were you?" Lucy repeated. "If you have an alibi, it would be in your interest to tell us."

"Taurus chatroom. I was answering questions from fans."

"At two in the morning?"

"Lots of gamers have early hour sessions," Adrian said. "And in Europe it's daytime. We have customers all over the world. If you don't believe me, check the company's data logs. We monitor all office traffic on social media."

"Except that wouldn't prove anything. It's all usernames and text. That's the trouble with the Internet. You can be anybody you want, but it also means anybody can play Adrian Pryce. Who's to say it was really you on the computer?"

She took a breath, and allowed herself a weak, lightly curved smile.

"But since I'm tiring of seeing you sweat..."

Lucy sat directly opposite him. On the observation room monitor, the interviewee's face was almost completely obscured. The positioning was near perfect, so exact it was either premeditated or amazing coincidence. She shifted something across the table. The object couldn't be identified through the window or on television.

"Let's say I believe you. A note with a distinctive letterhead. Left at the murder scene where we'd find it. And then there's the phone message. Somebody went to a lot of trouble to implicate your company, Mister Pryce. To implicate you. Any idea who it might be?"

"Take your pick," Adrian said, shoulders rising above Lucy's as he shrugged. "Holiday season's coming up, and that means major game releases. There's plenty of competition out there for Christmas number one spot. And we attract hordes of crazy fans. Want to see how many? Come to the expo."

"You'll have to excuse my ignorance. What's an expo?"

"Our annual trade show. A promotional get together. We're hosting it tomorrow at the office tower. It's the largest public event of the year for us, where we showcase our recent releases and titles still in development. All the big players will be there. The list's full up, but I'm sure I can get an old college friend an invitation."

His tone was more relaxed than earlier, bordering on playful. But Lucy remained businesslike.

"Unless you're planning to lock me up," he said. "Then I'd have to waste that phone call on my attorney."

She thought it over for a second. "You're free to go. For now. I'll escort you to the door."

"Keeping your eye on me?"

Lucy stayed quiet, acting professional as she led Adrian from the interview room. He looked at the mirror with apparent relief.

Ron watched his partner follow the interviewee out. "We're letting him walk?" he asked his black-suited superior. "Prime suspect says he didn't do it, and we just take his word. This is bullshit, Lieutenant."

"We got nothing on him," the boss said. "At least, not yet, but don't stop digging."

Ron headed for the exit. Frustration showed on his face.

"Wallace." The senior detective waited for him to turn around. "Does your partner know this guy?"

"Like you and I know the President. They were in the same year at college. Both studied locally. Drexel University. Different subjects, though. Pryce took computer science, and she did criminal psychology. Not even the same faculty."

"No personal history?"

"Personal? This is Duvall we're talking about."

The Lieutenant sucked his lips. "Call it an experienced hunch, but there's definitely a connection between these two. Could be minor, like you say. But if not... Conflicts of interest don't sit well with internal affairs. Do I have to remind you what happened last year with Killian and his brother? Our pals in the press are still banging on about that cover up."

Ron looked at his superior disapprovingly, but he

remained on topic.

"So watch Duvall closely. First sign something's off, any hint of this being more than an acquaintance, you call me."

"Sure, boss. But I'm telling you —"

A no-nonsense glare from the Lieutenant silenced him.

"Like you told me with Killian. You had a blind spot with your last partner. This time, keep your eyes open."

CHAPTER FIVE

The Adrian Pryce Fan Club

An army of teenagers had invaded the Taurus Studios roundabout, congregating in clusters near refreshment stands and temporary wooden souvenir stalls. Either it was a warmer day than usual for winter, or those in attendance were feeling especially brave.

The majority wore no coats over their short-sleeve T-shirts. Black was the commonest color choice, with many baseball caps and shoulder-slung rucksacks bearing printed images. Gold-horned Taurus bulls and downsized versions of *Crimson Shadow* posters outnumbered other designs, but computer games were the universal theme. Square-jawed heroes and suggestively dressed females featured prominently in the artwork. One fanatical group of messy-haired geeks had shown up wearing cardboard face masks of Adrian Pryce.

Burly security guards in blue-shirted uniforms were stationed along cordoned-off routes. Three men at a steel barrier checked credentials. The queue people outside the Taurus tower entrance was thirty deep, with a good number already waved through to a holding area.

A cloth banner stretched between the bull's horns boldly promised *"The Greatest Game Expo Ever."* A massive digital screen displayed a countdown. As the ticking clock reached *05:00*, an electronic chime sounded, prompting loud cheers from the crowd.

Lucy and Ron stood far back, watching the unmanaged chaos from a safe distance. They were close to a tripod-mounted plasma TV, one of several set up along the approach. Nearby, a Hispanic woman in a grease-stained, striped apron staffed a hot dog stand. Most attendees were eager to press forward, so business was slow.

Ron tucked into an unappetizing 'snack': a black-ended sausage sandwiched in a soggy roll, practically drowned in gooey ketchup.

"Sure you don't fancy some fine cuisine?" he asked in between two munches. "We still got four minutes until the doors open."

The empty-handed Lucy watched the TV monitor. A live broadcast came from outside the tower, where a shortish man in square-lensed, red-tinted glasses was talking excitedly to an unseen camera. His mohawk-style, spiky-blond hair resembled a saw blade, and unhealthy-looking warts covered his chin.

Unlike the teens waving from the queue behind him, the presenter's white T-shirt was plain and devoid of any graphical logos. A caption on a superimposed black footer identified him as *James Fitzroy, Chief Reviewer, Gamer Frontline.*

"Excitement at Taurus Studios' fourth annual gaming expo is mixed with tragedy," he announced, voice projected by loudspeakers above the television screen. "The community is still in shock at the brutal murder of Justin Norris, the musical pioneer known around the world by gamers and moviegoers alike."

"Never heard of him until we found the body," Ron said. "Talk about hype after the fact."

He swallowed the last of his food and cleaned his hands on a paper napkin. The cop glanced at the attendees, but they seemed far more interested in the countdown — now at *02:00* — than Fitzroy's eulogy.

"Yeah. They seem real shocked, don't they? No such thing as adverse publicity, I guess."

"Viewers will already know my opinions on the company and President Pryce..." Fitzroy continued.

"The way this guy talks, you'd think Pryce was the one in the Oval Office," Ron said to his partner.

"Adrian always had an ego complex. But the man we interviewed was broken. Unsure of himself. I don't believe he's our guy, Wallace."

"Even if he isn't, there are plenty of other nutcases around. Look at these people. Never seen so much religious devotion. Like a God damn papal visit. Pardon my blasphemy."

Fitzroy shouted louder, desperate to get the attention of the apathetic crowd.

"In the absence of any company announcements, it's only fitting that we at *Gamer Frontline* provide a tribute to the legendary composer."

He gestured to someone off camera, and waved both arms in a flowing, circular movement akin to a conductor before an orchestra. His overacting drew some laughter and snide comments from the expo crowd.

"Here is a collection of his greatest works," Fitzroy said.

Music blared over the speakers, fast in tempo, punctuated by many dramatic beats. But the countdown reached zero seconds later, and the tune was quickly forgotten amid cheers, excited chatter, and shrieks of excitement. Behind the frustrated commentator, the expo guests scrambled toward the open doors.

"And so the stampede begins." Ron rolled his eyes. "You good to go, Duvall?"

"Why wouldn't I be?"

Lucy marched across the roundabout directly to the security barrier. Once again, she was a woman on a mission, never wandering from the most direct route. She circumvented the cordon, ignoring complaints and nasty looks from the invitees. Before the astonished guard at the far end could object, she whipped out her detective's shield.

"Police business."

"You'll have to be more—"

"We already cleared it with your boss."

Lucy showed no sign of backing down.

"She's in one of her moods," Ron said. He budged between them to flash his own badge. "Detective Wallace. My partner, Detective Duvall. Best to let us inside quietly, unless you want to create a scene. And trust me, you don't."

The guard mulled it over — briefly — then waved the two cops through. Ron gave his partner a querying glance as they headed through the doors.

"That was edgy, even for you."

"We're investigating a murder. Why should I not be?"

* * *

The scene inside the Taurus lobby was more chaotic than outside. Employees in business suits stood behind display counters packed with high-priced souvenirs and official *Crimson Shadow* merchandise. Many tie-ins were on sale: a board game with oriental artwork and ninja weapon playing pieces, toy plastic samurai characters, and even replica red-garb clothing and masks. A cynic would label it a cash grab, but most customers were eager to spend their money.

A few security guards watched from the balcony, but almost everyone was on the ground level. The crowd was concentrated around a centrally located platform. Taurus' main stand was one of many displays, but by some margin the busiest.

Adrian stood on the stage-like structure, flanked by two women in *Crimson Shadow* outfits. Their wardrobe was a perfect match to the woman on the poster: tight martial arts robes dyed the color of blood, with sheathed imitation weapons.

The masks were absent, possibly so Sophie could woo the crowd with sexy eyelid flutters and frequently blown kisses. She was to Adrian's right, performing acrobatic feats. These included high kicks, karate chops at pretend targets, and crouched fighting stances. Her movements were clumsy and imprecise. Compared to the masked heroine shown in televised gameplay footage, who despatched seven armored samurai with one free-flowing attack, the cosplayer was an amateur.

The spectacled Asian woman to Adrian's left did much better with the choreography, though her frequent blinking, lack of empathy, and trembling lips suggested stage fright. She was tall for a female — two inches on Adrian and a whole foot on Sophie — with long, naturally soft black hair fastened into a jade-clipped ponytail. Her sandy brown skin was smooth and makeup-free, without a single bead of sweat on her lean cheeks.

An excited gamer — a teenage boy in a Taurus baseball cap — punched the air in triumph. "That was easy," he said, waving a wireless video game controller in his reddened fist. "I'm the master of the flaming forest, folks."

That was a reference to the "Stage Completed" screen. It showed an image of the ninja in a katana-wielding victory pose. She was surrounded by burning trees and impressive overlaid statistics.

Adrian reached over to collect the gamepad. "Anyone else fancy a go?"

A plethora of arms shot up, accompanied by squeals of delight. Then the noise dropped an octave, and the fan club parted to allow the two detectives through. Lucy held her badge high to ward away the teenagers. A chorus of boos greeted her.

Adrian lowered the controller, looking a touch miffed at the intrusion. He stepped down from the stage to confront her head on.

"I know you have a job to do, but you could be more discreet. This is the product launch."

"A discussion in private would have been better," Ron agreed, disdainfully eyeing his partner.

"But you're right," Lucy said, "we have a job to do."

She looked around the room, and the crowd by the stage, which had grown noticeably thinner since her arrival.

"Large turn out. See what you mean by interested fans. But why would a gamer go after a former employee? Seems to take obsession to a whole new level."

"Unless they didn't," Ron said, "and the motive was financial. Which brings us back to you, Mister President."

An attendee strutted toward the stage, pushing an Adrian-masked teen out of the way. It was Fitzroy, the game reviewer who'd given Norris a questionable tribute. Still wearing his cheap, red-tinted glasses, he thrust a microphone-fitted MP3 player in Lucy's face. The recording light was on.

"Any comment, Detective?"

Lucy appeared stunned at the interruption, and Adrian gave the reporter a mean stare of his own. The models on stage — Sophie and the Asian — looked at each other, perplexed. They had stopped the martial arts choreography, and nearly every guest in the lobby — plus the guards upstairs — was watching Fitzroy's unorthodox interview.

"Any leads? Are you linking the death of Justin Norris to Taurus Studios? Is there evidence to connect his brutal murder to the gaming community?"

Lucy opened her mouth to reply, but the commentator gave her no opportunity to speak. His eyes widened as he clenched his MP3 recorder tight, giving him the appearance of a lunatic on the verge of breakdown. And his questions were increasingly hysterical.

"Could this be the start of something bigger? Is a new terror about to grip the city of Philadelphia? Are we in mortal danger? Do you have any suspects?"

"I'm not at liberty to comment on an ongoing investigation," Lucy said. "Lieutenant Blake will give a press conference this afternoon."

"A textbook answer. Where's the originality?"

"Hey!" Ron stepped forward to intervene. "Leave the sarcasm to me, pal. This is a police investigation. There's no story for you here. Talk a walk."

Fitzroy acted as if the detectives weren't there. He thrust his MP3 recorder at Adrian, almost clubbing him on the nose.

"Do you think it was a mistake to part company with a top talent?" the reporter pressed. "Can we expect a further dip in quality from Taurus? More unoriginal games that pander to the masses?"

"Dip in quality!? Pander to—" Adrian lost his cool and didn't even feign diplomacy. "Who the hell are you to come here and chuck insults around? It won't wash, you asshole. Everybody knows you're biased against us. How much did our competition pay you to talk shit?"

"Now we're seeing the real Adrian Pryce, people. An obsessed control freak who only—"

Lucy placed a firm hand on Fitzroy's shoulder, adding a tight squeeze that made him flinch.

"I advise you to step back," she said, touching her holster bulge. "Or we'll have to take action."

"Is that a threat, Detective?" Fitzroy turned his attention to Adrian. "Same game, sexier clothes. You think you can hide the truth, Pryce? But it will come out. I know what you've done."

"What truth? You insinuating son of a bitch."

He snatched the MP3 recorder in anger, threw it on the floor so hard it broke, and grabbed Fitzroy's neck with both hands.

Lucy tackled Adrian from behind. Showing her upper body strength, she pulled him away and held him face down on the stage. Ron dragged Fitzroy a few paces back, applying brute force to separate the two quarreling men. The reviewer's shades came off and clattered against the marble floor. The Asian woman stepped aside, while Sophie looked on in shock. Security guards stormed down the nearest staircase.

"What the hell do you think this is?" Lucy said. "Amateur crime hour? Calm down and let us handle the detective work." She redirected her fury at Fitzroy. "And you need to leave. I won't ask again."

He quit struggling, but Ron kept his grip on him.

"Everybody getting this?" the reviewer yelled at the

captivated crowd. "Police brutality. The iron fist of the system suppressing us. I have rights. I demand an apology."

Digital cameras clicked and beeped as guests used them to take pictures of Ron forcibly restraining his accuser.

"What the hell for?" he asked, unperturbed. "Messing up that tuft of fur you call hair? That murder you're so interested in. To answer your earlier question… Yeah, we got a suspect. His name's Fitzroy."

CHAPTER SIX

Crimson Shadows

Seen from the balcony, Fitzroy appeared like a midget next to the heavies that restrained him. Expo attendees kept their distance, leaving a ten-foot circle of marble floor otherwise empty. With the reviewer now in Taurus' security custody, the two detectives had moved near the stage. They were close to Adrian, who seemed somewhat calmer and back in control of his emotions.

Loud cheers continued as the guards hauled the detainee toward the entrance. The ring of space followed the prisoner and escorts with uncanny precision. Once the three men had vacated the premises, the excitement subsided. The guests soon turned their attention to souvenir hunting and playing video games.

A well-manicured man leaning over the balcony was unimpressed. The wristband of his gold watch glinted as he tapped the chrome rail. Dressed in a pressed purple suit, firm-collared shirt, and polished Italian shoes, he was evidently wealthy. And at least twice, or perhaps three, times older than the teens he looked down on. Either the auburn-haired watcher possessed considerable power, or liked to pretend so.

The observer's dark green eyes focused on Adrian. He waited until the president noticed him and then inclined his head. Without waiting for a response — verbal or gestured — the man headed for a secluded, shadowy corner away from office foot traffic. The balcony screened him from the ground floor, and with the elevator tubes inactive, the four yard patch was effectively a blind spot.

The man raised a flat palm toward an approaching security guard as a silent suggestion to patrol elsewhere. Without a word of dissent, the sentry altered his route.

* * *

"Take a ten-minute break, girls," Adrian said, glancing over his shoulder at Sophie. "Once the excitement's settled down, we've got some promotion to do. When we're done, I want them all talking about *Crimson Shadow* and not that lunatic." He turned to Lucy. "Are you planning to arrest him?"

"We got a case for Fitzroy disturbing the peace. Enough to peg him as a definite suspect. But nothing to link him to the crime scene, and you assaulted him first."

"After he provoked me. So that's it? You're not even going to question him?"

"Oh, we'll question him," Ron said. "Once he calms down. But that could be a while yet. In the meantime, we got our eye on some other promising leads."

He let his piercing gaze unsettle Adrian for a moment, then gave him a false smile.

"I'm off to the men's room," the president said. "To take a piss. Unless you want to follow me there, too."

Adrian glanced up at the balcony. Only the briefest of

looks, but the detective noticed. He surveyed the upper tier, but saw nobody up there except patrolling security guards.

"Go ahead," Lucy said. "Nothing to see in there that would interest me."

"You haven't told your partner, have you? Don't worry, Detective Duvall. I can keep a secret."

Ron gave her a bemused look as the president walked off.

"He likes to play games," was her unconvincing explanation. "Pay no attention to what he says."

She wandered to the stage and flashed her shield at the Asian choreographer. The woman flinched, looking somewhat uncomfortable as she stepped off the platform. Lucy followed her round the side, to a cordoned off area away from the crowd. A gang of puberty-age boys stayed behind to drool over Sophie, who repeated her dance routine despite the boss' orders.

"Mind if I ask you a few questions?" Lucy asked. "Miss…"

"Tania Chin," she said. "I'm the lead programmer on Project Ninja." Seeing Lucy's perplexed reaction, she quickly elaborated. "*Crimson Shadow*. Project Ninja was the working title, when we were in the pre-production stage. It's been a three-year development cycle, and I was there from conception."

Instead of rejoining his partner, Ron tracked Adrian through the crowd. The detective noted the black-on-silver male and female restroom symbols. The president headed straight past them and carried on toward the stairs. His tail dropped off, careful to keep his distance.

Lucy bit her lip and continued to question Tania. "I always thought of programmers as desk workers. Doing the boring stuff in the back office."

"It's not boring. Not all the time, anyway. But I spend most days in back offices. We're the people the company like to forget at launch events."

"Is the dancing a sideline?"

Tania followed Lucy's gaze to Sophie, who was busy posing for her male admirers.

"They need women to be *Crimson Shadow*," the programmer said. "I could have managed on my own, but Adrian wanted someone else to work with me. Someone prettier. Apparently, beauty is more important than the skill set."

"Sounds about right," Lucy muttered under her breath, then quickly changed tack. "Your colleague over there doesn't seem to mind the attention."

Sophie kneeled down and loosened the belt around her ninja outfit. She was an unapologetic temptress, and the teenage boys were happy to be ensnared in her seductive web.

"Adrian..." Tania hesitated a moment. "...is fond of Miss Gallier, and few pretty women work at Taurus Studios. And I'm not as comfortable performing in front of a crowd as her."

"You did fine. At least you weren't falling over you feet every ten seconds. So what else does Miss Gallier do? Besides dancing and flirting with gullible teenagers?"

"Sophie's head of public relations, according to her e-mail signature. I don't really know her that well. She doesn't spend much time with the other team members."

"Too busy servicing the clients, I suppose."

Tania — looking uncertain how to respond to the snide comment — gave a shy grin.

"What's he like?" Lucy asked. "Adrian Pryce, as a boss?"

"All right."

Tania avoided direct eye contact, and there was no conviction in her reply. Lucy smiled and patiently waited for her to continue.

"He calls the shots." She adjusted her spectacles until they were level. "There's not a lot of room for creativity at Taurus Studios. Adrian likes us to follow his rules. But they don't always apply to him."

"Driven and obsessed. Sounds just like this guy I knew at college."

* * *

Adrian stomped heavily along the balcony and joined the purple-suited businessman in the shady corner. Ron, still climbing the stairs, watched from a distance.

"A little tacky, don't you think?" the manicured man said. "Dancing with two ladies? And a fistfight with a reporter. I've warned you about losing your cool, Adrian. Violent conduct is a story we can do without. Especially this close to the launch date."

"Fitzroy's a talentless hack, but he was right about one thing. Sex sells. Most of our fanbase are teenage boys. It's what they want to see. A male fighter in black might be more realistic, and could work as a secondary character in the sequel. But *Crimson Shadow* will get us to number one. Which you should understand the importance of, being our producer. The man with the money."

"Demographics change."

The well-dressed man peered over the railing. With the male heavy crowd, it took him a moment to spy a group of females.

"This is not the eighties, or even the noughties. There's a lot more accountability these days, examples to set. I just came from a meeting with our investors. They want us to appeal to a broader audience from now on, and venture into new markets. Which means we need to diversify. In plain English, less sex and more variety."

"How will pissing off our existing customer base help us expand?"

Adrian shook his head, stopping when he saw Ron turn off the stairs onto the balcony. The detective approached slowly, brushing past a security guard. He closed in behind the money man, like a predator stalking its quarry.

"Do I need to remind you we had three triple-A flops last year?" the producer said, unaware of Ron's presence. "Building our fanbase might — just might — allow me to revise our bleak profit projections. Less red and more black. The Norris situation hasn't helped the share price. Our stocks took a nosedive when Taurus Studios and murder got mentioned in the same report on the evening news. Those of us that live in the real world have to deal with the fallout."

"Bad news is good news. Isn't that one of your catchphrases, Miles?"

The producer clenched his fist, then apparently thought better of a second violent incident.

"Having the police nosing around our company and ask questions is hardly good business. Not for me, and definitely not for you."

"That's a shame." Adrian nodded towards Ron. "Because it seems there's a detective here who'd like to speak to you."

The policeman responded to Miles' sharp backward glance with an exaggerated hand wave.

"Why not put some spin on it?" the president said. "Use some fancy words. It's what you're good at."

Adrian walked off without a look back, leaving the cop

and the purple-suited financier alone in the secluded corner.

"Pretty shady. This sneaky cubby hole. Don't like to mingle with other guests, huh? Why do I get the impression you've been avoiding me? Oh, excuse me. Forgot the introductions. Detective Wallace. You are?"

"Miles Dawson. I handle the company's finances."

"Of course you do," said Ron, smile vanishing in an instant. "You must be Pryce's attorney, then."

"And producer." He cemented his upright stance. "That means I run the show. Money talks, despite what Adrian thinks."

"Have you told him that?"

The lawyer reached into his suit, pulled out a business card, and slid it into Ron's pocket. The detective kept his eyes on him the whole time.

"When you want to talk to my client, you go through me. Or I'll go through your boss, and claim police harassment along the way. You might find it a slippery path. Do we understand one another?"

Ron didn't seem unsettled in the slightest.

"I understand lawyers better than you think. Spent my entire career dealing with them." He took out his notebook and pen. "Nice peaceful spot you've picked out. Away from the crowd. It'd be a shame to let this opportunity to talk go to waste. So, if you don't mind, I'd like to ask you some questions."

* * *

The sun was about to set on Philadelphia. The expo had finished, and technicians worked on dismantling the last television screen. Some refreshment stands and trader stalls were still manned, their lights switched on since it was getting late in the afternoon. Few people were outside the Taurus Studios tower, which appeared like a black column against the orange-brown sky.

Ron walked alongside Lucy, crossing the empty, litter-strewn roundabout. "Weird bunch. Your old college pal has ruffled some feathers over the years. Fitzroy. His producer stroke attorney, plus quite a few of his staff."

"We're not pals," she said.

"Sure about that? You were awfully protective when that loon went after him. Thought you were going to toss in a few punches and his Miranda rights."

Lucy quickened her pace, moving ahead of Ron. She unlocked the unmarked car door and pulled it sharply outward. Then she got in, slammed it shut, and fastened her seat belt.

Ron took his time before joining her.

"Acting on impulse," he said while he strapped up. "That's not like you, Duvall."

"Are you done with the commentary?"

Lucy started the engine. Ron placed a restraining hand on the handbrake before she could disengage it.

"Just looking out for my partner."

His concern sounded genuine, with no sign of the usual sarcasm.

"You know, Pryce got pretty heated back there. He would have choked Fitzroy to death. If the guards weren't there, we'd be dealing with two murders. Maybe he lost his temper with Norris over some business deal. He could be our man, Lucy. Level with me. If there's something—"

"You're wrong. That guy may be a self-centered control freak, but trust me. He's not a killer."

* * *

Someone entered a restroom stall. It was a tiny, four foot wide cubicle with a white plastic door, ebony-tiled walls, and porcelain toilet. The mystery person, shrouded in shadow, wore a long-tailed, black leather jacket zipped up to the neck.

A sliding bolt clicked shut. There was a silent pause, as if the darkened figure was checking nobody else was around. The killer — or someone dressed similarly to them — took out a mobile phone and typed on its lighted alphanumeric keypad with gloved fingers.

The unknown person wrote a text message. For the few words that weren't in shorthand, they chose from the suggested autocomplete options with speed and accuracy.

Ungrammatical sentences appeared piece by piece. *Sophie. Would love to see U. My house. 2nite. 8pm.* The caller inserted a blank line and added a single word signature: *Adrian.*

The typist selected *S Gallier* from a list of contacts, and pressed the send button. A green tick by the message indicated success.

With the evening rendezvous set, the killer flushed the unused toilet, presumably a precaution in case somebody entered the washroom. They walked past three other lavatory stalls to the exit.

A mix of sounds — people talking, the bustle of activity, and video game sound effects — echoed around the room as the door swung inward to reveal a familiar scene.

A few seconds later, the faceless figure had disappeared among the Taurus Studios expo attendees.

CHAPTER SEVEN

Steamy Encounter

Suburban Philadelphia was a different world from the inner city. Compared to downtown in rush hour, the low-rise detached houses and leafy cul-de-sac lanes were peaceful. Except for the occasional SUV driving by and excited dog barks, it was a quiet evening in this wealthy area.

Moonlight pierced silvery clouds, adding a shine to the red bull that decorated the front garden. There were no signposts, but the layout of the road-encircled lawn and horned statue was identical to the scenic Taurus Studios approach. The estate with the classical-pillar facade, wrought-iron gate, and arched windows could only be described as a mansion. This was surely Adrian Pryce's house. If the palatial, white-brick home wasn't the private residence of the company president, it belonged to a *very* obsessed fan.

A picket fence enclosed the garden and swimming pool at the rear. The slatted panels were attached with rigid steel brackets, and the wooden planks were ten feet high with only hairline gaps between. Sharpened-to-a-point tips made it clear trespassers weren't welcome on the grounds. At night, the pool looked downright dangerous: a sheet of still, impenetrably black water within a lighter, tiled border.

A surveillance camera was fixed to the temple-like pediment that covered the patio doors. Motors whirred as the device swiveled in a pre-programmed arc, monitoring the back yard. It took roughly ten seconds to complete a full sweep of the outdoor pool area. After a three second pause, the reverse rotation started. And so the pattern continued.

A white plastic tarpaulin sheet flew up into the air, thrown by someone beyond the fence. It landed atop the spikes and flattened against the wood. The camera was pointed in the wrong direction. But the fleeting movement would have still been difficult to spot, even for the keenest-eyed observer.

The panels creaked. There was a grunt of exertion, faint and short. Two leather-gloved hands gripped the sheet. A balaclava-masked head came into view, slowly rising until the eye slits cleared the fence. Shrouded by darkness and almost impossible to see, the black-clad figure remained motionless as the camera rotated to face the tarpaulin. There was no alarm siren, or any sign the intrusion had been detected.

As soon as the lens turned away, the killer mounted the obstacle, used a powerful push to gain altitude, and swung a booted leg between two cushioned spikes for leverage. For someone physically fit, clearing the ten-foot barrier was no real challenge. The intruder dropped into the garden and sprinted across the frost-hardened grass to the patio. By the time the surveillance camera reversed its motion again, the masked figure was already standing in a blind spot under the pediment. Their well timed approach suggested a planned infiltration.

Pausing for the lightest of breaths through the

mouthpiece veil, the killer opened a metal box mounted on the exterior wall. An insulated cable linked it to the camera, making it obvious what the numeric keypad inside controlled. The intruder typed in a six-digit code. A green light flashed, then a message appeared on an LCD screen: *SYSTEM DEACTIVATED*. The whirring stopped, with the switched-off device pointed at the side path.

The killer closed the control box and threw a nearby electrical switch. Underwater illumination discs on the pool base powered up. With the gloom dispersed, the surface changed color from black to clear, turquoise blue. The intruder flipped a second lever beside the first. Steam rose from tiny vents around the pool's edge, generating a fog effect that reduced visibility to mere inches.

Dangerous but inviting, the scene was set for whatever the murderer had planned.

* * *

A flashy sports car — a sleek, yellow convertible with its roof covered — drove up to the Pryce residence, around the bull statue, and stopped outside the front porch. Sophie exited the vehicle, wearing a milky-white evening dress with a short skirt and string-thin shoulder straps. Her glittery heeled shoes and pearl necklace completed an outfit suitable for a high-class event. Her lips were so heavily coated in red gloss they appeared almost bloody.

She closed the car door and stopped to check her appearance in the side mirror. The guest made a minor alteration to her dress, pulling it tighter around her waist to expose even more cleavage. Sophie smiled in satisfaction and strutted up the porch steps, heels clacking the polished marble.

She reached for the buzzer, a simple button set in a carved brass bull's head fixture. Just before she pressed it, she noticed a rather-obvious note taped to the door frame.

The visitor gently raised the bottom to read the message typed on the yellow paper: *Waiting in the pool. Warmed the water up for you. A.*

"Adrian, you naughty boy." Shee peered into the security camera above. "All right, mister romantic. I'll play your game."

Sophie gripped the doorknob, gave it a slow, drawn-out turn, and pushed. She stepped into the hallway, a long arterial corridor decorated with silver-framed posters of Taurus Studios games. Candle-shaped bulbs glowed yellow in crystal pyramids, lighting a straight path from the entrance to the rear patio. The double doors at the far end were half-open, and the windows steamed up by the artificial mist.

"Out… here."

Adrian's voice came from the pool area, words broken by a jarring pause. Sophie seemed not to notice the odd speech. She stepped out of her high heels and slid them under a coffee table with a toe-prod.

"I'm coming," she said, walking barefoot down the hall. "Don't want to be late for an appointment with the boss."

Four sliding doors with black glass windows led to ground floor areas, and a chrome railed staircase to the upper landing. Sophie ignored all those and proceeded to the rear patio, dress rustling against her knees. Water vapor condensed on her face as she stepped through the swirling steam.

Sophie wafted the air and looked around the foggy garden.

"Adrian?"

There was no reply.

"Adrian?" she repeated, more apprehensive than before.

"Take your… things… off!"

Another inconsistent pieced-together response. The three snippets were all different volumes, the last word shouted dramatically as if part of an edited public speech.

Sophie jerked back. She looked round again, but the steamy mist made it difficult to see anything other than shifting, blurry shapes.

"Why do you sound so weird?" she asked. "So… scary?"

The only audible noise was her heavy, irregular breathing. Sophie's dress was wringing wet from condensation, sticking to her knees. Looking about nervously, she made no attempt to pull the material away.

"Welcome to… the last event… of your… lifetime."

The terrified woman walked along the poolside, mist thickening around her. Water dripped from her damp hair as she swiveled on the spot.

"Adrian! This isn't funny. And it's freezing cold." She shivered as if to make her point.

"Taurus Studios invites you to play a new kind of game."

It was Adrian's voice again, but the sentence sounded normal, with no gaps or change in tempo. Faint cheering was audible in the background.

"Stop it!" Sophie shrieked. "You're freaking me out."

"A game without checkpoints or continues."

The spoken words were louder now. The mist parted to reveal a dark, vaguely human shape. A black and hairless figure, little more than a silhouette. Then the steam became denser again, obscuring the mystery stalker.

Sophie slipped on the wet tiles and almost fell back into the pool. She clumsily regained her footing.

The shadow reappeared, larger and more clearly defined. The masked, leather-clad killer stepped through the vapors toward her, approaching from the house. Nerves becoming outright panic, the guest looked on, quivering in fear as a gloved hand lifted an object. It was white plastic, flat and oblong-shaped.

"A game with true consequences," the voice said, now obviously a pre-made recording. "Where death is permanent. Just like real life."

The killer stopped the playback and threw the MP3 player down on the frosty grass. Sophie backed away, mouth open in an expression of pure terror. Her bare feet were close to the drop-off. The menacing figure in black had her trapped, with the pool at her rear and the path to the house obstructed.

The killer's eyeballs moved around the oval slits — observing the environment — and then focused directly on their target. Sophie saw the wearer's lips press against the veiled mouthpiece. A cloth impression of a twisted and evil smile.

She screamed and made a diagonal dash toward the house corner to evade her attacker. The black figure crouched low, and mist soon enveloped them. Sophie approached the side gate, only to see a padlocked chain securing it. Slowing her sprint to look around, she retreated to the perimeter fence and rubbed the dampness from her face.

The masked killer rose behind her, grabbed her necklace, and yanked it taut. Gloved fingers pulled the pearls apart, forcing them along the threading.

Thin steel wire bit deep into the victim's windpipe. Her scream turned to a choked gasp. Eyes bulging, she squirmed in the killer's grasp. Her bare toenails scraped up frost and dry mud.

Sophie's hands flailed at the garotte, but she couldn't even get a firm grip, let alone pry it off her reddening skin. The killer was much stronger than she was. Their boot heels dug into paving stone cracks and barely moved despite her efforts.

After a hopeless ten second long struggle, the masked figure pulled the wire tighter, lifting Sophie's feet off the ground. They dragged the kicking victim over to the swimming pool, spun her about so her trailing legs dipped in the water, and then let go.

With the stranglehold released, Sophie screamed in terror. Then she landed with a splash, and her desperate cry for help was silenced.

She surfaced and coughed, spitting out water. The killer was there waiting, gloved hand already in position to snatch the necklace. The assailant inserted one arm through the loophole at the rear, their leather palm sliding down their victim's lubricated back. Increased tension made the wire twist round Sophie's neck and tighten into a noose. Loose pearls rattled together on the thread.

She pounded the killer's forearm, screams silenced once more. Her blows were timid, almost negated by water resistance. The smiling assassin forced their victim down and dunked her head underwater.

Air bubbled from the submerged woman's nostrils. She watched, helpless as the killer took out a tablet phone and used its camera to record her dying moments. After another failed attempt to loosen the necklace, Sophie reached up at the kneeling figure.

Her wet hand slipped on the leather jacket, unable to get a grip. She stretched higher still and pulled at the balaclava. It distorted out of shape, obscuring the murderer's eyes, and then came away in her clenched fist.

A large air bubble rose from Sophie's open mouth and popped on the surface. The shock of recognition upon seeing the killer's face was clear in her expression, every detail recorded by the phone's camera. Her continuous kicking created a whirlpool effect, but her head stayed in focus throughout.

Her limp hand slapped down on the paving stones, splashing water over the assailant's boot. Then it slid lifelessly back into the pool, and her struggles ceased.

The killer reached forward to reclaim the floating balaclava, then let go of the necklace. Sophie's face-down body drifted away from the edge, remaining afloat with her drowned black hair waving like tangled seaweed.

The unknown assailant placed a Taurus-logo-headed letter on the paving stones. Water soaked the paper, but the typed words were perfectly legible.

Sexual liaisons between Taurus employees are strongly discouraged and could bring the company into disrepute. You behaved inappropriately, Miss Gallier. Consider your employment terminated.

CHAPTER EIGHT

The Suspect

Sycamore Avenue was marked with a traditional white-on-green signpost. The side street was on the fringes of downtown Philadelphia, a few blocks from the landmark skyscrapers.

Windows in this neighborhood were far less clean, with many protected by metal bars. The few not obscured by dirt glowed pinkish-red, lit by sleazy neon advertisements. Available were hotel rooms, all-night liquor stores, and adult entertainment. The road was in poor condition, marred by cracked kerb stones and potholes full of muddied water. Luminescent graffiti was everywhere, from garage doors to shadowy alcoves.

Lucy looked out from a second-floor apartment window. Her blonde hair and shirt appearing amber-orange in the glow of the nearby street lamp. With no shutters for protection, she'd be an easy target for an opportunistic shooter.

But she didn't look afraid. The sole occupant stood there unflinching as she sipped from a plain-white porcelain mug.

There was little activity to see. Nobody walked the pavement except for an old, snowy-haired woman with a crooked walking stick.

Lucy turned away and sat down on a hard-cushioned brown leather sofa. It was typical of non-luxurious and practical apartment furniture, with sturdy wooden legs, flat-topped armrests, and a total lack of any cosmetic features. The mahogany table was basic, if spotlessly clean. Paperwork was filed in a sectioned brass rack. A folded suit top, wallet, handcuffs, and holstered handgun were laid out in a straight, tidy row. Compared to the outside environment, the functional abode could be regarded as fashionable, if not for the cracked walls and peeled-back carpeting.

Lucy lifted a plastic folder from the empty seat beside her. Her expression was unreadable as she rested the binder on her lap and opened the front cover. Inside was a photo album that showed her progression from a blonde, happy-looking toddler to a casually dressed teenager with sleepy eyes and purple lipstick.

On the next page, she appeared with Adrian. He looked far less professional than the present-day company president, and a lot more like a stereotypical, messy-haired computer nerd. As the album pages — and years — progressed, other people disappeared from the photos. Lucy morphed from the scruffy girl into a makeup-free patrolwoman. And finally, to a black-suited detective who proudly flashed her shield.

"How many times have I told you, Wendy?" a thuggish-sounding man yelled. Heavy footsteps pounded above. "You're such a lousy —"

"Hey!" Lucy projected her voice up at the ceiling. "Got a problem up there, Joe? Something the police need to deal with?"

Everything suddenly went quiet. She waited a few seconds and returned to studying her photo album.

A mobile telephone rang, playing a default factory-set tone. The detective put down the folder and walked over to the table. Mug in hand, she reached into her suit pocket and took out her cellphone. It was a dated, black-cased model with keypad buttons eroded from overuse. The caller ID displayed on the simplistic screen was *Wallace*.

"Duvall. You need something?"

"He called the cops," Ron replied. "Said he killed her."

"Who? Mind talking some sense? Who are you referring to?"

There was a brief pause before her partner spoke again.

"Take a good guess. Adrian Pryce told us to meet him at his place. Your old college buddy just confessed to murder one."

Lucy's grip tightened around the mug handle. "Send me the address. Do nothing till I get there. Promise me, Wallace."

"Sure. We're partners, aren't we?"

Lucy finished the call before Ron could say more. She covered her mouth to cough, then put her cup down on the table. It wobbled before settling. The liquid at the bottom was syrupy brown, too viscous and semi-transparent to be tea or coffee.

* * *

Floodlights shone on Adrian's backyard, leaving no part of the garden, pool or temple patio unlit. A dozen temporary generators had been set up near the picket fence. Engines chugged away, supplying power to the taped-off crime scene.

The police forensics team — the same personnel who'd attended Norris' warehouse — scoured the area for clues. Some moved across the grass, stepping carefully and precisely as they waved ultraviolet strip lamps. Others dragged poled nets and pinging sensor equipment through the pool, stopping every so often to check results.

Sophie's corpse had been removed from the water. The dead woman was laid face-up on a black plastic sheet, beside a body bag ready to be zipped up once the preliminary exam was done.

Her dress had partially dried, but still clung to her chest in several places. Damp, shiny skin gave her an artificial, almost mannequin-like complexion. The pearl necklace and soggy, Taurus-headed letter were sealed in evidence bags beside the deceased.

"The note has the same typeface," Doctor Vickers said. "Same logo at the top."

"So Pryce killed them both?"

"Somebody did. And that's a working assumption. We certainly don't know who."

Ron, peering over her shoulder from behind, browsed the bagged items. Then he walked around the body to study it from a side angle.

"You're starting to sound like Lucy."

"I've been doing this job for five years."

Vickers moved Sophie's tangled hair with tweezers and kneeled down to inspect her bruised throat.

"First thing I learned, stick to the facts. And those facts are we got a dead female. Strangled. Circular depressions to the side suggest the murder weapon was that pearl necklace."

"You mean the one we found around the victim's neck?" Ron said. "Looks like something you'd wear, Doc."

"Nothing traditional about this woman. Is that how ladies dress these days? She's practically naked."

"You think Pryce and this… Sophie were having a fling? Maybe he invited her over to his place for a little midnight date? Dancing. Sex. Murder. You know, the usual for a psycho killer."

In response to Vickers' despairing sigh, Ron raised his hands in apology.

"Stick to the facts. I get it."

Ron gave the forensics woman a mock salute and turned away. A car engine grew louder. Headlamps lit up the fence spikes, their beams moving past the hanging tarpaulin towards the front of the house.

"Here comes trouble," Ron said. "Wish me luck."

* * *

"I told you to wait for me."

Lucy looked flustered as she exited her car. Her ride was a plain, gunmetal-gray economy vehicle with a heavily scratched roof, missing left wiper, and luminous paint stains on the windscreen.

"There's no mystery to solve here," Ron said. "I was at the office when Pryce called to confess. Me and a dozen other cops heard him spill the beans."

"You still should have waited."

She staggered, quickly righting herself. Ron's eyes narrowed. He took a sniff, then leaned forward to smell her face. She pushed him away and straightened her suit top, but she was clearly unfit for duty.

"You drove here in that state?" Ron looked flabbergasted. "Are you insane? Why the hell didn't you call someone to pick you up? Or sit this one out at home?"

"Where's Pryce?"

Lucy moved toward the house, veering from her usual orderly path. Ron grabbed her by the waist.

"I'm calling you a cab. We'll do the interview tomorrow."

"I'll be fine."

She reached inside her suit and pulled out a tube of breath mints. She popped one in her mouth and gave her partner a reassuring, straight-faced glance.

"Really. I'm fine," she said. "I can handle this. We can't afford to wait until tomorrow. Not with a killer on the loose."

"The killer's in there, with three cops watching him."

Ron waved at the policeman guarding the door and took Lucy out of earshot.

"And no, you're not fine. This is about Pryce, isn't it? I don't know what the history is between you two..."

"There is no history," she said defensively. "We knew each other at university. Briefly. That's it. Hardly a relationship I need to declare."

"Briefly? I don't think so." There was a moment of awkward silence before Ron continued. "You dated the guy, didn't you? When you were at college. How far did it go? Did you sleep with him?"

Lucy brushed back her hair and avoided direct eye contact. She was a different woman now, a nervous wreck who couldn't stand still.

"Jesus!" He lowered his voice to a hushed whisper. "You realize the shit you're in? That you've put me in? If Blake finds out that there's a conflict of interest —"

"There is no conflict!"

The policeman looked over as she yelled. Lucy smiled innocently and waited until he turned his attention elsewhere.

"Trust me," she said. "It's over between us. Has been for years."

"Hard to trust someone who drink drives. Or a cop who keeps the truth from her partner."

Lucy ate another breath mint. The tube's top almost flipped from her unstable fingers as she replaced it.

"I know this man, Ron. I can read him."

"No, you can read the statement. Once I've taken it down and spoken to Blake."

He turned toward the policeman, about to call out to him. The jittery detective grabbed her partner's shirt sleeve.

"I'll let you do the talking," she said. "But I have to be part of this."

"Not a good idea. There's a dead woman in his back garden. You remember the receptionist at Taurus? The flirty one? Her name was Sophie Gallier. It looks like she was Pryce's lover, too. Seems things don't end well for them."

"You're right about that. I got burned by that bastard, too. Don't tell me you didn't sense the animosity at the interview. The only feelings I have for that man are hatred and contempt. And he knows it."

Ron looked at the policeman, then back at Lucy. "This morning with that reporter…"

"Game reviewer," she corrected him. "Pryce struck first. I stopped him. Simple as that. I was doing my job, like I've always done. You go in there alone, and he will just close up. Wait for his creepy attorney to show. With me in the room, he might get edgy and say something. Maybe it won't be incriminating, but he'll talk. What have you got to lose?"

Ron chuckled in response. "How about my career and pension?"

He paused for a moment's reflection, then gave Lucy a

concerned look. A hard-faced "don't mess with me" expression.

"I do the talking," he said. "Let me be the bad, serious cop for a change. You be yourself. The silent, jilted ex-lover. And tomorrow, when you've sobered up, you tell me everything. Deal?"

* * *

Adrian's living room resembled a teenage boy's dream world, with yet more framed posters of video game characters. Computers were everywhere: an extensive, history-spanning collection from early 1980s machines with thick keyboards and brick-like power units, to the latest, sleekly designed consoles. The chairs, rib-shaped tables, and pyramid lamp shades were ultra-modern. Opaque, black glass panels and chrome frames were consistent with the architecture of the Taurus Studios tower.

Adrian sat on a semicircular, five-cushioned futon that surrounded an inactive, sixty-inch plasma television and gaming suite. Dressed in a maroon bathrobe, he had two broad-shouldered, uniformed policemen for company.

The suspect suffered in silence between them, perspiring face buried in his cupped palms. He had a nasty wound on the right of his forehead, a deep cut that had stopped bleeding and scabbed over.

None of the cops seemed sympathetic to Adrian, and his living room was crowded with them. Two butch females flanked the sliding door to the hallway, and an unfriendly older guy slouched by the closed window curtains.

Lucy stared at the suspect from behind the television, arms folded. The giant screen obscured everything below her hips. Ron was much closer. The tall, imposing figure toyed with his handcuffs, watching Adrian squirm in discomfort.

"Let's hear that crazy story again," he said, "just so we're clear on what happened."

"I've told you. When I came home…"

"There was a man in my house!"

Ron quoted the famous line from *The Fugitive* with mocking gusto. Nobody laughed, except for the older cop.

"Don't forget to mention the artificial arm. Or that you're innocent."

"I never mentioned an artificial… There *was* somebody here, dammit. He was wearing a mask. I didn't see his face. It's the truth!"

He looked at Lucy, who stared back indifferently.

"He knocked me out," Adrian said. "When I woke up, I found Sophie's body floating in the pool. She was already dead."

"And that would be when you called us to confess. Makes sense."

"That wasn't me! Right after I found her, you guys showed up. I never had the chance to make a call."

Ron stretched his handcuff rings so hard the chain clinked.

"This mystery guest. Did he turn off all the cameras? Let the girl in? It seems the killer was somebody who knew the security code and had a key to your front door. Let me think who it could be."

"Anyone can find out a code if they want to. Maybe this guy has a friend who works for the alarm company. Or he's been watching me. And copied my key while I was at the office. Wait. What if this guy's a Taurus employee?"

He stared pleadingly at Lucy. She took out her breath mints, slowly unscrewed the cap, and swallowed a couple straight from the tube.

"Could be," she said neutrally.

"Or maybe he already knew the code because it's his house," Ron said. "Sounds more plausible to me."

He held up an evidence bag. Inside was a mobile phone: an advanced model with a wireless Internet connection and a flashy, touch-sensitive screen. The device used in the Taurus restroom.

"Recognize this? The last number dialed from it belonged to the dead girl. You don't need to confirm that. We already did. Funny thing about these modern phones. Whenever you send a text message, it records the sender, date, and time. Does all our detective legwork for us. Isn't that fantastic?"

"Obviously, someone stole my phone."

Adrian sounded increasingly desperate, legs squirming like an animal trapped in a cage.

"Obviously," said Ron. "No signs of a struggle inside. Forensics found heeled footprints in the hall. Which means the girl walked into your house willingly, to join her host for a late night swim..." He leaned closer to Adrian, face twisted in an unpleasant sneer. "Only you had something else in mind for her, didn't you? A date with murder."

Dawson entered from the hallway, an expensive overcoat buttoned over his purple suit. The two women officers barred his path.

"Say nothing more," the lawyer said. "You'll only incriminate yourself."

"He doesn't have to." Ron backed away. "We got all the evidence we need."

"I didn't do this!" Adrian screamed. Once again, he looked at his former lover. "Lucy! That phone isn't mine. Somebody planted it. You have to believe me."

She stepped around the television screen and nodded at the two men beside the suspect. They stood up and hauled him to his feet.

"Adrian Pryce," she said. "I'm placing you under arrest for the murders of Justin Norris and Sophie Gallier."

Ron slapped his handcuffs on the prisoner, who offered no resistance.

"I want to talk to my client," Dawson said. "Now."

One of the female officers led the attorney away while Lucy approached Adrian. His eyes burned with hatred.

"You know how the phrase goes," he stated through clenched teeth. "No good deed —"

Ron twisted the handcuffs, showing no remorse as Adrian grimaced in pain.

"You have the right to remain silent." Lucy's recital of his rights was emotionless, almost robotic. "Anything you say can and will be used against you in a court of law."

CHAPTER NINE

Lifesaver

Quite a few nosy neighbors watched from upstairs windows as the police escorted Adrian to a waiting patrol car. A beady-eyed woman in daffodil-patterned pajamas talked excitedly to a much older man who yawned in response. She whispered in his ear despite being indoors, doing her best not to stare too hard.

Lucy opened the car's rear door. Adrian gave his ex-lover a grumpy, bitter-faced glare as Ron herded him past. Keeping the suspect's wrists on a tight leash, the detective forced his prisoner's head underneath the frame. The caged-off compartment used to transport prisoners had more than enough space for one.

Ron slammed the door shut and pulled Lucy to one side. With Adrian out of their sight, the neighbors seemed to lose interest. One by one, the bedroom lights switched off and curtains were drawn.

"So you and Pryce were…"

He trailed off, leaving his partner to fill in the blank.

"We were," she said. "And now we're not. Let's leave my

past where it belongs. Okay?"

Lucy turned toward the patrol car. Ron grabbed her shoulder, but she shrugged him off without slowing her pace.

"Yeah, I get it." She headed round to the passenger side. "You're driving."

"You did the right thing by arresting him," he said over the vehicle roof. "The professional thing."

"Did I? The evidence seems far too convenient. Too obvious. What if he was telling the truth, and this is a frame up?"

"Sure it is." Ron chortled in amusement. "A phantom intruder broke in, shut off the security, drowned a girl, and left without leaving a single trace. That's as hard to believe as you going all soft. This is real life, Duvall, not television. Sometimes the answer is obvious."

He clambered into the driver's seat and adjusted the rear-view mirror so he could monitor the prisoner.

"Best get used to the accommodation, pal," he said, buckling up. "You live a long way out of the city. It's a good half hour's drive to the precinct. Why don't you relax back there and make yourself uncomfortable?"

Lucy got into the passenger side, facing forward as she fastened her seatbelt. She closed the door, and Ron followed two other police cars down the leafy street.

Neither of the detectives spoke as they set off on the long drive toward Philadelphia. Distant skyscrapers towered over suburban homes, shining like beacons in the pitch black sky.

"I thought we were friends."

Adrian leaned across to Lucy's side. A tow truck passed in the opposite direction, casting light on the squad car interior. The prisoner didn't blink, not even when the headlamps shone straight into his eyes. He sat motionless as the barrier's latticed shadow moved over his face.

"We were a lot more than that." Lucy kept her gaze on the road ahead. "But being told you're special to a guy, only to come home and find another woman asleep in his bed… That doesn't leave much room for interpretation. Still can't believe I fell for your charm. But I won't make the same mistake twice."

"All right," Adrian said. "You win. I was seeing someone else four years ago. What does my love life matter now?"

"A great deal," Ron replied, "since we discovered your latest girl's body floating in your swimming pool." He spoke quickly to keep up the pressure. "Your admission of guilt's refreshing. Got anything more to confess? More employee terminations?"

"No. What's the point? You both think I killed her. I'm not saying another word until I've spoken with my attorney."

He leaned back in resignation and turned his neck to peer through the side window. All was quiet except for the rumble of tires on the tarmac. Ron glanced at the suspect's reflection in the mirror and took advantage of a break in traffic to whisper in Lucy's ear.

"Whatever happened between you two, it's over. You proved that tonight. If Blake comes after you for this, I got your back. We all have our secrets, partner. So, about our deal. As long as your past doesn't cloud your judgement, I'm quite happy to leave it buried."

"That's okay, Wallace." Lucy made no effort to talk quietly. "Once we've processed this two-faced creep, I could use some downtime. There are things I need to get off my mind. Coffee sound good?"

* * *

Kelli's Open All Nite Diner was the name written in bold yellow on the grease-stained, laminated, single sheet menus. The fast-food joint on the downtown street corner was as cramped as one might expect. Plastic, low-backed stools bolted around the central bar left a little legroom, and sixty people could squeeze in the booths if the place were busy. At this early hour of the morning, it wasn't.

Other than Lucy and Ron — who'd chosen a table near the back — the only customer was a bald, bearded redneck who wore a lumberjack-style checkered shirt, ripped jeans, and cowboy boots. He spat saliva into his coffee cup, ate a rash of bacon with his hands, and wiped his palms on the tablecloth. The young waitress working the night shift timidly approached his seat, standing as far from him as she could while she poured a refill.

Ron gave the poor-mannered customer a no-nonsense glare and moved his jacket flap to expose his holstered sidearm. Upon seeing the weapon, the redneck turned away with a bearish grunt. The waitress thanked the two detectives with an appreciative nod and made a speedy return to the bar.

"I was in my freshman year," Lucy said.

Ignorant of the confrontation, she absent-mindedly plopped a sugar cube in her coffee and watched it dissolve.

"A carefree teenager on her own in the big city."

Ron sipped his drink. "I imagine that was scary."

"I should have been more scared. Then I wouldn't have got into the trouble I did." Lucy dipped her spoon into her cup, stirred the liquid, and observed milky trails spiral around. "The crowd I got mixed up with... For them, fitting in was a big thing. Maybe the only thing that mattered."

"Lucy Duvall was a sorority girl?" Ron frowned, as if struggling to visualize his words. "Out chasing boys. Clubbing, drinking. No wonder you kept it a secret. Doesn't match the ice queen persona at all."

"We didn't just drink," she said without looking up. Her voice was heavy with regret. "There were other pressures. Bad habits I shared with the rest of the girls."

"You're talking about drugs. And not only the odd bit of weed. You mean the hard stuff."

He spoke the last part slowly, phrasing his deduction like a question. When Lucy didn't reply, he placed a consoling hand on her wrist.

"That's all in the past, though. Right?"

She nodded and wiped a tear from her eye. Her partner offered her a napkin, but she shook her head.

"Yes," she said, all traces of iciness melting away. "But it was bad, Ron. And I mean real bad. I can't remember when I took the first pill. I must have been drunk. But I do recall taking three that night four years ago."

Lucy slurped her coffee, gulping heavily enough to be heard across the table. The saucer wobbled as she replaced the cup, spoon rattling on the unbalanced porcelain.

"I could barely stand when I left the bar. I was on my way back home, stoned out of my skull. Completely wasted. It's mostly a blackout, but somehow, I got lost and ended up in the local park. That's when it happened. When I first met Adrian Pryce."

* * *

With trees and shrubbery in full, summery bloom, the park could be mistaken for the open countryside. Rap music shattered the peace, rapidly spoken lyrics indecipherable except for frequent, uncensored profanity. An unseen car sped off into the night, rubber tires screeching on a nearby road.

As the noise faded, two conifer branches parted, blown to the side by a fierce breeze. Then a modern office tower became visible through the gap, shattering the illusion. The grassy lawns, cobbled footpaths, and freshwater lake were merely a nature reserve in the wilderness of a nondescript American city. It was somewhere the locals might go for an evening jog to escape the bustle of the business district.

Only one person was in the park. Young Lucy was a teenage brat, wearing a bright pink, sleeveless top, PVC miniskirt, and platform-heeled shoes. The purse strapped on her shoulder was less than an inch thick, barely large enough to hold an identity card.

The delirious girl zig-zagged along the footpath, struggling to stay on her feet. Her eyelids were half-shut, her pupils dilated. Long blonde hair blew across her cheeks as she stepped onto the grass.

"Don't mess with me!" she said, hiccuping drunkenly. "I'm one of the girls."

Lucy held her arms out wide and looked up at the starry sky. The wind picked up, whistling through the trees. The teen staggered back and forth. Her shoe soles slipped, leaving soft, light brown mud marks on the turf.

She was still stargazing when the breeze turned into a fierce, howling gale. Her dress pressed close against her skin, sinking into the gap between her bare knees. With no solid foothold or the alertness to react, the gust of wind blew the dazed girl across the grass. All the way to a low, single-roped fence at the water's edge. Her lower ankle caught the cordon, and she toppled over backwards into the lake.

The splash Lucy made was tiny, but her scream was

ear-piercing. Her eyelids sprung open, as if she'd woken from a daydream. Her shrill cry turned to spluttering coughs as water poured into her mouth.

The teenager struggled to stay afloat. Within seconds, her flapping arms and kicking legs had slowed to where she hardly moved at all. Even in summer, the lake was icy enough to induce numbness.

Lucy clawed at the lakeside grass, varnished fingernails digging tiny trenches on the slippery mud. She screamed one more time and then went under. Darkness encroached on Lucy's vision. From her perspective, the shore was a dark, ripply blur. Black streaks spread to all four corners, obliterating finer details until only vague outlines remained.

A white light appeared, rays spinning around its blinding center. The imperiled girl squinted and discerned the faint, mirage-like shape of a man riding a pedal cycle. The featureless stranger dropped his bike on the lawn, sprinted across to the shoreline, and thrust a helping hand down into the lake.

Lucy — finding strength from somewhere — reached out and grabbed the lifeline. The helper gripped her wrist and pulled the drowning woman to the surface. Water trickled down Lucy's cheeks. She looked on the verge of death, eyes fluttering as she cleared her throat to speak.

"Thank you. I don't know what would have—"

"Hang on!" the man said, dragging her to safety.

Lit by the cycle's headlamp, the teenage Adrian Pryce was dressed much untidier than the businessman he'd one day become. His dirty shirt hung out of his tracksuit pants, and the zip of his bomber jacket was bent out of shape.

Lucy blushed and looked up at her brown-haired savior with sweetness and affection. He removed his coat and wrapped it around Lucy's wet, mud-stained body. She might have been freezing cold, but the blossoming relationship was warm.

* * *

Ron nodded thoughtfully and finished his coffee. The redneck had left the diner during Lucy's story, and the detectives and waitress were the only people present.

"A lifesaver," he said. "Wondered why you cared so much for the guy who dumped you. Now it makes sense. Actually, it doesn't. But it's good to know my partner wasn't being totally irrational. Turns out the ice maiden is the genuine Lucy, after all."

She looked uneasy, perhaps troubled by the flashback. "I nearly died in that lake. I should have died. If not for Adrian, I would have."

"Hey." Ron reached over to lift his partner's chin up. "That was then. This is now. One act of kindness doesn't make the man a hero. Not when he grew up into a woman-hating scumbag."

"I suppose you're right." She didn't sound that convinced. "It's just... When someone saves your life, you feel obligated to them."

"You almost drowned. Sophie Gallier wasn't so lucky. Maybe it's not a coincidence. Maybe Pryce still has feelings for you, and wondered what if. And maybe drowning that poor girl in his backyard pool was his way to live out a personal fantasy."

Lucy smiled. Only a faint lip-twist, but her shell was cracking.

"That's a lot of maybes, and you know that..."

"Detective Duvall only deals with facts. Well, how are these for facts? Adrian Pryce messed with the wrong woman four years ago. Made the mistake of his life by saving that drunk, drugged-up college kid. And his bullshit, cooked-up story won't stop her nailing him to the wall."

"We can agree on that."

CHAPTER TEN

Conflict of Interest

Lieutenant Blake bit down on the filter stub of his cigarette, outer teeth grinding together. He sucked in deep, then exhaled. His cheeks swelled as smoke puffed through his nostrils, clouding the two-way mirror. The bald policeman resembled an angry caricature, with a pumped-out chest and twisted eyebrows. Either he was building up to a bollocking, or — more likely given Lucy's unsettled expression — was still in a foul mood after giving her one.

"I should have said something," Lucy apologized. "Told you about our history."

"But you didn't." Blake removed his squashed cigarette and threw it in an ashtray. "You let your personal feelings for a suspect interfere with a murder investigation. And now, I'm not sure I can trust you."

Adrian was in the interview room, wrists handcuffed to the chair. A sticky plaster covered his head wound, but he still appeared distinctly uncomfortable. Ron, sat opposite him, set up the recording equipment. Every click and button press came through clear over the intercom.

"I don't have personal feelings for Pryce," Lucy said. "Not anymore."

She stood beside the Lieutenant, just beyond arm's reach. They both looked forward at the interview room. Neither of them had turned to face the other during their uneasy conversation.

Dawson joined them in the observation booth. The attorney wore another expensive suit, this one olive green with ivory buttons. He carried a fine, chocolate-brown leather satchel with MD monogrammed in gold under the handle.

"Morning, Mister Dawson."

Blake delivered the greeting with no hint of kindness. It was a formality, not a peace offering. The lawyer rolled up his sleeve to check his Cartier wristwatch.

"Time is money, Lieutenant. Since you're wasting both mine and my client's with these trumped-up charges, I expect to be compensated in due course. Not to mention holding an innocent man. You should be out there combing the streets. A Taurus Studios employee was just murdered. What are you doing to find this nutcase?"

"Questioning the prime suspect. Getting to the truth. You may want to check all the evidence stacked against your client before you make any more threats. Are you so sure he's innocent?"

"I'd hardly call the evidence stacked. It's a stretch to even call it circumstantial. What about the cut on his head? Mister Pryce was assaulted in his own home, and he's the one being interrogated. Is this how the police department normally treats victims of crime?"

Lucy drew her index finger across her forehead, cutting skin with her sharp nail. She showed a flattened drop of blood to the astonished Dawson.

"Not that hard to hurt yourself," she speculated. "What if he planned the whole thing?"

"If you're looking for psychos, check the mirror. There's a couple of them right here at the police station."

He sneered at Lucy and stormed out of the viewing chamber, letting the door slam behind him. Blake lit another cigarette and watched Dawson enter the interview room. The attorney bent forward to whisper quietly in Adrian's ear.

"What was that about?" he asked.

"Just taking him out of his comfort zone."

"Before you get cocky, Duvall, the only reason you haven't been canned is because your partner vouched for you. I believe things are over between you and Pryce. Doesn't mean I want you in the box together, but this case has gotten messy. Last thing we need during holiday season is a serial killer. The mayor's office has put us under pressure to get a quick result. If that means giving you one more chance..."

The unfriendly manner in which Blake spoke implied it was to be Lucy's *final* chance.

"You think he'll talk to me with his lawyer present?" Lucy studied Adrian, who appeared a lot less nervous with Dawson beside him. "Doubt it, boss. Like you said, things are over between us."

"It's worth a shot. As of now, Wallace is the lead investigator. You support him, and offer any information you feel is relevant."

* * *

Lucy walked into the interview room carrying a portable cassette recorder. It was a bulky item, an inefficient relic by present-day standards. There were so many scratches the black plastic appeared almost gray.

"Our forensics woman doesn't like modern equipment," she said. "Can't say I blame her. This is a recording she made of a 911 call. A little crackly, but I'm sure you'll recognize the voice."

Lucy spun sharply on the spot, eyes boring into Adrian as she pressed the play button. She held the device above the table, with the speaker side angled down slightly.

"She's dead," the caller said. It was clearly the suspect speaking, despite whiny interference. "Sophie. I... killed her."

The sentences were mismatched in style and volume, with a lengthy pause between the snippets.

"Sir?" asked a confused male dispatcher. "You claim you've killed a person? Who are you referring to?"

"This is... Adrian Pryce. I'm at home... waiting for... the authorities."

Lucy stopped the tape. Ron leaned across and put himself right in Adrian's face.

"Seems to be a habit of yours. Calling 911 after a murder. Like the attention?"

"Come on, Detective." Dawson laughed at their conjecture. "I'm no computer whiz, but even I can tell that recording has been doctored. Somebody's being creative, editing audio fragments to put words in my client's mouth. He never made that call."

"I think he did," Lucy said. "And this obvious tampering is a trick to throw us off his trail. Who'd murder somebody in their own home and dial 911 to confess? A crude diversion, but that's your style, isn't it? Crude."

"I'm being set up!" Adrian flung his fists on the table. "I didn't kill them. What does it take to convince you?"

A cellphone rang, playing a vibrant rendition of classical Italian opera. Everyone in the interview room looked at the lawyer. Not fazed at being the center of attention, he removed the phone from his inside suit pocket, glanced at the screen, and accepted the call.

"Dawson."

He cupped one hand around his ear. The person on the line was inaudible, and the only clue the attorney gave was a solemn-faced nod before he ended the private conversation.

"I have proof."

"You don't sound that happy about it," Ron said. "So I'm assuming this proof of yours isn't very concrete."

Dawson lifted his satchel onto his knees, sprung the locking catches, and removed a laptop computer. He placed the bottom keyboard section on the table, opened the top, and turned the unit sideways so everyone could see the raised screen.

"Show us," Lucy said.

"That was my assistant Lisa on the phone," Dawson said while his machine booted up. "She told me the footage is horrifying. Apparently it was only uploaded a minute ago, so the site administrators haven't had the chance to block the transmission. This video is being streamed all over the Internet."

"What video?" asked Adrian.

His attorney clicked on a Web browser icon, then a search bar. He typed in *Pryce Pool Murder*. On two occasions, the shaky-fingered lawyer backspaced after making a typo. The suspect swallowed as he saw his name appear, while Ron looked on apprehensively.

Lucy kept her cool. "Go on."

Dawson pressed the enter key, and a video window

opened automatically. The footage began with a scream. Sophie — trapped in Adrian's swimming pool by the gloved, off-camera assailant — fought bravely to free herself. She fell silent as the killer tightened the pearl necklace around her throat and forced her underwater. The victim flapped her arms wildly about, and liquid droplets showered the lens.

Adrian turned his head away. "God. Turn it off!"

"You're a genuine piece of work." Ron twisted his face in disgust. "Uploading a snuff video to the world. How sick is that?"

Sophie's gurgles came across the laptop speaker. Ron's hands clenched into fists. Lucy gave her ex-lover a spiteful stare, doing nothing to calm her partner.

"The only reason you're not sitting on the floor right now," he said, barely containing his fury, "is because I'm taking you down for this the proper way. So your lawyer won't be able—"

"Detective!" Dawson interrupted. "The screen..."

The attorney gesticulated to the laptop. Ron turned to see a second window open inside the first.

It was a local news feed, with a pretty blonde presenter reading headlines from behind a studio desk. A digital clock superimposed in the corner showed the time as *10:14*. Dawson held out his wrist. According to his Cartier watch, it was correct.

"Wallace," Lucy said. "It's live. This video is being transmitted now. Adrian's not our guy."

Ron looked at her disbelievingly. "What if he set—"

"He's not our guy. We screwed up."

She unlocked Adrian's handcuffs, pausing afterwards to look down regretfully at the freed prisoner. The lawyer closed the laptop, stowed it away in his briefcase, and gave his client a comforting pat on the shoulder.

"I screwed up," Lucy added.

"Satisfied, detectives?" Dawson inserted himself between her and Adrian. Then he glared at the mirror — and the unseen Blake. "You charged in and arrested Mister Pryce with no thought for his wellbeing. Gung ho and amateurish tactics. Well, you can expect a formal complaint from my office. And a lawsuit to follow in due course."

Lucy walked to the door, paying little attention to his outburst. "The killer played us all for fools."

"You got that right, Ms. Duvall. The fools you are."

"He wanted us to arrest you," she said. "This all revolves around you. First Norris. Now Sophie. He's going after your company. This isn't over. You're still in danger."

Adrian looked into her eyes. There was a moment of understanding, though not reconciliation, before the attorney pulled his client away.

"We're all in danger from you lunatics," said Dawson. "If you need to talk to Mister Pryce, you know where he lives."

"Not so fast." Ron met Dawson's glare with his own. "Sophie Gallier worked on the *Crimson Shadow* project, right? Like Norris. That loophole... the lucrative contract you had with the musician. Now that she's dead, do her royalty payments also default to Taurus? Maybe we got hasty and jumped to the wrong conclusion. Thanks for setting us back on track. Suppose this isn't about revenge or love, but money. That would be your department."

"You don't know when to quit, do you?" Dawson confronted Ron face-to-face. "Expect me to file for damages by the end of the week. You should worry about your own money, Detective."

"Wallace!" Blake shouted across the intercom. "Enough!

Let them walk."

"Listen to your boss," the attorney said, with a threatening glance at Ron. "While you still have jobs."

He escorted his client to the door.

"Adrian!" Lucy yelled after them. "I'm sorry. You probably don't want to talk right now, but if you think of anything relevant, anyone who might have reason to hate you or your company, you call me. Okay?"

He turned around and gave her the gentlest of nods. His expression was somewhere between unfriendly and lukewarm.

"Start by questioning my employees."

"For routine enquiries, of course," Dawson was quick to add. "We run background checks on everyone we hire. None of them have a criminal history, unless you're worried about parking tickets."

"Why them?" Lucy asked. "And not an outside rival?"

"The Web address, the one that came up when Miles accessed the video. I recognized it. That footage was transmitted from the Taurus Studios server."

"Adrian," his attorney said. "You need to think carefully about what to disclose."

"Nobody can access our system from a remote location. That means the person who arranged the broadcast, and whoever killed Sophie, was in the Taurus building. You were right about someone holding a grudge against me. And the killer works for my company."

* * *

A silhouetted man hunched over a work desk, his gender betrayed by the thick hair sprouting from his wrists. His creased, red-and-white-striped shirt was drenched in sweat, his left kneecap visible through a nylon-spanned hole in his black jeans.

The junk-cluttered room was dark, faint sunlight filtering through tears in the dusty curtains. Virtually every newspaper clipping pinned to a cork notice board was an article relating to Taurus Studios and/or Adrian Pryce. The few that weren't provided commentary on computer games or historic Pennsylvania serial killer cases.

The seated man used rusty-bladed scissors to cut around the front page of a local paper. Its lead story was *"PR EXEC FOUND DEAD IN PRYCE'S POOL."*

He added the latest cutout to a pile on his desk. There were seven of them, all about the Sophie Gallier murder. Among the blunt, direct headlines were more imaginative attention-grabbers: *CRIMSON SHADOW FALLS ON PHILADELPHIA* and *IS THE GURU OF GAMING THE TAURUS STRANGLER?*

The hairy-armed man's unshaven cheeks glowed a soft blue. The light source was a television mounted above an unmade, coffee-stained bed. Or more specifically, the flashy title sequence of *Philly Lowdown with Kristina Malloy*. The man pulled a remote control from under the news clippings and unmuted the volume.

Music blended into applause as the on-screen titles faded and a glamorous female presenter appeared in close up. She had shoulder-length blonde hair and gleaming white teeth. The camera panned back slowly to reveal smart, casual clothes. Kristina's honey-brown shirt was fitted with a wireless microphone, and her loose dark gray trousers stopped at her ankles, just above low-heeled, practical shoes.

The glamorous woman was young, probably mid-to-late twenties, but projected confidence as she addressed her viewers.

"With me today in the studio is James Fitzroy, chief reviewer for *Gamer Online*."

She finished the rehearsed introduction with a gesture to her right. The camera angle changed to a wide shot of her and the guest. Dressed in the plain T-shirt and red-lensed glasses he'd worn for the Taurus expo, Fitzroy teetered on the edge of his leather recliner.

He waited for the applause to die down. "Thank you, Kristina. It's a pleasure to be here today. To share my thoughts with the world."

"I wish it were under better circumstances," she said, adding a serious note to the interview. "But once again, life has imitated art. With two murders and speculation rife that Adrian Pryce is the so-called Taurus Strangler, do you think it's finally time that publishers took another look at violence in computer games? That perhaps the medium should set a more positive example to society?"

"The Taurus Strangler. Such a glorious name. Brilliant and edgy. Simple, but with an aura of menace. He's out there right now. Watching, ready to strike again."

Fitzroy thrust his hands forward, palms and thumbs bent into an unbroken ellipse. The presenter retreated into her chair, mortified, as her guest tightened his grip around an imaginary person's neck. He shook about, seat legs vibrating as he throttled his pretend victim.

"If you could answer the question, Mister Fitzroy," Kristina said assertively.

He relaxed and placed his hands on his still knees. "Just making my point. Humans are a violent race, capable of the most heinous crimes. We always have been."

In the darkened room, the seated individual opened his desk drawer. Inside it was a semi-automatic pistol. The gun was the cleanest item in view, its black barrel polished and free of dust.

The mysterious male lifted the weapon and closed his hairy hand around the handle. He aimed at the notice board and lined up a newspaper photo of Adrian in the sight.

"Our ancestors battled it out in arenas," Fitzroy said to Kristina. "We battle it out online, but the idea is the same. Have games become more realistic? Yes, and their themes maturer. Greed, sex. Death, hatred, revenge."

He recited the list like a salesman pushing a product, with increased emphasis on each successive word. The interviewer looked increasingly uneasy as he went on.

"It's not society that copies games, but games that copy society. Do you believe works of fiction are truly responsible for the Taurus Strangler? What about the Boston Strangler? Or the Hillside Strangler? There were no video games then."

"What's your explanation, James?"

"They are a smokescreen put forward by politicians, and by people like you. To hide the truth. There's a killer inside us all. A demon. All it takes is a strong enough reason to release that monster from its cage."

Kristina gave a reassuring smile to the studio audience, fearfully eyeing Fitzroy. "Thank you for your insightful input. We'll continue after the break."

The man seated in the dimly lit room lowered his gun. He reached deep into the open drawer and pulled out a laminated identity card. His fingers obscured the photograph and employee name, but the imprinted company logo on the upper right was a familiar, golden-horned bull.

CHAPTER ELEVEN

Security Risk

Motorists steered aside to allow the convoy of police vehicles past. There were two patrol cars and an armor-plated, dark-windowed van in the middle. The cops proceeded directly to Taurus Studios, only taking detours to avoid parked traffic, a fenced-off construction site, and the roundabout at the very end. The bull statue horns reflected the emergency lights as the transports approached their destination.

On the last stretch, the two squad cars slowed down, allowing the van to overtake. Siren wailing, it jerked to a stop outside the main entrance. Both automobiles parked sideways, establishing a temporary roadblock with one vehicle on either side.

A large contingent of police officers — a dozen uniformed cops plus the detectives — exited. Those who emerged from the transport wore full tactical gear. For these troops, black body armor, visored riot helmets, and automatic weapons were standard issue equipment.

Heavy boots pounded basalt as the squad marched to

pre-determined locations around the Taurus building. A strong-armed officer — it was difficult to tell whether it was a man or woman — uncoiled police tape from a reel and threaded it through a line of concrete-based posts. An efficient operation, and the cordon was established within minutes.

The tower doors slid open. A male teenage employee wearing an ear-mounted cellphone and rucksack took one look at the police and then made a hasty retreat. Other workers in the lobby conversed nervously as the cops sealed off all potential escape routes.

An overweight African American man dressed in a slightly lighter blue uniform than the rest tossed a half-eaten, napkin-wrapped doughnut in a trashcan. He met the detectives just outside the entrance. The guard's name badge, covered in sugar grains, identified him as *Gordon Levitt, Head of Security*.

"I'm in charge of security here."

"Yeah, we gathered that," Ron said. "Part-time job? Didn't see you at the expo."

"Because I was busy watching the cameras. Your Lieutenant Blake phoned ahead. Said we had a breach of some sort."

A shiny silver SUV pulled up to the roadblock. The vehicle's frame spanned the width of the lane, and its tires were better suited to cross-country travel than city driving. Embossed on the five-inch wide front bumper was the model name: Road King. The windows were transparent, giving onlookers a clear view of expensive dashboard features, plush leather seats, and a satellite navigation system.

Dawson jumped down from behind the steering wheel, calmly closed the door, and marched toward the police cordon. Adrian followed from the passenger seat, quickening his pace to catch up. The attorney didn't so much as glance at the officers that allowed him past the barrier.

Levitt stood at attention as the producer approached. "Everything's set up as you asked, sir."

"I trust you'll complete your business here swiftly," Dawson said, addressing the detectives. "Our afternoon shift's over. People want to go home."

"Apologies for the inconvenience." Ron was his usual insincere self again. "And condolences on the loss of Miss Gallier. I can see she meant a lot to you."

"Yes, she did. She meant a lot to everyone at Taurus, but life goes on."

"Not for her, it doesn't," Lucy said. "And someone who works in this building sent that video."

She turned to face Levitt, who snapped awake from his daydream-like state.

"Where's the server room?"

"It's…" The security chief looked at his boss.

Adrian stepped around Dawson to mediate. "Downstairs." He gestured toward the entrance. "We're holding a memorial service for Sophie later. You're welcome to come along and pay your respects. But before that, I believe you wanted to check our computer system."

* * *

The Taurus server room was a dark, windowless box, illuminated by low-wattage strip bulbs and countless blue and green indicator lights. Hard drive banks were arranged in numbered sections, and accessed by a futuristic, hexagonal console in the center.

An airtight-sealed door separated the contained

environment from the exterior corridor. Ventilation systems whirred away, recycling the air through narrow, rectangular slits. The seamless metal walls, floor, and ceiling all looked the same: dull, silvery, and dust-free. The storage lockers — tall, featureless black containers with keypads — would work as props in a science fiction movie. According to a digital thermostat with a double readout, the temperature was fifteen degrees Celsius or sixty Fahrenheit.

This was Tania's territory. The programmer typed on keyboards under six identical monitors, working her way clockwise round the control console. Her spectacles reflected long streams of green text, binary data, and code fragments that only a computer expert could comprehend. An athletically fit female cop watched from behind, looking completely out of her depth.

The policewoman's attention went to the airlock as it opened with a pressurized hiss. Adrian entered, closely followed by Dawson, Lucy, Ron, and finally a fidgety Levitt. The security guard remained near the door while the entourage spread out. Even with six people inside, there was plenty of standing space among the databanks and lockers.

Levitt appeared in a hurry to leave. "I'll get back to the control room. I've got… uh, things to be checking. The technical expert can take it from here."

He squeezed sideways through the closing door. Tania continued to work, moving from one screen to the next. She was lost in her own world, and paid no attention to the police as she typed away. Occasionally, she glanced at the detectives, but the console was her primary focus.

"Whenever you're ready," Ron suggested.

"Someone hacked in," she said over her keystrokes. "From outside. They were using our server as a relay."

Adrian's jaw lowered at the revelation. The technician

pre-empted his question.

"I've run a full diagnostic of our systems. Rebooted the mainframe. The scan showed no trace of malicious activity."

"How the hell did they get through our firewalls?"

"I'm not sure."

The president's gaze hardened. He stepped over to the console, casting a shadow over Tania's bent back.

"You're in charge of server security, aren't you? You told me that our systems couldn't be accessed remotely. But it seems like somebody managed it. How is that possible?"

"Adrian," Dawson intervened. "It's not her fault. Go easy on her."

His stance softened a touch.

"What happened?" he asked Tania. A little more gently than before, but still miffed.

"Whoever did this had excellent IT skills and detailed knowledge of our systems. We use advanced encryption. In theory, we're secure against the latest intrusion techniques. No hacker could have broken through the firewall. Not without knowing the setup."

Lucy took a moment to ingest Tania's explanation. "So you're saying the person responsible works for Taurus? But they weren't in the building when they hacked in?"

"That would be..." Tania seemed frightened by the conclusion. "The logical assumption."

"We have to widen our net," Ron said, moving closer to Adrian. "Perhaps include suspects we'd previously ruled out."

"It was a *live* news bulletin. Which means the sender opened the second window on their end. When the footage was being streamed, I was busy answering your questions. I'm sure you remember."

"Did I mention your name?" Ron circled around and

took up a position beside the console. "But we will need a list of people who work in this building. And, assuming a hi-tech company like Taurus keeps tabs on its employees, their shift patterns."

"When was your security system last updated?" Lucy asked Tania.

"Five months ago," Adrian said.

He looked at the programmer for confirmation. She gave him a shaky nod.

"Then it could be an ex-employee we're looking for. That list needs to include those people, too."

Adrian headed for the door. "Miss Chin will provide you with the details."

"And send me a copy when she's done," Dawson said. "I'm heading over to the office. To prepare an official statement before the press speculation gets out of control. If anything comes up in the meantime, I expect you'll inform me straight away."

Adrian stopped and turned to face Lucy. "We're holding that memorial service for Sophie, if you want to join us."

"I'd like that," she said with a warm smile.

They left the room together. The door closed behind them, leaving the programmer alone with the police.

"Sure," Ron shouted at the hissing airlock. "Why not? Somebody has to do the boring stuff."

Tania typed away, engrossed in her work. He looked at the policewoman, who stood there in total silence.

"And that would be the three stooges."

*　*　*

Other than more advanced computers, the main development office had few features to distinguish it from any other business. Staff cubicles were tiny rectangular zones segregated by plastic dividers. Employees were issued only the basics: an L-shaped, metal framed desk, a terminal, two rather shallow drawers, and an adjustable swivel chair.

The workers shared a communal kitchen area with vending machines, coffeemakers, and water coolers. Translucent signs, fixed to the ceiling with chrome struts, identified the various departments. On this level were *Finance*, *Quality Control*, *Human Resources*, and *Public Relations*.

Taurus employees gathered in the central aisle, heads bowed toward the black wooden floor. A giant *Crimson Shadow* poster — one with Sophie as the unmasked ninja — was mounted on an easel surrounded by bunches of flowers and sympathy cards. Office lights were dimmed except for those directly above the memorial, giving the artwork a surreal, almost angelic glow.

Quite a few people shed tears, and one woman used a soggy handkerchief to blot her cheeks dry. Adrian led the service from the front, with Lucy at his side.

"We'll miss Sophie's beautiful face. Her soft, comforting voice. But most of all, we'll miss what she gave Taurus Studios. Sophie didn't just play a fighter." He paused for effect. "She was a fighter. This was a woman who fought for this company every single day. She was on the front line working with the media and the customers. Thanks to her, our marketing an edge that will be sorely missed."

Someone arrived late and joined the employees at the back. His face was obscured by the crowd, but his striped shirt identified him as the man who'd cut out the newspaper clippings on Sophie's murder.

The newcomer forced his way through the mourners, angering quite a few of them, and dodged into a cubicle. He placed his rough fingers on the divider, squeezing so hard it wobbled. In his other hand, hidden below the plastic screen, was a supermarket carrier bag. The white polythene sagged, and a gun-outlined object was visible at the bottom.

"How best to put this?" Adrian said, continuing his eulogy. "Sophie Gallier gave us a leg-up on the competition."

The joky play on words lightened the mood, generating chuckles that spread through the audience. While the mourners shared a rare moment of laughter, Striped Shirt reached into his carrier bag and lifted the object out. It was indeed a gun, the same one he'd handled in the apartment.

Careful to keep the weapon hidden below the divider wall, the man wrapped it up in the empty plastic and tucked it underneath his arm. At the memorial, Adrian's expression turned serious.

"Goodbye, Sophie."

Many who'd gathered to mourn repeated his words. One group at a time, they left the others and shuffled back to their cubicles. Striped Shirt moved from aisle to aisle, brushing past employees returning to the desks. He reached the kitchen, and hid round a corner as the office lights switched on.

"You spoke well," Lucy said.

She joined Adrian by the poster and pointed out the names listed at the bottom, credited in small print.

"Justin Norris. Now Sophie Gallier. Can't be a coincidence. I need to check out this project. Do we have time for a studio tour?"

"I think we can manage that."

Lucy moved closer to him. She stepped within touching distance, but kept her hands to herself.

"How about an apology?" she asked. "Will there be time for that?"

"We're not at that stage yet. But you could make a

start."

* * *

 A color printer hummed and deposited a letter-sized sheet of paper into the output tray. Tania collected the printout — a rather mundane list of names in spreadsheet cells — and handed it to Ron. The female officer tapped her shoes, looking none too thrilled with her guard duty assignment.

"Quick, accurate, and detailed," he said, checking the hard copy. "Ever thought of joining the cops? You'd be an improvement on our researchers."

"And work for a government salary? Better to rot in this dark hole."

"Definitely not for you, then. You're much too smart."

Ron's jest brought a smile to Tania's face. She looked sheepishly about, as if fearful someone had overheard her comments.

The detective gripped the paper tighter, crumpling the corner. "Didn't know that nut job used to work here."

"Who?"

Ron turned the sheet so Tania could see the text written in the row above his pointed finger. *James Fitzroy. Beta Tester, Development Team. Resigned.*

* * *

Fitzroy watched from the kitchen. The carrier bag crinkled as held the wrapped pistol tight. His tinted shades appeared flamingo pink under the bright office lights, convex lenses reflecting Taurus' staff at work.

Tips of employees' heads jutted above cubicle dividers. Someone passed a cardboard folder down an aisle to a colleague. By the furthest-away wall, near Sophie's memorial, were Lucy and Adrian. They shook hands in a gesture of renewed friendship and headed toward the exit doors.

Fitzroy set off in pursuit, only to bump into a worker who rushed around the corner. The staff member was a blond, tired-looking, boyish man in his early twenties. His black shirt was tight against his stomach, and his slacks were half an inch too short. The clothes looked as if they belonged to someone else, and he'd probably borrowed them for the memorial.

"Hey," the employee greeted Fitzroy. "Didn't know you were back at Taurus. Then it was you I saw you at the expo earlier."

"Just for today."

The gatecrasher held the bag behind him as the blond man filled a plastic cup at the water cooler.

"Surprised you came. I thought you hated Sophie."

Fitzroy's lips twisted at the mention of her name.

"The woman was a parasite who fed off the lifeblood of Taurus Studios," he said. "I didn't come to mourn her. I'm here on business. This company was once great, but people like her and Adrian Pryce have sucked its soul dry. Look at that poster. She was a sex object, a tool Pryce used and abused."

The cup crumpled slightly in the employee's nervy fingers.

"Colorful language." He took a long sip. "Reminds me of the fan fiction you used to write. Did that ever catch on, Fitz?"

"No, because the best of my work got stolen. Now I spread the truth. The truth employees at this company are too blind to see. But that will change. I tried to share my findings through my game reviews, but nobody listened."

Fitzroy was so hysterical the other employee took a pace back.

"Only revealing the devil's treachery shall release you from your shackles. You might not realize it yet, but I'm the Taurus savior. You will all thank me when this is over."

He turned and walked away, marching almost robot-like to the exit. A few of the staff recognized him and exchanged questioning glances, but most were too busy working to notice the ex-employee pass the cubicles. Or the polythene wrapped pistol he openly carried.

The only person who said anything was the man he'd spoken to.

"Yeah, I'll thank you. Thank you for leaving me in peace, you crazy bastard."

He crushed his empty cup and pressed the broken plastic flat.

"The Taurus savior…" He froze on the spot, his grip suddenly looser. "The Taurus Strangler. My God. It's him. He's here!"

Other employees turned to stare. The squashed container dropped from his open palm and slid across the kitchen floor.

CHAPTER TWELVE

Exposed

The project room was structured like a beehive honeycomb, with computer workstations facing inward along three concentric, hexagonal tiers. Programmers and designers worked with touch-sensitive screens, manipulating cinematic images and character models. Some graphics were still in an early development phase, little more than wireframe men and concept sketches. Others were fully textured 3D constructs, realistically animated to every individual grass blade and hair strand.

The eponymous Crimson Shadow might pass for an actual woman if her outfit wasn't so outlandish. The skin-tight red catsuit looked just as impractical as on the game posters, but the bizarre supporting cast of samurai giants, ghostly creatures, and geisha girl assassins suggested authenticity was a low priority.

A thin-limbed gymnast hung in mid-air above the center of the room, suspended by four steel cables. The woman wore a black, one-piece Lycra bodysuit fitted with electronic transmitters. There were literally hundreds of the tiny devices. Glowing red diodes extended from her toes all the way to the crest of her head. With her plastic imitation sword, the motion capture artist was a real-life facsimile of *Crimson Shadow*. Her ninja mask even had the same elongated gap across the eyes. The only differences were the clothing colors and the breathing vent over the woman's mouth.

Her harness belt was the only part of her outfit connected to the cables. Other than that, she had total freedom of movement. Wire lengths - and therefore waist height - were controlled by winches integrated into black, disc-shaped suction pads. There were four anchor points altogether, arranged in a diamond pattern on the ceiling.

Digital timers on the discs ticked down the seconds. Whenever they reached zero, a loud beep signified the end of one gymnastic routine, and the beginning of the next. A giant television screen below mirrored her movements in real-time. Sensors picked up even the smallest details. The wireframe avatar mimicked every subtle muscle flex and chest heave.

The staff were engrossed in their work, too absorbed in bringing *Crimson Shadow* to life to notice Lucy enter from the corridor. Her eyes widened in awe as she watched the harnessed woman execute a perfectly timed sliding kick. The gymnast's outstretched foot shot forward in a straight horizontal line, creating the illusion of ground below her. Then the artist 'leaped' up and slashed her katana in a sideways arc.

Lucy was so fixated on the Lycra-suited acrobat she didn't spot Adrian come in behind her.

"This is the project room," he said, glowing with pride, "where the little people bring my ideas to life."

"The little people? Is that how you see the rest of us?"

"Of course not. That was a joke."

He followed up with a smile, but Lucy's expression was cold and unimpressed.

"You haven't lost your sense of humor completely since joining the cops, have you? What... You think I don't value my staff?"

Lucy walked down the aisle and observed sketches on the tables. One was a series of musical notes on lines, quavers and crotchets drawn in classical style.

"Do you?" she asked. "Norris worked on the project, and you fired him. You two obviously had issues."

"Norris had *financial* issues. I have no control over how my employees spend money."

Lucy glanced up at the gymnast, who performed another somersault and katana slice.

"And you like to have control, don't you? Over peoples' lives? Your workforce, your women. It's all one big game to you."

"If only it were that easy." Adrian gazed wishfully at the artist above. "We are living in the twenty-first century. The modern woman is tough." His eyes dropped to Lucy. "Independent. Quite prepared to dump men she doesn't approve of."

Right on cue, the gymnast kicked high, a powerful strike at an imaginary opponent. With uncanny synchronization, a *Crimson Shadow* character on a designer's screen sent a robed bald monk flying off a sheer-faced cliff. With nothing to break his fall, he plummeted into a roaring river below.

"Nice analogy," Lucy said. "Not sure I buy the changed man act, but I am impressed with your people. The girl has excellent form. Who is she? I didn't see her at the memorial."

"That's because she never knew Sophie. The lady performing miracles up there is Jenna, a professional motion capture artist. We had to pay extra to hire her on a temporary contract, but she's worth it. Our usual woman's got more important things to work on."

"Another healthy young lady that wears a catsuit to work? I may as well quit now."

"Don't be silly. The other girl—"

Adrian stopped when he saw Lucy's grin and responded with one of his own.

"So you've remembered how to enjoy yourself. Or maybe it's your partner's sarcasm rubbing off. When you're done making fun of me, we should get back to the tour."

* * *

Gordon Levitt sat before a wall of monitors that streamed live surveillance footage. CCTV covered almost every area of the Taurus tower, including the lobby (with views from four different angles), elevator tubes, the server room, and a whole series of near-identical cubicle workspaces. The middle screen, larger than the rest, showed the president's office. Some images remained static. Others changed as cameras swiveled or moved along rails. External recordings included the front entrance, roundabout approach, and emergency exits.

Such intrusive security measures would probably horrify conspiracy theorists and civil liberties activists, but Levitt was more interested in munching his doughnut than voyeurism. He put his feet on the coffee-stained desk, reclined back, and took an enormous bite of pastry.

He was still licking sugar from his lips when Ron stormed in and rushed to the security screens.

"Where's Lucy?" he asked.

"Who?"

"She's my—" The detective gave Levitt a repugnant

glance and watched the guard calmly chew his doughnut. "Forget it. You tuck into your second lunch."

Ron turned his attention to the monitors and moved a pointed finger from left to right. He stopped and slapped the screen when he spied a familiar man in red-tinted glasses walking down a corridor.

"Fitzroy. So he is here. That bastard was under our nose this whole time."

"Hey." Dough melted in Levitt's open mouth. "I know that guy. I think he works here."

"He used to, which gives him a grudge and motive. Which part of the building is that?"

The subject turned left at a T-junction. He vanished from the monitor and almost immediately appeared on the one to its right. Levitt watched the footage, forehead creased in thought.

"I think that's the project office. Where they do… Really strange techie stuff with graphics."

"The security budget must really be tight if they put an airhead like you in charge."

"Huh?"

A report came through a two-way radio on the desk. "We got a dude acting crazy," a hoarse-voiced man said. "Making threats against the boss. Someone named Fitzroy."

Levitt went for the walkie talkie, but Ron reached it first.

"Detective Wallace here. You sit tight. Me and Sergeant Dumbbell are on the case."

Fitzroy marched down an otherwise-empty corridor, unwrapping the plastic bag while he walked. The camera panned to the left, past him. Ron glimpsed something black and metallic, but the object was unclear. He tapped the monitor impatiently. When the image rotated back to its former position, the suspect was gripping his pistol.

"Gun!"

He tossed the walkie talkie to the security chief and drew his own weapon in one swift move.

"Tell your men to seal off..." He checked the time and location stamp on the screen. "Floor eleven."

Levitt sat there, unresponsive. His greasy palms smeared the radio.

"Now!" yelled Ron.

* * *

Lucy and Adrian concluded their tour of the project room, and finished up at the door. They stood close together, side by side.

"Well," she said. "You've given me a few leads that are worth pursuing."

"Which of them is most promising?"

The president propped his back against an empty desk. Lucy weighed up her response. Before she could reply, Fitzroy burst into the room and waved his gun in the air.

"Nobody move!" he screamed. "You think you can just get rid of me? Is that it?"

A male employee jerked upright, almost falling off his seat. The motion capture artist gasped in terror and lost concentration. Steel cables ensnared her legs as she spun around helplessly.

Lucy reached for her sidearm and moved across to shield Adrian. Fitzroy trained his weapon on her. She froze, hand still inside her suit.

Nobody wanted to risk vacating their chair. Jenna let gravity take over and swung upside down as the timer beeped. The screen captured her uncontrolled somersault.

"We can talk about this," Lucy said.

Fitzroy's sweaty fingers twitched. He side-stepped to get a clearer shot at Adrian, and aimed at his exposed head. Despite jittery spasms, the gun stayed surprisingly steady. He'd dropped all pretense of sanity, mouth watering in pure rage.

"Why did you let this man go free? He's guilty. I can prove it to you."

"This guy's crazy," Adrian said. "He's been hounding me ever since he left Taurus. You should read some of his reviews, or his fan fiction. It's garbage. A load of dramatic hyperbole."

Fitzroy's finger half-squeezed the trigger. He breathed out through closed teeth. Jenna clamped her palm over her mouth filter, suppressing whimpers.

"That's enough, Adrian," Lucy said. "No need to provoke him. I'll hear the guy out. Where's the proof, Mister Fitzroy?"

"All around you. Can't you see it?"

His glasses reflected her poker face. Hand on her holster, she was ready to move should the slightest opportunity present itself.

"Look at his work!" the crazed reviewer yelled, though Lucy didn't comply. "It's all sequels and clones. Pryce is killing the industry."

The main door swung inward. Black glass throbbed as it slammed into the wall. Ron charged in, weapon drawn. Scared gasps echoed round the project room. Steel cables creaked around Jenna.

"I've got you covered, Duvall. A clear shot at the suspect. Just give me a reason to take it, asshole."

Fitzroy kept his pistol aimed at Adrian's head. He showed no sign of backing down.

"Wallace!" Lucy shouted. "Stay out of this. You say there's no originality. What about *Crimson Shadow*? Looks very original to me."

"Recycled trash. It's a cash in, nothing more. Another game sold with sex and violence. That's all Taurus does. I sent letter after letter to Pryce. Published review after review. I offered him guidance, told him how to save himself. But he ignored me. He chose to remain on his dark path."

Fitzroy's hand shook with rage. Adrian remained silent in the face of the accusations. Jenna and the avatar had both stopped moving, limbs twisted at awkward angles.

"Norris saw the truth!"

Fitzroy sounded delirious as he continued his manic rant.

"That's why he left. The girl — Sophie — Pryce was in love with her. But they both rejected him. And so he killed them. Can't you see? This man's the devil."

He took off his spectacles and threw them away. His exposed eyes were wild as a rabid dog's.

"Tell her what you did," he demanded, stepping within point blank range of Adrian. "Tell her!"

"All right! It's true. I killed them."

Jenna and several employees all gasped at once. Lucy stared in disbelief. Ron kept his aggressive stance, watching the suspect step away.

"I was right." Fitzroy lowered his voice, in partial shock himself. "I knew he was guilty. Now you can arrest him. I solved the case. I'm a hero."

Overcome with emotion, he relaxed. Adrian took advantage and grabbed the pistol. The two men struggled and twisted around. Each attempted to redirect the gun.

With the other man in the way, Ron's view of Fitzroy

was blocked. Lucy's suit flapped as she swiftly drew her weapon. She had a direct line of sight to the target, but seemed reluctant to fire.

"I lied!" Adrian said. "It's a trick. Shoot him."

Fitzroy kicked the president in the knee and shoved him against the wall.

Lucy fired before Ron, emptying three bullets into the assailant's chest. Jenna screamed as blood oozed from the wounds and dyed the white shirt stripes deep crimson.

Fitzroy squeezed his weapon's trigger as he fell back. Adrian ducked instinctively. But there were no gunshots, only a high-pitched laser sound effect.

The dying man landed beside his replica weapon and smiled up at the light overhead.

"I showed you the truth. I'm a hero."

He lay still, eyes frozen in a deathly stare. Ron slowly lowered his gun. Jenna spun back upright and untangled herself from the cables.

Adrian ran to the shell-shocked Lucy, but she couldn't look away from the dropped 'pistol'.

"It was just a toy," she said, mortified. "I killed him over a God damn toy."

"You couldn't have known. The gun seemed real enough from where I was standing. You saved my life today. Never mind what that nutcase told you. You're my hero, Lucy Duvall."

Adrian threw his arms around his ex-lover and embraced her in a tight, appreciative hug. She patted him weakly on the back, struggling to hold on to her firearm.

Ron looked on with concern. Behind him, a Taurus employee snapped a picture with her cellphone camera.

CHAPTER THIRTEEN
Off the Case

"Detective girlfriend saves murder suspect. Sound about right?"

Lieutenant Blake slammed the morning newspaper on his tidy, traditional desk. The actual headline was much kinder: *HERO POLICEWOMAN RESCUES TAURUS PRESIDENT.*

"That's not what it says, sir."

Lucy wore a clean slate-gray suit and trousers, and her hair was freshly combed. She stood on the green carpet, arms behind her back. There was only one chair: a throne-like, leather-backed antique with intricately carved wooden legs. That belonged to the boss.

The office could be mistaken for a library with its varnished oak panel walls, marble corner pillars, and brass lamp fixtures. Ceiling-high bookcases stocked police procedural manuals, city guidebooks, and gumshoe detective novels. The Venetian window blinds had been lowered, lead-ball-weighted cords dangling at the sides.

Detectives in the office beyond the closed door were

distorted to polygonal blurs by frosted glass. Only Blake's name and rank — etched in gold — were clear.

"I was reading between the lines," he said. "That's what people will say. And once the honeymoon is over, it's what reporters will write. That stunt you pulled yesterday made you a celebrity, Duvall. The press like to dig up dirt on celebrities. How long before they find out Pryce saved your life four years ago? That you two were already lovers?"

Blake gave the newspaper a forceful prod. The picture under the headline showed Adrian hugging Lucy, her head nestled behind his.

"Integrity. Professionalism. Honesty. Common sense, and the code we're supposed to follow. Do you understand what the words mean?"

She had no answer.

"What were you thinking? Palming the legwork off on your partner while you rekindled the fire with your college sweetheart. I've read the witness statements. Twice. I can't believe they're talking about Lucy Duvall. Acting all warm and cuddly with the prime suspect in a murder investigation."

"He provided us with an alibi, sir. It checked out."

"What if he was lying? Computers can do crazy things these days. But it seems your... *intuition...*" Blake put condescending emphasis on it. "...about him was correct. That's what you bet your life on, Duvall. Intuition, not evidence."

Lucy's chin fell. Confidence drained from her cheeks. She had no excuses to offer in her defense.

"I don't get it. You've always been career first, focused one hundred percent on the job. You had no time for socializing, romance, guesswork. No soft spots for bad guys to exploit. Now you're acting all soppy. On top of that, I have to explain why we shot a guy armed with a toy gun."

"With respect, sir, it looked real."

Blake leaned forward across his desk.

"Well, with respect, you're not the one who has to deal with the press and internal affairs. Luckily Fitzroy was a white kid, so the networks can't play the race card. And it's the season to be jolly, so we might avoid rioting in the streets. But I've still got to answer some uncomfortable questions, and so do you. Maybe if you'd had your head in the game, we could have detained that psycho before he caused all the panic."

He held out his hand, palm face up.

"You know the routine, Duvall," he said. "I need your badge and gun."

Lucy stared back in disbelief. "You're suspending me? In the middle of a murder investigation?"

"The investigation's over. We got our guy. Thankfully, there's an impartial witness who can testify to him threatening Pryce. Forensics are analyzing Fitzroy's computers. There were a lot of them in his apartment, so it may take a while to find something to tie him to the murders. It'll work out, but his gun was still a toy, and a Philadelphia PD detective shot him. Somebody's head has to roll for this, and it won't be mine."

Blake beckoned impatiently. Lucy kept a stiff expression as she removed her weapon from its holster.

"He doesn't fit the profile," she said. "Or the M.O. The guy we're looking for used a computer cable to strangle his victims. Fitzroy was deranged, completely out of his mind. Our killer's precise, calculating. He wouldn't barge into a building swarming with cops, announce he was about to kill somebody, and wave a gun around."

"A toy gun," Blake reminded her. "Thank you for your

psychological profile, *Ms.* Duvall. But I'd rather get an opinion from a qualified professional."

Lucy slapped her weapon down in the Lieutenant's hand. She took out her wallet and looked at her reflection in the shield before she unclipped it.

"You're making a mistake," she warned. "The killer's still out there."

Blake plucked the badge from Lucy's fingers. "I don't think so, but if that's what your intuition tells you, go be the armchair detective. Just get your ass out of my office. I've got a press conference to prepare for."

* * *

Lucy walked through long shadows cast by the setting sun. Light never shone on her once, not even a glimmer, but she kept her chin up as she strode along the pavement outside the precinct. There were no tears, nor any feet stomps. No angry glance up at Blake's office window. If the off-duty detective had any feelings, she didn't show them.

Ron waited by her trashy car, obstructing the path to the driver's door.

"Sorry if you got chewed up in there," he said. "It's a raw deal. Some lunatic aims a gun. What are you supposed to do in a situation like that? Wait to see if it fired real bullets? This is all political bullshit, Blake vying for his promotion."

"Guess I asked for it. This charming personality. Being the amiable woman on the team. It doesn't really suit me."

"This will all blow over. Trust me. Soon as folk find something else to complain about, you'll be back. The ice cold bitch. Who thought I'd ever miss her?"

Ron gave Lucy a complimentary pat on the shoulder.

She responded with an unconvincing, half-hearted nod, but he saw the unease that lingered in her body language.

"You're gonna keep seeing him, aren't you? Pryce, the same asshole who cheated on you. Geez. You got a death wish?"

"He's not the man he used to be."

Lucy took out her car keys and inserted the bulkiest one in the driver's door.

"No, he's not," Ron said. "Now he's a filthy rich, cheating asshole. You think you were ever anything special to that guy? He'd screw any woman daft enough to fall for him. Like Sophie Gallier. Remember her, the girl who drowned in his pool? There are far too many connections to your ex-lover. What if you're right about Fitzroy not being the killer?"

"You still believe Adrian's guilty."

"If not, then he's a target. Neither scenario bodes well for you, does it?"

The car door unlocked with a clunk. Lucy pulled it open so fast she almost knocked Ron over.

"What do you want me to do?" she asked. "Bug the guy's house? Go through his e-mails?"

"I want you to stay the hell away from him! Before you get killed. Is that really such a hard ask?"

He yelled so loud a nearby tramp looked up from his collection tin. Before Lucy could climb into her vehicle, he placed an obstructive arm across the open door.

"Fake gun or not." Ron lowered his voice to a quiet, but firm, whisper. "You were there for him. He saved your life, then you saved his. Now you're even. You don't owe that nerd a damn thing. If the killer is still out there, let the rest of us catch him. You go home and chill out. Enjoy your suspension. Okay?"

"Okay," Lucy said grumpily.

Ron gave her a warning stare, then lifted his arm away.

"And don't take any of Pryce's calls. His safety's a police matter now."

* * *

A fierce argument was going on in the apartment above. An irate man chastised a distraught, whimpering woman. A bottle smashed, she sobbed, and everything went quiet. Lucy took no notice of the disturbance. She sprawled across her sofa, leafing backward through her photo album.

"Police have named the hostage taker as James Fitzroy," Kristina Malloy said, "a name my regular viewers will recognize."

Wrapped in a maroon cloak and flowery scarf, she presented her evening report from the Taurus Studios roundabout. Her head filled the center of the television. Vibrant light from the screen splashed across Lucy, adding multicolored patches to her shirt.

"Many would agree Fitzroy was a disturbed individual, especially after my interview this morning. But nobody could have imagined the horror he would inflict. Thanks to the efforts of our city's finest, the murderer's campaign of terror is finally over."

Lucy turned another page and scanned photos of her and Adrian in their college years. She lifted a bottle of malt whisky from her table and poured the last drops into her glass. The rim was stained with dark brown lipstick impressions, signs of heavy drinking.

"Speaking this afternoon, the officer in charge provided his reassurance to the public," said Kristina.

The image brightened as it cut to footage recorded

earlier in the day. Blake gave his press conference from outside the police precinct, bald head tinted dark orange in the sunset.

"We should never forget our role is to protect and serve. The department can confirm reports about the shooting of James Fitzroy, and the hostage situation at Taurus Studios. To avoid media speculation, I can also confirm the suspect used an imitation firearm."

He stopped to swallow. A few bulbs flashed in the unseen crowd behind the TV camera.

"This was a high-pressure scenario. But impeccable standards are what citizens rightly expect from our police officers. I guarantee there will be a full investigation into this incident. We are co-operating with internal affairs and have nothing to hide."

Lucy drank her remaining whisky and slammed the glass hard on the table. It was only through sheer good fortune it didn't shatter.

"We also believe James Fitzroy was responsible for the murders of Justin Norris and Sophie Gallier. That he was the so-called... Taurus Strangler." The Lieutenant looked uncomfortable saying those words. "As for his motives, I will not speculate. I have nothing further to add at this time."

Lucy grabbed the remote control and pointed its infrared lens at Blake's face.

"I'll add something," she said to the television. "He didn't have a motive, because he's not our guy. While you're busy hanging those vultures a scapegoat, the real killer is getting away with murder."

She jabbed the standby button, and the picture flickered to black. The angry woman sat in near total darkness, illuminated only by a faint, pinky-neon glow from her apartment window.

"Time for the armchair detective to stop pitying herself. And to do some unofficial police work."

* * *

There was a loud, high-pitched beep. A computer monitor screen switched on, and a thin, green-lined grid faded into view. The squares were all empty except for a flat, slightly thicker, horizontal white line along the middle.

"Adrian."

Lucy's voice was clear over the speaker, if somewhat slurred.

"It's me. I think you might be in danger."

The white line vibrated in tandem with her speech, creating sinusoidal waves over the display. Every syllable generated a distinct spike in the pattern.

The computer operator, a shadow-shrouded figure wearing black leather gloves, pressed a function key. A message flashed in red under the grid: *President Office Phone - Recording #32.*

"Don't go home. I'm coming over to the Taurus building. Officially, I'm not on the case any longer, but we can talk. Just wait for me."

Lucy ended the call, and the white line flattened out. The unseen operator moved the computer mouse across a smooth, black glass table. Red laser light shone through finger gaps onto the sleeve of a leather coat.

The arrow pointer stopped over a floppy disk icon in the lower left corner. There was a faint click, and another flashy message appeared in place of the first: *Recording Saved.*

"We're about to finish for the night," someone said.

It was a female voice. Footsteps approached from

behind the figure.

"Unless you two want to get locked in."

Multiple strip lights turned on, illuminating the honeycombed desks in the Taurus project room.

The woman who'd just entered removed her hand from the switch. It was Jenna, dressed in her transmitter-tagged bodysuit and ninja hood.

"Anybody in here?"

The central screen picked up data from the motion capture suit. Like its wearer, the wireframe avatar walked slowly forward. The digital woman's head moved from side to side in perfect sync as Jenna checked the desks.

Crouched behind a workstation, the gloved figure reached up. They unplugged a cable from the desktop phone and coiled it into a repeated circle. Unseen by the approaching employee, the leather-clad intruder yanked the cable's other end and snapped it off the clear plastic connector.

Jenna stepped past the desk. She relaxed when she saw the person kneeling there.

"What are you doing here so late?" she asked, unaware of the cable stretched behind their back. "Here for my cooldown routine?"

The computer user moved the laser mouse, and used it to click on a right-pointed, triangular icon.

"Adrian," the recorded voice said. "It's Lucy."

Waves appeared on the green grid, in the same sequence as before. Jenna bent down to inspect the monitor and waited until the rest of the conversation had finished.

"That woman. Isn't that the cop who shot—"

She paused as a shadow moved across the keyboard: a tallish figure, closed fists far apart with something thin and curved between. Before the gymnast could scream, the strangler swiped the bent phone cable over her head and tightened the deadly noose.

The killer dragged Jenna back, muscular arms pulling the Lycra-suited woman below the desk. She could no longer be seen, but every kick, hand-swipe and gasp was transmitted on the giant monitor.

The wireframe model writhed about, an open-mouthed victim in the grip of an invisible strangler. She desperately clawed at her throat. The avatar thumped the space behind her, then resumed scratching her neck. Her struggle for survival against the unseen enemy continued for a full minute. Then the woman relaxed, her head tilted back.

Released from the assassin's hold, the digital model collapsed in a heap. Soft footsteps receded, strip lights went dark, and a door clicked shut.

The only source of illumination that remained was the connected green lines on the big screen. A 3D graphical replica that traced the still outline of a female body.

CHAPTER FOURTEEN

Attack at Taurus

Horizontal gray lines and static covered the monitor screen. The only discernible information was a caption displayed on the footer: *Project Room, 20:58*. The corresponding surveillance camera had been disabled, but Levitt wasn't paying the slightest bit of attention. His eyes were glued to his mobile phone, which streamed televised footage of a basketball game in progress.

The men in yellow jerseys went on the offensive. A seven-foot giant, his embroidered name illegible on the small screen, passed across the width of the court. The receiver out-jumped an opposing player in blue, caught the ball, and dribbled toward the basket. Roared on by the home crowd, he skillfully feinted and dodged by two defenders.

"Go on," Levitt urged him. "Take the shot. You can do this."

The phone volume was so high that macho grunts and bounces were audible over cheering spectators. Absorbed in his play-by-play commentary, the chief of security didn't see the strangler sprint across a four-way junction. The balaclava-masked, leather-clad figure was only on camera for half a second. Then the fleeting shadow was gone.

Twin headlights blinded the building approach monitor. A battered vehicle turned side-on and slowed to a stop. Its exhaust pumped out fumes. The driver — possibly Lucy, though the blonde's face was mostly obscured by window condensation — tapped the wheel, as if contemplating what to do.

"Damn it!" Levitt almost lost his grip on the phone. "Why didn't you shoot!?"

Murmurs of discontent rippled round the arena crowd. The guard reached for the security desk behind and took an iced doughnut from a plastic bag. That left him only one more to consume, but the bread crumbs scattered on his trousers suggested he'd already stuffed a few down his throat.

"Idiot! He laid it on a plate for you. All you had to do was dunk it in the basket. We don't pay you for fancy footwork. We pay you to score points."

Levitt wolfed down the doughnut. He tapped on his phone screen and scrolled down a page of overlaid statistics. Icing sugar had melted in his fingers, leaving sticky finger marks he struggled to wipe off.

Half-way through the list, the guard chief reached for the plastic bag again. It was no longer there. Loose breadcrumbs had been swept into a long, narrow pile, and a typed letter placed beside them. The company bull logo was visible in the top corner.

"What the hell?" Levitt coughed, still munching his unfinished doughnut.

He used his feet to push the swivel chair across to his desk. In the poor light, he had to squint to read the note.

All Taurus Studios employees are expected to present a good image of the company. We encourage healthy eating, particularly for security guards. You failed to meet these standards, Mister Levitt. Consider your employment terminated.

The shopping bag dropped over Levitt's head. Crumbs rained on his shirt. The guard tossed his phone and scrambled to get up. The Taurus Strangler — who'd snook up on him unnoticed — tightened a computer cable around his throat and yanked it taut to secure the bag in place.

A film of clear plastic stretched over the terrified guard's face. His chair wheeled about as he desperately tried to escape the killer's grip. Salivated dough spread across Levitt's mouth and cheek, flattened to a thin, mushy paste.

He clawed between his lips and attempted to rip the polythene, but only dirtied the bag with sugary finger marks. His suffocated groans were lost amid cheering from the basketball arena.

Levitt opened his upper desk drawer. A magnum revolver — a wild-west-style, high-caliber handgun lay inside — just beyond reach. Aware of the danger, the strangler pulled the computer cable and dragged both the man and the chair away. The victim's boot soles squeaked across the floor as he failed to get a foothold.

Tipped backward, the guard saw his attacker stare at him through the balaclava's eye slits. He thumped the killer's chest, his blows far too weak to do any harm. Convulsing at the mouth, Levitt sank into the seat cushion. Arms flopped on limp, crumb-strewn knees. The intruder kept a tight grip on the cable and turned to view the security monitors.

Lucy — it was clearly her now — exited the parked car and walked toward the office tower. The murderer breathed heavily as the entrance doors slid open. Slitted eyes followed the woman's progress on the screens.

The killer unwrapped the cord from Levitt's neck and slammed his head on the desk. The polythene bag was still tight around the dead man's face, stuck to his cheek by soggy doughnut residue.

* * *

Lucy walked past the unstaffed reception desk and continued toward the elevator tubes. Her footstep clacks echoed round the empty hall. The pyramid-framed lights underneath the balcony lit up hung *Crimson Shadow* posters, but all the television screens were dark. Surveillance cameras fitted with sensor dishes tracked the visitor's position, turning silently on support axles.

"Anybody here?" she called out, but received only a time-lagged echo in reply.

Lucy pressed a darkened elevator call button. When nothing happened, she pushed again and held it in. The shaft doors remained closed, and the disc-shaped platforms were stationary on upper levels.

She gave the glass tube a frustrated fist-pound, then turned her attention elsewhere. Almost immediately, she noticed a slightly ajar opening with a thin sliver of light down the middle.

Lucy groaned and held her head. After she recovered from a dizzy spell, she shoved the door open. The corridor beyond was a square-shaped tunnel. Regular spaced wall lights gave the black marble a gray striped texture. All the office keycard readers had red padlock indicators, and nobody was around at this late hour.

Lucy stopped to rub her forehead again, righted herself, and pressed on. Whenever she stepped through a well-lit segment of the passage, disheveled clothes were revealed.

Her shirt collar was undone, pants creased, and shoe caps dirty. An empty gun holster stuck out from under an unbuttoned suit.

The visitor came to a T-junction. Interest piqued by loud cheering from her left, she staggered in that direction. The noise increased in volume as she approached a signposted door. She rubbed her fluttery eyes and focused on the silver-on-black typeface. *Security Room.*

The half-drunken Lucy lurched through the threshold in a trance-like state. She took no precautions as she entered. On the wall opposite, the bank of monitor screens showed empty Taurus offices. The project area camera was still faulty, displaying only flickery lines and static.

Seeing the garbled footage jerked the suspended cop into alertness, but she didn't notice the masked intruder enter behind her.

The Taurus Strangler snook closer. Security images were projected across the killer's balaclava. Their exposed irises reflected reversed surveillance videos. Those were replaced by solid, unbroken black as the stalker moved into Lucy's shadow.

She saw Levitt's tensionless legs on the floor, but the chair backrest concealed the rest of him. The upturned cellphone at his feet transmitted the closing minutes of the basketball game.

Lucy stepped further into the room. She recoiled when she discovered the security chief's body. Smeared sugar had solidified over the polythene bag. White streaks partially obscured Levitt's compressed face and dough-clogged mouth.

She staggered back, her eyes now wide open. She went for her gun and muttered a quiet curse when she realized the holster was empty. The killer moved behind her and raised a stretched computer cable. The strangler's lips were stationary against the mouthpiece veil. There was no noise, not even the slightest breath, to alert Lucy to the impending danger.

She stepped back from Levitt's body, head passing under the wire. In the static-filled monitor screen, she saw a fuzzy reflection of herself and the masked, shadowy figure about to garrotte her.

Lucy instinctively raised her hand, reacting just in time to block the inrushing cable. The plastic strip tightened across her palm and slid down the inside of her wrist.

"Shit!"

The expletive was barely audible over the roaring basketball crowd. The killer applied more pressure and dragged her away from the desk. She dug her heels in defiantly, doing much better than Levitt, but it was a losing proposition. Despite failing to noose Lucy's neck as intended, the strangler had her trapped.

Lucy stamped on the masked assailant's foot and rotated her hips into a twist. Her spirited fightback took the killer by surprise. They careered into the swivel chair. It wheeled aside, and momentum carried the struggling duo into the security desk. Levitt's unbalanced, top-heavy corpse dropped on the floor behind them.

Shrieks from the basketball crowd went up an octave as Lucy spied the revolver in the drawer. She reached for it. The strangler tried to pull her away, but tripped over the dead guard's outstretched leg. The would-be victim took advantage of the stumble and grabbed the weapon.

Lucy aimed blindly over her shoulder. The killer ducked and yanked the computer cable to jerk her off balance. Wrong-handed and slipping, the opening shot went well wide of her target. A screen shattered, and the image blacked out, leaving a smoking hole in the glass. Sparks flew from damaged, shorted-out circuitry.

Lucy checked the revolver's chamber. Five of the six partially exposed slots were empty, and a single bullet left. She pressed the gun's barrel into the stretched computer cable and pulled the trigger.

Her shot severed the wire in two. Free from restraint, she dived forward, rolled over onto her back, and aimed the revolver up at the Taurus Strangler's chest. Out of ammunition, she could only bluff.

"Take the mask off, Adrian! I know it's you. You were the only one who knew I'd be here tonight. I want to see your head before I blow it off."

Lucy's calm, unflinching aim and ice-cold gaze revealed nothing. There were no telltale panic signs to suggest her gun was empty.

The killer, apparently buying the ruse, retreated to the desk. They reached up and started to pull off the balaclava.

The neck of the mask had barely lifted from the leather coat when the strangler kicked the swivel chair into Lucy to block her aim. While she was stunned, the attacker sprinted from the room. Soft footsteps receded to the right.

Lucy let out a relieved sigh. Keeping the revolver aimed at the door, she stood up, removed three spare bullets from the drawer, and reloaded the weapon. The firing chamber snapped into position.

She took the phone in her free hand, shut off the Internet broadcast, and used the numeric keypad to dial a local number. An automated directory matched it to a name. *Philadelphia PD - Homicide*. There was a basic dialing tone, and then three complete rings, before someone picked up.

"This is Duvall," Lucy said. "Who am I speaking to?"

"Ron Wallace. Career advisor."

"Quit joking around, you moron. And get your ass over to Taurus Studios."

Liquid splashed in the background. Porcelain rattled.

"You went back there!?" Ron said. "To see Pryce. On your own. Unarmed. What part of our conversation did you actually listen to?"

"The security guy's dead, and the killer's still here. I got myself a gun."

"Sit tight. I'm on my way. Where in the building are you, exactly?"

Lucy scanned the monitors. She located the Taurus Strangler in the server room. Left arm off-screen, back to the camera. The killer ripped cables from a hard drive, then sabotaged another.

"I'll be in the basement. Bastard just tried to kill me. Now he's destroying evidence. I'm going after him."

"Don't be stupid, Duvall! Wait for backup to—"

Lucy switched off Levitt's cellphone and threw it on the desk. Revolver in hand, she edged forward, and turned the gun in a wide, sweeping arc as she stepped into the corridor.

* * *

The light bulbs in the server room had all been shattered, cracked tube sections left in live sockets. Sparks fell off disconnected ends. Between those, the blue text on the computer screens, and blinking indicators, there was just enough illumination to see the data banks. Removed hard drives cluttered the aisles between, dumped in a sea of glass fragments that sparkled like diamonds. The temperature had risen to twenty-three degrees Celsius and a red triangle symbol flashed.

The airlock door slid open. Lit from behind, Lucy was a

faceless shadow aiming a silvery magnum revolver. The gun followed her observant eyes as she scanned the room from outside. There was no sign of anybody else. Only flashes of light, fizzing electricity, and the occasional beep from a computer terminal. Darkness clouded much of the scene, which left plenty of potential hiding places for a killer.

Lucy advanced through the airlock and turned continuously. Glass shards cracked under her shoes. Smoldering sparks landed on her shoulders as she neared the central console. She ignored the distractions and continued her search.

The detective spied a glimpse of movement and spun sharply to her left. At first, she saw nothing but sabotaged computer equipment. Then creaky metal alerted her to a black-clothed figure perched on a storage bank.

A thrown hard drive knocked the revolver away. The Taurus Strangler jumped down. Two thrust feet struck Lucy in the chest. She fell on her back with a thump. Broken glass scattered from her.

The floored victim had no opportunity to recover before the killer wrapped a replacement garotte around her throat. Like the cables that powered the few still-active hard drives, the plastic cord was half an inch thick.

Trapped under the assailant with her neck pinned down in a noose, Lucy's efforts to escape were hopeless. A shower of sparks rained from above, adding a yellowy glow to the strangler's balaclava. The eyeballs — isolated ovals in an otherwise black void — shone with psychotic intensity.

Lucy gurgled and feebly groped at the mask. Her fingers slipped into the veil and sunk into a narrow gap between the killer's parted lips. The strangler pulled her head closer, sucked in deep, and exhaled on her face. Strands of blonde hair, trapped under the tension-creaky cable, lifted off her neck.

"Lucy!" Ron called out. His voice was quiet, still a good distance away.

She tried to reply, but no words came out. Her hands relaxed as she succumbed to unconsciousness. Her body dropped on the fragmented glass. The sparks stopped falling, and darkness obscured the strangler in mid-assault.

CHAPTER FIFTEEN

The Aftermath

The police arrived at Taurus Studios in force. Ron spearheaded the charge through the tower lobby. The team moved quickly but carefully to the open double doors. The detective kept his gun steady, aiming forward while three uniformed cops — two short-haired, brutish-looking men and a lean Hispanic woman — provided backup.

As they checked the floor for hostiles, the quartet stayed close together, almost shoulder to shoulder, with all directions covered.

"Lucy! Lucy!"

Ron repeated the frantic call every thirty feet, undeterred by the lack of reply. When the police reached the corridor, he signaled the woman officer to take point. He protected her from the front while the uniformed men watched the rear.

It looked as if he'd memorized the route. He navigated the maze of corridors without stopping and reorganized the assault formation at junctions so nobody could approach unseen.

The team soon arrived at the security office. The patrolmen remained in the corridor while the other cops checked inside. They came out ten seconds later, gloomy-faced with the woman suppressing a gulp.

"Server room's that way." Ron pointed at a left turn ahead. "The killer could still be in the building. Keep your guard up."

The others followed his lead. The close-knit group proceeded down a flight of steps and through the basement corridors to a darkened airlock.

Sensors flashed green as they approached, and the pressurized door slid open. Ron peeked around the corner, but observed only black shapes, sparkly glass, and a faint gaseous wisp that could be smoke.

He nodded to the Hispanic woman, who took out a pen-size flashlight and held it under the barrel of her pistol. The cops all moved at once. As the men breached the threshold, the female followed to provide light and potential cover fire. They all stayed close to the server room walls, negating any threats from behind.

The focused beam swept from left to right, and then back again, illuminating discarded hard drives. The searchlight stopped, directed downward at the floor. And a familiar blonde woman.

"Lucy. God, no."

The circle of light shifted violently across her still body. Ron placed a steadying hand on the Hispanic cop's wrist. He signaled the two men to keep watch over the entrance. Then he dashed over to Lucy and checked her pulse.

"She's alive. Call an ambulance!"

He pulled the loose power cable off her neck, revealing a red mark where she'd been choked.

"You're one lucky bitch."

A cough came from somewhere opposite the airlock, whiny and suppressed. Ron took the flashlight from the female cop, held it alongside his weapon, and used the beam to search the room.

Something glinted in a storage locker, distorted by a narrow-barred grille. The numerical keypad symbol was a green opened padlock, unlike the others, and the door was a quarter-inch ajar.

Ron placed a finger to his lips and handed the flashlight back to the Hispanic. He approached from the compartment's left side while the three beat cops covered the front and right.

The lead cop held his breath, steadied himself, and tugged the handle. He kneeled down as the locker opened, prepared to squeeze the trigger.

"Don't shoot!" the woman inside yelled.

Ron exhaled when the light shone on Tania's face. Perspiration dripped from her hair onto her already-damp shirt, and her dislodged spectacles were about to come off. One legging was rolled up to her knee, the other stuck in her shoe. She looked as if she'd hidden there for a while.

"Don't shoot."

"It's all right." Ron holstered his weapon. "You're safe."

He approached the girl and extended a hand. She took it, giving the detective a gentle hug once she left the cramped confines of the locker.

"I heard a gunshot from upstairs," she said, "so I hid in there. I saw somebody come in, a man in black. He's gone now, but..." She stumbled back and stared at the prostate Lucy. "Your partner. She's not..."

Tania hesitated to finish her sentence. Lucy coughed as she came around. Her eyes slowly opened.

"No," Ron said. "But she damn well ought to be. You did

the right thing. Some people aren't so sensible."

He beckoned the Hispanic woman across. She helped reposition Tania's glasses and comforted her while he joined Lucy.

"Did Pryce invite you over? Or was this your shitty idea?"

"Adrian wasn't here," Lucy said, voice quiet with exhaustion.

"You sure about that?"

Ron walked away and shook his head in disgust. He stepped over a damaged hard drive.

"What was stored on these?" he asked Tania.

"Archive footage." She winced as she stood up. "All the cameras transmit data here, as well as the security control room. We keep digital copies of all surveillance."

"Which someone didn't want us to see. Do these cameras cover every area of the building?" Ron glanced over at the recovering Lucy. "Even the president's office?"

Tania seemed reluctant to answer the question at first. After a lengthy pause, she gave the slightest of nods.

"Pity. Bet there'd have been some interesting stuff to watch." He turned to the policewoman. "Take the girl somewhere cozy. A safe place out of the way. You get me?"

"I understand."

The Hispanic officer escorted the unsteady Tania to the airlock. Glass cracked as the two women made their way past the wreckage. No sooner had the door closed than a radio crackled into life.

"Go ahead," the man nearest Ron said.

"We found another one."

The woman on the police frequency spoke with morbid flatness.

"Another body. She's been strangled too. Jenna McCoy, a

video capture artist who worked on the projects team. I know her name because... Because I talked to her yesterday afternoon, when I took her statement. She was looking forward to spending Christmas with her family." Anger crept into her voice. "And he left her like this. That sick bastard."

Ron snatched the radio from the policeman. "All units," he said grimly. "Complete your sweep of the building. Take extreme care. This is a double homicide. There could be a killer lurking around, so watch it."

He gave the receiver back and returned to Lucy, hands squarely on his hips.

"Two of Pryce's female employees are dead. Seems dangerous to get close to him. If we'd shown up a few minutes later, you'd be joining the other lovers in the morgue. You seeing a pattern yet?"

"The gymnastics lady wasn't his lover. She just worked for him."

"Right. Like Miss Gallier used to," Ron said. "Seems being his girlfriend isn't healthy. Unless you're into being choked."

He removed a surgical glove from his trouser pocket and slipped it on. He reached down to collect the computer cable.

"I'll take that. It's important evidence in a murder case. Not to be handled by civilians."

Ron kneeled by her side and pretended to check her neck. He spoke quietly so the others wouldn't overhear.

"We got an anonymous tip from a passer-by who saw a suspicious character outside the Taurus tower. Wearing a mask, dressed in black. We came to investigate. That's when we heard gunshots and radioed for backup. You were never here."

"Thanks," Lucy said. "Look Ron, I..."

He sniffed at Lucy. "And stay off the booze. So you know, this is a one-time deal. Fall off the rails again, and there won't be anybody to catch you. You'd best disappear before Blake shows up. He's not going to be happy when he finds out Fitzroy wasn't the strangler."

Lucy stood up to leave.

"Duvall," Ron shouted to get her attention. "I know you'll ignore every damn word I just said. So when you see Pryce, be sure to ask why he left the office early tonight. I'm be interested in what business he had that was so pressing."

He coiled up the computer cable and dropped it into a sealable plastic bag.

"You might want to hide any wires before you go to bed with him. Thought I'd share a useful tip with my old partner. You know, while she's still breathing."

* * *

The elevated highway connecting central Philadelphia to the suburbs was quiet. An occasional car sped by along the repetitive, six-lane stretch of basalt, mileage signs, and glaring street lights. Music pounded from a seedy, brown-bricked bar in the slums.

None of the vehicles took the exit that led to the urban labyrinth. Graffiti-smeared tenements, gravelly basketball courts, and poorly lit alleys formed an underclass neighborhood. The district around the concrete pillars was a rough, unwelcoming wilderness most commuters steered well clear of.

Lucy had pulled over into a lay-by, close to a gang-tagged emergency phone booth. The car engine was running, and exhaust fumes dissipated into the night air.

She took a long, blank look at herself in the rear-view

mirror. The strangulation bruises around her neck, shadowed by her chin, had turned deep purple. She was a total wreck. Sweating profusely, her blonde hair was all tangled up, and her vacant eyes were those of a sleepwalker.

Lucy lowered the driver's side window and leaned back as a gusty breeze dried perspiration from her face. She took out a half-full bottle of scotch from the glove compartment.

The thick, brown liquid swirled round the glass. As she shook the container, miniature waves crashed and ripples died out. Lucy unscrewed the tin cap — a precise, almost mechanical rhythm — and held the rim to her lips. Liquor filled the neck as she tipped it back.

She was about to drink when she stopped to glance at the passenger seat. Her photo album rested on top, open at the page with the university pictures of her and Adrian Pryce.

The breeze picked up strength, whistling as it blew Lucy's hair over the bottle. Caught in the wind, laminated paper sheets flipped across the album's binder rings. Snapshots of her life flashed before her. Her later years as a maturing student, her induction into the police force, the promotion to detective. Then blank emptiness.

"Get a grip, Duvall," she said.

Lucy lowered the bottle and let the scotch collect at the bottom. After a moment to compose herself, and another glance in the mirror, she stuck her hand through the open window. The discarded container smashed on impact. Fluid settled in its jagged, broken-off end.

Lucy reversed out of the lay-by into oncoming traffic, ignoring horns and screechy tires. A speeding minivan veered into the next lane. Its furious driver waved a clenched fist at the reckless cop.

With steely, unflinching determination, she stopped her

car, shifted gears, and drove forward over the broken bottle. Badly damaged by the front tire, it was pulverized under the rear, shards ground to glassy dust on the tarmac. Runny scotch trickled into a drainage gutter.

* * *

Doctor Vickers took a photo of Jenna's body from underneath. She had little choice regarding the angle. The corpse was suspended in mid-air, harness cables arranged so her death pose was decidedly erotic.

The gymnast's legs, tied around the ankles, had been spread wide, kept apart by suction-padded winches. Her form arched back, with her waist and neck secured in tight steel nooses. Jenna's upside-down head and breasts faced the entrance. Stripped half-naked, she hung in her underclothes: elasticated gym shorts and a rosy-pink bra. Her Lycra motion capture suit was nowhere to be seen.

Ron walked past a visibly shaken policewoman and joined Vickers by the giant screen. Footage of the murder ran in a continuous loop, acted out by the 3D wireframe avatar. The hopeless struggle with the invisible killer, both hands scratching her neck, and dropping to the ground dead. A message underneath the video pulsed green with an outer-glow effect.

Your contract was only temporary, Jenna. With the project nearing completion, we have no further need for a model or motion capture artist. The sensor suit is the property of Taurus Studios, and will be retained for later use. Consider your employment terminated.

"No written letter?" Ron said. "Was this guy in a rush or something?"

Vickers stepped on a computer desk to snap another photo. She was all businesslike, with no trace of a smile.

"Duvall didn't get a note at all. Perhaps those two only got in the killer's way, and the security guard was the intended victim."

"Thought you dealt in facts."

"I usually do. But I don't think we're going to find any here to help us. For an improvised crime scene, if that's what we're dealing with, it's remarkably clean."

Ron watched another replay of the murder. It looped back to the beginning, with the avatar looking anxiously around. The animation showed Jenna's last movements as she hunched over the unseen computer.

"If you inspect this part, you can see the girl turn away right before the killer attacked. She didn't flee. She was at ease. Which means she knew her assailant, and he wasn't wearing a mask. That would explain why he stuck around to wipe the surveillance videos. What if there was something else on those recordings? Footage that incriminated Pryce."

"You're basing a lot on computer graphics. That's what I don't like about modern technology. It's too easy to manipulate. DNA and fingerprints I can work with, not some jazzy drawing on a screen. Sorry, but there's nothing here that directly links anyone specific to the crime."

"This is his damn building, isn't it?" Ron gave himself a moment to cool off. "Look, I'm just worried about Lucy. She's convinced herself he's innocent."

"Maybe he is," Vickers said. "We don't have any proof. For all we know, this whole sequence is a fabrication."

Ron looked up at Jenna's body and eyed the harness cable fastened around her neck.

"What if Pryce is the strangler? And he's planning to finish what he started?"

"If he and Lucy are as involved as you say they are,

you'd better find some actual evidence quickly. Before she becomes the evidence."

CHAPTER SIXTEEN

Watchful Eye

Lucy parked across the street from Adrian's luxury abode and observed the front gates from a distance. Since her previous visit, residents had draped glittery silver tinsel from their porch coverings and mailboxes, and hung shiny baubles on tree branches.

The president's house was the only one without festive decorations. Curtains were drawn over every window. Glowing red bulbs in the bull statue's eye sockets gave it the appearance of some mythical, horned beast guarding the garden path. With the taller-than-average picket fence and blanket camera coverage, the estate was virtually a fortress.

Lucy stepped out of her car and hastened toward the gate. She seemed to have shaken off her hangover. There were no wobbles or head-rubs along the way, and no sleepy eyed stumbles. She had the expression of a soldier deep in enemy territory, constantly on the lookout for unexpected trouble.

She approached the barred entrance, stared directly into the camera above, and gave the electric buzzer a firm press. It beeped in acknowledgement, then fell silent. After five seconds, Lucy tried the doorbell again. And then a third time.

"Are you alone?" Adrian asked through the intercom.

"You've got enough eyes out here, haven't you? See for yourself."

The security camera rotated to the extreme right — past her — then the other way.

"Worried I brought the cops with me? Is there some reason I should have?"

"Thought you might be with that reporter. Kristina Malloy. She's been leaving messages on my phone all evening. She wants my perspective on Fitzroy. Why I hired him to work at Taurus, whether we did a background check. Don't know what I'm supposed to say. It's not like I knew the psycho personally."

"It's her job to ask tough questions. I wouldn't worry about it." Lucy spoke with soft-voiced innocence and presented a disarming smile to the camera. "I came alone, Adrian. Are you going to let me in?"

There was a loud buzz, and the electronic lock disengaged. She stepped through the gates as soon as the gap had widened enough and walked past the statue to the gloomy front porch. She was already at the entrance when he unfastened the catch.

Adrian wore his work clothes, minus the suit, with his silk tie hung loose around the unbuttoned collar. Lucy shoved by him without asking for permission.

"Come right in." He waited for the gate to fully close before he shut the door. "I don't mind at all."

He followed Lucy into the living area. Television and computers were switched off, and so were most of the lights. She circled around the futon and touched the squashed down cushions.

"So this is where you were, sweating away in the dark. Why weren't you at the office? Something been bothering you?"

"What? Like having a gun pointed at me?" Adrian said. "That might be a normal day for you, but for me, that was intense stuff. I thought I'd take a break. Work from home."

He opened a cabinet — black glass with a chrome handle, matching the other furniture — and took out two long-stemmed glasses. The crystal decanter was an exact copy of the one in the Taurus president's office, except with red wine in place of water.

"Not for me," Lucy said. "I've quit. But if it makes you feel better about things, have a drink."

She leaned against a wall. From there, she had a full view of the living room.

"It's not like you to leave someone else in charge. You've always had a more... hands-on approach."

Adrian stopped pouring, with only a tiny amount of wine in his glass. He put down the decanter and turned around slowly.

"What's going on?" he asked. "Something's happened."

"What makes you say that?"

"Stop playing games, Lucy. You storm into my house. Give me all these suspicious looks. Ask where I've been tonight. Make cryptic comments about my hands. Whatever you've found—"

"Gordon Levitt's dead." She did nothing to soften the news. "So is Jenna."

"What!?"

Adrian staggered back into the cabinet. He looked as rattled as the glasses and decanter. Lucy stepped past the futon and positioned herself between him and the exit.

"They were both strangled," she said. "Tonight. In your building. Someone tried to kill me, too. Only he screwed up."

Adrian gripped the cupboard to steady himself. "But I thought Fitzroy…"

"He didn't do it. But we know the killer works for Taurus." Lucy's eyes bored into him. "Or still does."

"You don't think…" He gasped without finishing the question. "You're wrong."

"I'd like to believe you." A quick blink, then her penetrating gaze returned. "But with all the deaths at your company, we're running out of suspects. Do you have an alibi?"

Her host was rendered speechless. The cabinet wobbled as he pressed harder.

"Can I take that as a no?"

"If it makes you feel safer, then arrest me. How did that work out the last time? I thought we'd made a connection. Obviously I was wrong."

"Where were you, Adrian?"

His steely resistance seemed to collapse under her scrutiny.

"Right here," he said weakly. "I've got cameras all over my house, but you'll just say they prove nothing. Because I could have altered the timestamps. I realize this looks bad, but I didn't kill Jenna. Or Sophie. Or the others. All I'm asking for is a little faith."

"Don't know if you saw the news, but I've been taken off the case. After I saved you from Fitzroy, I got suspended. Faith's in short supply right now. I'm uncertain whether the man standing in front of me has genuine feelings, or if he's playing a twisted game with me. So until the investigation is over, we should—"

"Wait a minute," interrupted Adrian. He paced about in

thought, hand on his chin. "You say the killer attacked you?"

"He took me by surprise, but don't worry. It won't happen again."

"But there was a struggle?"

Adrian kept his mouth open when he'd finished, as if he wanted her to elaborate.

"I got in a few blows here and there. Took a shot at him with a magnum. Unfortunately, I ran out of bullets."

Adrian ripped off his tie and discarded it on the cabinet. Lucy, looking somewhat perplexed, remained still as he unbuttoned his shirt. He pulled his left arm through the sleeve and gave it a sharp, powerful tug to force his hand past the cuff.

"I want to show you something," he said, breathing quicker.

Lucy watched Adrian go through the same routine with his right arm. With nothing to bear its weight, the sweaty shirt slipped off Adrian's hairless, smoothly toned back, and floated down to land behind his feet.

When viewed in dim light, his naked chest had a bronze-brown, waxy texture. Moisture had collected around his firm nipples and shallow belly button. He was a perfectly healthy man, with no sign of scarring.

"Seen it all before. There's no point in looking for bullet holes. Like I said, I missed."

"But you hit this guy. Can you see any bruises?"

Adrian turned round and bent forward so the light spread to his curved back. He placed his hands on the cabinet shelf corners and lowered his waist so Lucy had a full, unrestricted view. There wasn't a single mark on him.

Lucy's glare softened a little. "No, but I need more evidence. Take off the rest of your clothes."

"It's been a while since you asked me to do that."

Adrian was smiling when he turned to face her, but she remained deadly serious. She stepped away to put a few feet between them.

Her former lover followed her instructions, beginning with the laced black shoes. He unfastened his leather belt, dropped his pants, and shook them off. His genitals bulged under his golden-yellow briefs.

Lucy back heeled the trousers behind her and stamped down firmly on the belt.

"Don't get too excited. Just taking precautions. That's a potential murder weapon in the wrong hands. Your right leg. Lift it up."

Adrian looked bemused, but did as she requested. She grabbed his ankle and felt the ridge of his foot. First soft prods, then probing flicks with her index finger, and finally fierce backhand slaps.

Lucy gauged Adrian's reaction the whole time. She squeezed his toes for a few seconds when she'd completed her tests. There were no squirms. No sudden reactions. Nothing at all to suggest she caused him discomfort or triggered any pain.

Lucy released her grip. Though still wary, she appeared satisfied. Adrian exhaled sharply and rubbed his swollen skin.

"Don't tell me you kicked this guy in the balls, too."

He cringed as he gave his privates a nervy grope.

"You can put your clothes back on now." Lucy stepped off the belt. "I've seen everything that I need to."

Adrian collected his trousers. "But not everything you'd like to?" He pulled the pants above his briefs. "You know, there's still enough wine left for both of us."

"I should stay alert. I'm not drinking while there's a killer out there."

"Just when I thought I'd softened you up, out comes the ice maiden."

"Two people died tonight," Lucy reminded him. "So forget the flirting. This isn't one of your damn games, where you can press a button and they magically spring back to life. Jenna and Levitt are *dead*. That makes it four this bastard's killed. It could have been five. Because I let my emotions get the better of me. So forgive me for keeping this strictly professional."

Adrian left his shirt off and edged closer to Lucy.

"I wouldn't call it *strictly* professional. A visit in the early morning hours to give a suspect a strip search. Officially, this isn't any of your business. Now that you're suspended."

"Oh, I've got a personal interest in the strangler case. It started when he tried to kill me. And you seem awfully cool about his latest victims."

"This is just my way of coping." He looked down guiltily. "I've been thinking about it all evening. And that was before you told me Fitzroy wasn't the killer. When that reporter finds out about Gordon and Jenna… I should get some rest. I'll walk you to your car."

Adrian headed to the door. When he realized Lucy hadn't followed, he turned to see her leaning against the futon backrest.

"Somebody should watch the house," she said. "Since we're both targets, it makes sense for us to stay close until this is over."

"Then I should show you the security room."

He escorted Lucy out into the hallway and directed her to the left. "So we're clear about the situation… you're staying overnight at my place for professional reasons."

"For professional reasons," she confirmed, though it

didn't sound wholly convincing.

Adrian smiled in response. He took her past a framed *Crimson Shadow* poster, opened a black glass, chrome-handled door, and extended a flat palm to show his guest inside.

"Just like at Taurus," she said.

Except for the smaller scale — approximately four to one — and more limited camera coverage, Adrian's home setup was a carbon copy of Gordon Levitt's.

A wall of monitors displayed live feeds from various interior rooms, the front garden, swimming pool, and cul-de-sac. The desk and swivel chair were identical to those in the Taurus security office. The only notable differences were the missing guard and weapon. When Lucy checked the drawers, they were all empty.

"A facsimile right down to the furniture. Is this an empire building thing?"

"When I find something works well enough..." Adrian remained near the door and looked at Lucy affectionately. "I prefer to hang onto the idea. I learned that from a mistake I made a long time ago."

She ignored the thinly veiled compliment and watched the streamed images. "You like to keep duplicates. Are there are any backups of the server room drives? The killer wiped the security footage."

"I asked Tania to do some analysis. Based on her findings, I concluded it would be too expensive and impractical to store multiple copies."

Adrian noticed a disdainful glance from Lucy. Then his anger flared once more.

"How was I supposed to know someone would sabotage my company from within? Go on a killing spree? Whoever the strangler is, he knows everything about me. The night he killed Sophie, he deactivated the security system at my house. Now he's done the same thing at Taurus. This guy knows I don't keep backups. Any evidence that was on those hard drives is gone for good."

* * *

Tania slid her Taurus Studios ID through a reader just inside the server room door. Unseen locks clunked within the frame. Pressurized air hissed as vacuum seals expanded at the top and bottom. An indicator light changed color from green to red. There was a prolonged beep, and text replaced the temperature readout. *Environment Secure.*

The technician made her way past the damaged hard drives and stepped over a snaking power cord. Smashed glass fragments had been swept into tidy piles, and the strip lights refitted. Despite repair work, electronic systems were barely functional. Wires criss-crossed all over the place, clipped to exposed circuit boards.

Tania checked an orange-red cable that connected a mostly intact data bank to the central console. With a nod of approval, she ducked through a kennel sized between two power lines and moved around the controls to the only active terminal.

"All right," she said. "Time to open a back door."

Faced with a flashing prompt, she touch-typed a series of complex commands. Abbreviated instructions, followed by alphanumeric filenames and separating slashes.

Tania's eyes alternated between the monitor and the sealed entrance. Even when the programmer wasn't looking at the screen, she rattled off keystrokes without making a single error. When she finished, she pressed the enter key with a self-satisfied smile.

Icons appeared: floppy disks for executable files, paper sheets for documents, and folders to designate directories. Tania moved the mouse pointer over a symbol labeled *SECURITY SYSTEM BACKUP,* double clicked to open it, and selected a CCTV camera numbered *320.*

"What have you been hiding, Mister Pryce?"

A captioned window opened on the screen and played surveillance footage of the president's private office.

The camera was above the door, with a forty-five degree, front-down angle of Adrian's desk. A slight greenish tint suggested the images had been recorded at night, and a low-light filter applied.

"Who are you shouting at?"

Adrian paced around the room and yelled at a mobile phone. He stormed off to the left, then back into view. With no audio, the context was a mystery. After a lengthy monologue, the president threw the cellphone on his desk.

Tania paused the high-definition video and used a zoom-in function to center on the phone's screen. Before it went dark, a person's name was clearly visible under a thumb-sized Taurus Studios logo. *Miles Dawson.*

CHAPTER SEVENTEEN

Games Versus Reality

Lucy snored, shirt sleeve fluttering under her nose. Her squashed cheek nested in the crook of her armpit, offering some cushioning from the hard-surfaced desk in Adrian's security suite. Her discarded shoes lay under her stretched out legs. The plastic heels jammed beneath the wheels acted as wedges and prevented the swivel chair from rolling back. Her buttocks were literally on the edge of the seat.

The monitor bank emitted a series of chimes, a classic burglar alarm sound effect. Lucy stirred, still half asleep, as she scratched her chin. Then she sat upright and almost fell off her chair.

Grabbing the desk for support, she lifted herself back onto the cushion. Her eyes were wide open now and focused on the screens.

Red text flashed over the image of the swimming pool: *Motion Detected.* The same message was on another monitor that showed the side path. A ground-floor window was ajar. Chipped wood and splintered paintwork suggested the intruder had forced the frame.

Sunlit patches brightened the surrounding bricks. Lucy checked the time on the screen caption: 07:52.

"Shit."

She sprang to her feet and opened her mouth, about to yell. She stopped when she saw the frenzy of activity out front. News vans — identifiable from painted network logos, roof-mounted satellite dishes, and antennae — were parked outside the gates. Reporters in winter coats stood beyond the fence, backs to the security camera as they talked into cordless microphones.

Lucy scanned the other monitors. Adrian was sound asleep in bed, and her anxious face reflected over the dark backdrop, but there was no sign of any intruder. She checked the kitchen monitor. A rack of sharp, gleaming knives was on the black, L-shaped counter, with all utensils present. She glanced down at her shoes, but opted to leave them behind.

"All right, you bastard. I'm ready this time."

Lucy stepped into the hall. Her nylon stockings insulated her footsteps. The burglar alarm dropped in volume as she slid the security room door closed. Careful to breathe quietly and tread on her tiptoes, she began her search for the intruder.

* * *

A flashlight beam moved across an obsidian, altar-like computer desk. The simplistic, solid glass cuboid had eight chrome-handled drawers, four at either end, and a carved-out recess for extra legroom, but was otherwise featureless. Loose paper, sketches, and spreadsheet printouts were scattered around the luxurious, leather-cushioned office chair. Beneath the strewn litter, the wooden floor was a black sheet that seemed to absorb any stray light.

The intruder — a hunched, cloaked figure wearing dark clothes and surgical gloves — rifled through the upper left drawer. More papers piled on those already dumped. So did plastic document wallets, a sticky-note pad, and miscellaneous stationery.

Wind whistled through the open window, followed by a wooden clack as the damaged frame swung shut. Once the disturbed items had settled, the burglar gently closed the drawer and moved onto the next.

"Freeze!" Lucy yelled.

Light shone from the hallway, giving the knife she carried a silvery glint. Its serrated blade looked sharp enough to cut through bone. She held it edge-on, angled across her chest. Her stance was menacing, her knees slightly bent. If provoked, she was ready to strike a deadly blow.

The intruder didn't move a muscle as Lucy flipped the light switch. A row of wall lamps, milky-white pyramids in chrome settings, illuminated Adrian's study. Momentarily blinded, the detective saw a crouched silhouette point a handgun.

She blinked as her eyesight adjusted. Then a mustached man behind the desk stood up.

"Knife to a gunfight," Ron said. "Not the most advisable approach. Is there some reason you don't have a weapon? Oh yeah. That's right. You're suspended. This isn't your case any longer."

Lucy slid the hallway door closed. "What the hell are you doing?" she hissed.

"Just making sure you didn't mistake me for a psycho." He quickly lost his smile. "Ah, you meant *here*. In the prime suspect's house. I was checking computer cables. Thought

Pryce might be missing a couple. So, did you get a semen sample from him yet?"

"You're out of your mind. If Blake finds out you came here..."

"Listen to the angel preach. You should take a look around your boyfriend's private office. He's got some interesting stuff."

Lucy lowered the knife and took in the spacious study. Almost everything was made of silvery chrome, dark glass, or both. The modern furniture included storage cabinets, backless stools riveted before a sturdy design table, and simplistic pedestals.

She strolled around the exhibits on display. Adrian's collection was a mix of memorabilia and merchandise that traced the history of Taurus Studios. The journey through time began with early logo concepts — red hornless bulls — and ended with contemporary *Crimson Shadow* toy figures.

"This place is like a museum. The story of his company."

She looked admiringly at a fifty-inch television screen embedded within the wall. It switched on automatically as she approached.

A muted, late-night action movie reached its dramatic climax. An African-American woman in a scruffy brown jacket — a fictional detective with a short ponytail and Los Angeles PD lanyard — stormed through a decrepit warehouse. She took out a small army of street punks with a laser-sighted colt pistol. The cop never missed a shot and emerged from the one-sided gun battle without a scratch.

"The modern action heroine," Ron scoffed. "Load of bullshit, if you ask me. Nobody could be so reckless or dumb in real life. When I said interesting..." He waited for Lucy to turn around. "I meant Pryce's private collection. That he keeps hidden away. Pretty gruesome stuff."

He placed a wad of papers on the desk and spread them out in a row. Lucy seemed unnerved as she viewed the pastel-drawn sketches.

Crudely shaded figures battled each other on plain white backgrounds. The recurring character was an early version of *Crimson Shadow*: a ninja in garish red, sashed martial-arts robes with blocky hands and penned curves for breasts. Fighting alone, the warrior woman was depicted as highly skilled and ruthlessly proficient. She slaughtered a horde of low-detailed, masked men with her katana and shurikens.

The last image was of someone entirely different: a black-garbed male ninja holding a stretched piano wire.

"Look like anyone we know?" Ron asked.

"It's just a picture. Make believe. He probably did it years ago."

He pulled the strangler's sketch away from the others and pointed to the garotte. It was drawn in various shades of gray, simulating a shiny glint.

"Almost looks real. As if it's based on personal experience. And this drawing paper seems brand new to me. I don't see any curls at the corners. Do you?"

"It's concept art," Adrian said.

His sudden appearance at the door startled Lucy. She spun around, her trailing suit scattering sheets of paper.

"For the planned *Crimson Shadow* sequel. The *Dark Hunter*."

"Thanks for clearing that up," Ron said with a sarcastic smile. "I feel a lot better now. For a moment there, I was convinced you were a psychopath."

Adrian stepped into his study. Slipper soles slapped on the wood tiles.

"Another guest I didn't invite. Is this how you do things

in the police? Invade people's privacy? Violate their rights? I thought that to enter someone's property without their permission, you required a warrant."

He walked over to a hi-tech videophone on the desk and picked up the cordless receiver.

"Perhaps I should give your boss a call. Get him to clarify the law."

"Wouldn't bother. He's at home sleeping."

"Or maybe I should phone my attorney instead! And tell him there's a smarmy cop poking his nose into my business. Who doesn't seem to give a damn about probable cause or people's rights."

"Please," Lucy said soothingly. "Don't humor him."

Ron stacked the papers in a neat pile. "I think I've seen everything I need to, Mister Pryce. It's really quite easy to explain. I was concerned for your safety, so I decided to check up on you after the two murders at your office. You heard about those, right? When I got here, I saw the lights on at four in the morning. And Lucy's car parked outside. Naturally, I was worried about my old partner. Thought she might be in over her head."

"As you can see," she said. "We're both safe and well."

"Then I'll let you get back to whatever you were doing. It would probably be best if I left quietly. With all the commotion out there and all."

Ron walked foxily to the television and tapped an upward-pointed arrow icon on the screen. At his touch, the channel changed. Kristina Malloy appeared in center shot.

She was standing by the front gate, in a near perfect position for a news broadcast. The bull's head was behind her. Horns and red eyes shone in the camera spotlight.

Ron touched a loudspeaker symbol to deactivate the mute function.

"We can confirm there have been two additional victims in the Taurus Strangler case," Kristina reported.

Adrian clenched his fist when she mentioned the killer's nickname. His angry reaction went unnoticed by Ron, but not Lucy. Her pupil movement was slight, lasting only a moment. She returned her attention to the TV screen and kept her thoughts private.

"It appears Lieutenant Blake's comments yesterday afternoon were premature," Kristina said. "And that James Fitzroy may not have been responsible for the murders. With Philadelphia once again in the grip of fear, and two more employees of Taurus Studios dead, the spotlight is now firmly back on Adrian Pryce. I'm outside his house, where several witnesses have reported a blonde woman matching the description..."

Lucy tapped the loudspeaker icon, silencing her in mid-sentence.

"Real life soap opera." Ron walked to the broken window. "I can see why you might want to switch it off."

"You think I'm just going to let you walk out?" yelled Adrian. "After you broke in here?"

"Yeah, I reckon so. Unless you'd rather cause a scene, and give Miss Malloy something really juicy to comment on. A scuffle with a cop would be quite sensational."

Ron left the study with no further challenge. He winked at Adrian as he shut the window and jogged away into the night.

Adrian's unfriendly glare remained etched on his face. "I'm calling Dawson right now. We'll need to prepare a statement for the press. Put whatever positive spin we can on the story while my company's still worth something. Then we should discuss Detective Wallace's unorthodox methods. His total disregard for procedure, his baseless insinuations. How the hell do you stomach working with someone so slimy?"

"Don't get too worked up. Ron is—"

"Lucky I won't be making a formal complaint."

* * *

A pale ray of sunlight shone across Lucy's forehead, tapering to a blunt point on the bridge of her nose. It widened to a full inch as she parted the living room curtains. She took a discreet peek through the window, long enough for news camera lights to converge, then pulled the drapes together.

"They still out there?" Adrian asked.

He entered from the hallway, carrying a steaming cup of coffee. The enamel was atypically bright and flashy in design, with a Taurus Studios bull on a creamy yellow background.

Lucy stepped away from the window. "Yeah," she said with a tired yawn. "And multiplying, as vermin do. I'm tempted to take Lieutenant Blake's advice and go on a long vacation. Were you able to get through to Dawson?"

"Tried his private number three times. No answer. I left a message on his machine."

Adrian scraped his thumbnail down the cup's side, applying so much pressure it scratched the paint.

"I just watched the morning news. More of that Kristina bitch talking through her ass. She used that name again. The Taurus Strangler. She made it sound like this freaking nutcase has official ties with my company."

"Well, three of the four victims worked for Taurus. And the other used to." Lucy gave him a placative smile. "Just saying."

"Jenna was a temp!"

Adrian hurled his mug away. It spun upside down in mid-flight and bounced on the futon. Coffee splashed over the cushions.

"I spoke to the girl once. Maybe twice. There was never anything between us. Why kill her?"

"Why kill any of them? That's what we have to figure out. And we will, if we work together. Which is why you need to calm down and think."

"I built Taurus from nothing." Adrian pointed angrily at the window. "Now those damn news crews want to drag my reputation through the dirt. No, I won't fold to the pressure. I'm not going to run away because some disgruntled employee has it in for me. I worked too hard for this."

He bit his lower lip. Raw fury burned in his eyes. He was a walking time bomb, ready to explode. Lucy approached with care, hands in her trouser pockets.

"Relax, tough guy," she said. "The strangler tried to bump me off too, remember? I'm not about to skip town either." She watched circles of light sweep over the closed curtains. "But I wouldn't mind some privacy. I know this run down place where the press won't be so welcome. How about some breakfast?"

* * *

"Any more reporters show up?"

The old-timer looked somewhat comical in his cartoon-strip pajamas and *Mickey Mouse* slippers. White hair and sunken eyes hinted at a man in his seventies or beyond. He stooped to pick up a newspaper off his front doorstep. Folded in two, the top section had a pessimistic headline printed above a cropped picture of Lieutenant Blake. *TAURUS STRANGLER OUTWITS POLICE - WHO CAN PROTECT US?*

"Hey, pal! I'm talking to you. And this isn't your parking space, asshole."

He directed his comments at an anonymous motorcyclist parked across the way. The helmeted rider was a hundred yards from the news vans, in a tree-sheltered spot with a narrow, but clear, angle of the Pryce residence gates.

Dressed in a zip-up black leather jumpsuit, studded boots, and padded gloves, the biker's body was completely covered from the neck down. They — it was impossible to tell whether it was a man or woman — had kept their silver-colored, reflective face plate lowered, and no hair protruded from the helmet.

The motorcyclist turned their head. Sunlight reflected off the visor, a blinding glare that forced the senior citizen to cover his eyes. He mumbled something incoherent, stormed into his house, and threw the door closed.

A yellow taxicab caught the biker's attention. It stopped in front of the news vans, reversed into an empty driveway, and turned back. Some reporters gave the car a passing glance, but nobody surrendered their spot outside the gates.

Only the motorcyclist spotted two people climb the picket fence with the help of an aluminium ladder. They were both dressed in thick, blue jeans and trainers, winter coat hoods pulled across their faces. The leather-clad biker watched their not so discreet getaway. Reflected in the visor, the couple argued.

The female who led the escape was relatively inconspicuous, but the male behind her seemed a lot edgier. He glanced around nervously, face framed between two ladder rungs. The woman beckoned three times before he leaped into her arms. The biker watched the misfits creep into the next garden, exit through a wooden gate, and get into the cab. Once inside, Lucy and Adrian lowered their hoods.

The motorcyclist squeezed the throttle to rev the engine. Camera lights flashed across the silver visor as the rider did a sharp, one-eighty-degree turn in front of the duped reporters.

As the taxi moved off, the couple shifted closer together, shoulders within an inch of touching. Both passengers appeared relaxed, unaware they had a tail.

CHAPTER EIGHTEEN

Home Visit

Adrian cautiously sniffed the food on his plate. The pancake was more brown than yellow, batter covered with burned grease. There was very little meat on the fatty bacon, and the pickled onions were shriveled. He hadn't eaten a single scrap, or even touched his meal. Lucy sat across the dining table. She was either famished or not too choosy about her diet, since her plate was almost empty.

"When you said breakfast at your place, you made it sound so romantic," Adrian remarked. "Thought you'd eat healthily."

He rolled a pickle with his wood-handled fork. The reverse side looked no more appealing. He let the onion spin back, played safe, and stuck to his creamed coffee. Lucy sliced a thick strip of bacon from her last portion, speared it, and gobbled it down.

"I messed up the timings," she said. "Guess I'm not used to cooking for two."

"You didn't need to go to all this trouble." He prodded his pancake to test its hardness. In most places, he had to force the fork in. "I'm sure there's a diner around here."

"In this neighborhood? That's not a good idea. Anyway, I thought you wanted privacy."

Adrian mustered some courage. He cut off a thin piece of pancake, chewed for a few seconds, and then swallowed it. A silent concession of defeat.

"So, *Crimson Shadow...*" Lucy looked up. "Who else was on the team?"

"Besides Sophie and Norris? Dawson was the chief producer. Tania did most of the coding. It's this year's marquee title. Pretty much everyone in my company has worked on it at some point."

Adrian paused, tapping his knife handle against the table.

"But not the security guy. He has nothing to do with the project. Neither do you. And Jenna wasn't technically a Taurus employee at all. Are you so sure that's the connection?"

"I just got in the killer's way. But Levitt... Could he have seen something on the cameras?"

Adrian laughed. It turned into a cough as he choked on a pickle.

"A bunch of security staff left Taurus. When we went over budget last Christmas, we made a lot of adjustments. Job cuts, if you want the blunt truth. Levitt wasn't great. Or even average. He was a low paid rent-a-cop, but someone we could afford."

"And now he's off your payroll altogether."

Adrian gave her a distasteful glare. It was unclear whether it was her comment or the food that had made him queasy.

A loud thump came from the apartment above. Glass smashed. A door slammed.

"God damn it, bitch!" the man upstairs yelled. "If I have to tell you again."

A woman cried. Whimpers soon faded to quiet sobs. Adrian looked about nervously, first at the ceiling, then at his host.

"Excuse me." Lucy placed her cutlery on her half-eaten food and pushed her chair away from the table. "There's this jerk I know. Been waiting to punch him for years."

Lucy collected her suit top from a clothes hook on the way out. She paused, then replaced it. She rolled up her shirtsleeves to expose tough-skinned forearms. Ready for a fight, she opened the door and left her dwelling with a distinctly mean streak.

Adrian pushed away his plate, having barely touched his breakfast. He took only the coffee with him as he wandered around the apartment. Saucepans and dirty spatulas were piled by the kitchen sink, next to empty plastic packaging. The visitor avoided them as if they'd been contaminated with a fatal disease, and stuck to the lounge area.

His first steps were cautious. Transparent facial expressions swung between unimpressed and total dislike. Adrian's demeanor improved when he spied the photo album on Lucy's credenza. He flicked the pages back, browsed through the police force pictures, and stopped at the section of them together at the university.

There was a wood-splitting crack, followed by a violent thud. Light shades shook. Stomping feet moved from above the apartment window to the door area.

"What the hell—" the male resident said.

The resulting commotion began with a slap, possibly a punch, and ended shortly after with a high-pitched, just about masculine groan. Adrian flinched in discomfort and looked down at his groin.

"You… You bitch!" the guy cried.

"Don't touch her ever again."

Lucy's voice was deafeningly loud. Everyone in the building could probably hear her.

"Not unless you want me to come back. Next time, it won't be a gentle prod. I might decide you're not man enough and chop them off."

Adrian looked up at the ceiling and tracked her footsteps to where the door would be. He smiled as he gazed out at Sycamore Avenue.

A sleek black motorcycle sped by, its helmeted, leather-clad rider a blurry, motion-distorted figure. Adrian pressed his cheek against the glass to get a wider viewing angle. There was no sign of the vehicle, only rusty-hooded junkers parked on the kerb and some punks loitering.

Five tones rang out, the start of a tune. Its high-tempo, adventurous theme was like Justin Norris' music, possibly one of his compositions.

Adrian took his cellphone from his trouser pocket and tapped the screen to read a just-arrived text message from *Miles Dawson*.

My office. Urgent. You know why. You better have answers. Come alone.

Alerted by footsteps on the outside landing, he put the phone away. Lucy entered her apartment to see his hand move swiftly from his pants and a thin, oblong-shaped bulge in his pocket. Her knuckles were redder than when she'd left, but she looked in good health.

"Thought you'd been suspended from the force," Adrian said, a little hastier than usual.

"I was."

Lucy walked to the dining table and collected the two

plates. She balanced them expertly on one hand and laid the cutlery on top.

"Wouldn't have done that wearing a badge. There are lots of rules for cops. Not so many for concerned residents. But it felt good to disobey the guidebook for once."

Lucy stepped on her waste basket's pedal to open its steel lid, scraped the food into a black plastic bag, and dropped the plates and utensils in the sink. She sponged them down in a bowl of bubbly water.

"Leaving me all alone in your apartment to deal with domestic abuse," Adrian said. "I take it you've finally crossed me off the suspect list?"

"Every relationship has risk. Sometimes the danger is obvious." Lucy scrubbed grease off a plate. "Other times, it's hidden beneath the surface. A woman needs to be careful who she gets involved with. So, who was on the phone?"

"What do you mean?" He feigned surprise, but dropped the act after she gave him an all-serious look. "Oh, that. It was only junk mail. Nothing important."

"Relationships are built on trust, Adrian." Lucy cleaned a second plate. She scrubbed hard until she'd removed every bit of grease. "Wallace thinks you're guilty, and right now he's the one with the badge and gun. I still believe you're innocent, but keeping secrets from me stretches that belief. Whoever called you, you need to come clean and tell—"

There was a click, the sound of a lock mechanism snapping shut. Water splashed over the sink bowl as Lucy dropped the plate. She turned around, hands dripping wet.

Adrian had left her apartment.

* * *

Lucy, with her soapy shirt sleeves still rolled up, exited her tenement to see a Philadelphia taxicab drive off. She stared at the passenger's head in disbelief. Adrian had his mobile phone out and looked apprehensively at the unseen text. Then the vehicle veered around a corner and vanished from sight.

"You stupid bastard."

A high-powered engine alerted Lucy to the motorbike coming from behind. She instinctively turned and grasped the railing of a nearby fence. Her shoe heels lifted off the ground. Like an athlete in the starting blocks, she was ready to sprint.

She kept her eyes on the leather-clad biker, but saw little except for her own anxious reflection in the mirrored visor. The rider slowed down on approach, booted foot easing off the footrest. Dipped headlights shone on Lucy's trousers as the vehicle stopped a few feet from her.

"Detective Duvall!"

The crash helmet muffled the biker's voice, but it was definitely a woman.

Lucy kept a firm grip on the railing as the motorcyclist lowered the bike's support stand. She raised her visor, exposing brown Asian skin, loose black hair, and spectacles that fit snugly within an inlaid cushion.

"Tania." Lucy relaxed, but only a little. "You've been watching us? Following us?"

"I need to talk to you. About the security footage at Taurus."

"I thought the killer wiped the hard drives. Adrian said there were no backups."

Lucy eyed her suspiciously and came to a speedy deduction.

"But you made one without his knowledge. That's why you waited to get me alone. Either that or... What did you find?"

Tania stepped off her motorcycle, leaving the detective to ponder the answer. She opened a storage box behind the seat strut and removed a computer laptop from protective padding.

"The murderer," she said. "I'd better show you inside."

* * *

Lucy stood behind Tania as she booted her computer. The laptop had been placed on the cleared dining table, with its raised screen flat against the wall.

The technician had left her helmet on the kitchen counter. Dressed in biker leathers, the Asian seemed a different woman to the shy programmer from Taurus Studios. With her thick-soled boots on, she rivaled the detective for tallness and conveyed an aura of confidence.

"I'm not sure I can help," Lucy said. "They took me off the case. If you have proof that Adrian's the killer..."

"Here. Take a look."

Lucy studied Tania's figure as she stepped aside, noting her lean-but-powerful thighs, leather gloves, and coat that gave her an almost masculine appearance. Convex spectacle lenses magnified her irises, making them seem unnaturally large.

Tania used the laptop mouse pad to click on a CCTV camera icon. A media player opened in a separate window, its interior totally black except for a progress bar. The percentage done statistic increased from zero, and incremented by a few points every second.

"Does it come with a cable?" Lucy asked. She kept her hands in front and viewed the screen from a distance.

"A charger, but I haven't got it with me."

She seemed oblivious to the insinuation — and Lucy's wariness.

"Bit of an oversight. What if you need one? Things don't always go according to plan. Sometimes you run into unexpected trouble."

Tania's confidence appeared to ebb away, and her hostess kept the pressure on.

"It just occurred to me. Doctor Vickers, our forensics woman, said something very interesting at the first murder scene. I could have done it."

Tania's eyes shifted slightly to the side. "Done what?"

"Killed Justin Norris."

The technician stared back in disbelief. Lucy gave her an obviously phony, Ron-like smile.

"Is it so implausible? He was too pissed to put up a fight. Levitt was fat on doughnuts. The other victims were both female. Sophie and Jenna weren't strong women."

The progress bar stalled at 68%. Tania took her trembly fingers off the laptop pad.

"Are you saying—"

"Just thinking. People assume the killer's a man, but the Taurus Strangler could easily be a woman. A woman with knowledge of the computer systems. It's quite easy to falsify video evidence. Especially when you're the only person who knows it exists."

Tania shook her head, almost in tears. "Is that why you think I came here? To set up your stupid boyfriend?"

"Love and hate. Both make good motives for murder."

"Okay, I hate the bastard! But not enough to hurt him. Or Sophie. Or the others." She removed her spectacles to rub her watery eyes. "I know you care about Adrian. But I can't understand why. He's always exploited his employees."

Her assessment was scathing and resentful.

"I never told him about the backups because I thought I might need proof someday. Or maybe show the world what the head of Taurus is really like. After the last two murders, I searched my files, hoping to prove Adrian was the killer. That he'd wiped the data to cover his tracks. But I found something else."

"What did you find?" Regret crept into Lucy's voice.

"Footage from five days ago." Tania directed the detective's attention to the laptop screen. "The president's office camera."

The progress bar was gone. Security video in the window showed the same images Tania had viewed the previous night. A downward shot of the Adrian's desk, seen through a green low-light filter, and his angry argument with Miles Dawson over the cellphone.

"More like his guilt," Lucy said. "Don't see how this helps him."

Tania wiped her nose dry and used the laptop mouse pointer to click on a bookmark icon.

The footage changed to an empty office, another recording from the same camera on a different date. Lucy watched as the video played.

Her hands pressed on the dining table when a round-headed shadow fell across Adrian's desk. The Taurus Strangler stepped into view, their leather outfit and balaclava seen from the back.

Lucy stiffened and looked over at Tania. Her leggings were vaguely similar — though noticeably tighter — and her gloves were a good match, but the jackets were different. The programmer's was a lot shorter around the waist and shinier.

Tania read Lucy's gaze. "That's not me."

"I know that now. But I had to consider you a suspect."

She returned her attention to the laptop. The strangler vaulted onto the desk, reached up, and removed a ventilation grille from the ceiling.

"What's he doing?"

Lucy clicked to expand the image to full screen size.

"Isn't that an assumption?" Tania asked with clear bitterness. "How do you know it's a man?"

The detective ignored the personal swipe and pointed to an object in the killer's hands.

"Any idea what that is?"

"You'll see in a second."

The killer turned to face the camera, booted feet placed to avoid disturbing items on Adrian's desk. In the low-light filter, the Taurus Strangler's eyes appeared as bright green rings around black dots.

A gloved hand rose into view, holding a thumb-sized plastic box with a shiny aerial sticking up. A glassy glint from the opposite end created a brief lens-flare effect.

"That's a camera," Lucy said. "Fitted with a transmitter. Why plant a camera in Adrian's office?"

"Look at where it was pointing. Down at his computer keyboard."

Working quickly, the masked intruder refitted the grille over the device and stepped down out of sight. With the cover back in place, the room looked undisturbed.

"The killer saw everything Adrian typed," Tania said. "All his e-mails. Even those he deleted. His login details, passwords. Nothing was private."

"So the strangler could access his account remotely. To post the video of Sophie's murder online. And who knows what else?" She exhaled. "Tania, about what I said before..."

"I get it. Near death experience. Then I show up on your doorstep wearing leather. I'd be suspicious too."

She closed the laptop and stowed it underneath her arm.

"Adrian would already know the passwords to his computer. He could have deleted the files discreetly. So if someone broke into his office to erase the footage. It means..."

"Means he's not the killer," Lucy said, invigorated with relief. "Tania, you're a genius."

CHAPTER NINETEEN

Cutting Losses

The ornate-handled, glass double doors swung inward, and urban Philadelphia briefly came alive. A chaotic mix of ambient sounds told the tale of a busy metropolis during rush hour: shoes clacking on the pavement, flapping coats, innocent everyday chatter, and slow-moving traffic.

Pedestrians scurried past, ignoring the frosty-cheeked man who'd just entered. If any of them had glimpsed under his winter coat hood, they might have recognized Adrian Pryce. The new arrival stepped through the threshold and shrugged off the cold. He waited until the door fully closed — and the sounds stopped — before he revealed his face.

The lobby he'd walked into was from a different century than Taurus Studios. Instead of modern chrome, there was varnished wood and polished brass. White-gray marble tiles formed the floor, with classical Roman pillars and ruby-red carpets for decoration. Silver letters were engraved on a twenty-foot-long, mahogany reception desk: *Frank & Bennett, Attorneys at Law*. Facing the entrance doors, it resembled an oversized plaque.

Adrian ignored the receptionist, a white-haired, librarian-like lady with horn-rimmed spectacles. He headed towards the elevators, pressed the call button, and impatiently watched the floor indicators.

One of four black-iron pointers rotated anticlockwise around a semicircle of Roman numerals, moving slowly from XIII to I. The elevator arrived with a bong, closer to a clock-tower chime than a traditional ping. Then the hand-crafted pine doors opened to reveal a watercolor painting of Colonial-era Philadelphia. That was mounted on the far side in a solid gold animal-engraved frame. The other walls were plainer, with only recessed panels and brass buttons to select a floor.

Adrian stepped in, pressed XIX, and turned to face the closing doors. Cogs clanked as unseen motors pulled the elevator up, but there were no rusty screeches or jittery shifts to suggest the machinery was unsafe.

The Taurus president stared ahead like a nervous candidate attending a job interview. It took roughly a minute and a half to reach the nineteenth floor, even though there were no additional stops en route. A bong signaled the elevator's arrival, and the doors slid open.

"Mister Dawson's expecting you, Mister Pryce," the petite, blonde secretary said. "You can go right in." Her somewhat awkward, formal introduction was eloquently spoken.

"Thank you, Lisa."

The waiting room was furnished with traditional wood and leather, like the lobby, but the equipment was modern. The secretary's desktop computer, headset phone, organizer, and printer-photocopier combo were all state-of-the-art, rivaling those at Taurus Studios. Lisa's pearl-white blouse, sandy-orange skirted suit, and diamond-studded earrings gave her the appearance of a high-salaried professional, and she was evidently capable of multi-tasking.

Adrian inhaled and walked past her desk. The electronically sealed doors ahead of him were opaque, black glass like those in the Taurus building, except with golden contact strips in the middle.

Lisa tapped a touch-sensitive button beside her organizer while she loaded fresh paper into the printer. The doors opened soundlessly. Adrian stepped underneath a security camera and into Miles Dawson's private office.

The attorney waited under a gold-plated, six-branched chandelier with candle-shaped bulbs. He didn't bother to shake hands with his business partner, and his grim face suggested the meeting would be anything but cordial. Adrian turned to see Lisa lift her finger off the door release button. The black-glass panels slid together, sealing off any potential retreat.

"I wanted to keep this matter between the two of us," Dawson said. "Give you an opportunity to explain yourself."

Adrian broke off eye contact to glance round at the collection of fine antique furniture. Besides the beautifully-restored writing desk and chairs, the bookcases were stocked with leather-bound law journals dating back to the early 1900s. And the watercolor portraits looked even more expensive than the one in the elevator.

"You mentioned it was urgent," Adrian said.

Dawson walked to meet him, eyes aflame with fury.

"So, this is what it's come to. We've not always been friends, but I thought we were at least colleagues. You show up at my office dressed like common street trash. Is that some ploy to convince me you're innocent? That you had nothing to do with this mess?"

"I didn't. I don't know who killed them, Miles, but—"

"Stop playing games!"

Dawson returned to his desk and slammed his fist down. He scrunched up a piece of paper and thrust its floppy end toward Adrian.

"What did you do with it?" he asked.

"Do with what?"

He plucked the sheet from Dawson's hand and flattened it. His expression became puzzled as he scanned the text.

It was a bank statement that showed transactions for Taurus Studios in December 2015. Most amounts were small for a major company, rarely in five figures, but near the bottom was a withdrawal of thirty million dollars. *Adrian Pryce* was listed as the recipient, next to an international financial code as a reference. Subsequent balances were all negative.

Dawson shifted over into Adrian's view. "I don't know how to put this in legal terminology you'd understand. So I'll try plain English instead. Where the hell is our money?"

"I... I have no idea," stammered Adrian. "I didn't make the withdrawal. Somebody must have hacked our account."

"Like they hacked our impregnable server? I thought you'd deny it, so I asked Lisa to prepare a statement in advance."

Dawson stormed around his desk, opened a drawer, and presented his client with a letter. The typescript was identical to the termination notices left by the Taurus Strangler. Same font, point size and margin width, with the bull logo at the top.

"What the hell is this?"

The two men eyed each other with suspicion. After an awkward pause, it was the attorney who spoke.

"Want me to read it to you?"

He pushed the document across the desk and recited the

text from memory.

"Because of an inexplicable accounting error, Taurus Studios has filed for bankruptcy. The company president Adrian Pryce has accepted full responsibility and has decided to suspend trading until the matter is resolved. Preorders of *Crimson Shadow* and all other studio titles will be canceled, and refunds provided. We can only apologize to our fans and customers."

Dawson sat down. His fingers flexed as anger boiled over.

"All employees should consider their contracts terminated with immediate effect. Sound familiar? I took that last part from your letters."

"I had nothing to do with those! Miles, you've got this all wrong."

"That's for a public defender to argue. I don't think you can afford my services any longer, or those of any other reputable attorney. Unless you have money in a *private* account to cover my retainer."

Adrian responded to the accusation with utter incredulity. He gaped at Dawson, open-mouthed. No words came out.

The lawyer's stare was unforgiving. "Then we have no more business to discuss." He tapped a button on his desk. "Consider our partnership formally dissolved. Lisa's already called security at my request."

The glass doors opened. Two strong-armed giants stood in the receptionist's office. Dressed in black shirts and carrying side-holstered automatic pistols, they resembled mercenary thugs. There was none of the apathy and laziness that typified guards at Taurus Studios. These men were trained killers.

"I've also instructed my secretary not to take any

further calls from you," Dawson said. "We've known each other a long time, so I hope to God you're just a conniving, backstabbing thief and not a murderer. But either way, we're done."

* * *

Taurus Studios employees streamed out of the company's tower, a mass exodus that showed no sign of slowing. Quite a few gave angry glares or stuck their fingers up at the security camera on the way out. A good number marched across the roundabout, deliberately trampling the grass, and one particularly irate woman kicked her stiletto heel into the bull statue base.

Nobody stopped to give an interview, despite constant efforts by marauding reporters. The news vans that had been outside Adrian's house were now parked along the approach. Press vehicles stretched so far back they obstructed late morning traffic on the cross streets. All local stations and many international were represented.

Kristina Malloy led her camera crew toward the building. She reached the bull's head before any of her rivals. With a satisfied smirk, she turned to her assistants, took a steel-framed comb from her coat pocket, and hurriedly tidied her hair.

Her cameraman gave an approving nod and directed the lens at her. A spotlight shone past Kristina onto the statue's golden horns. The second assistant held a poled microphone above her head.

"I want the building in shot." She waved him back. "And the employees. This is the story of the year. Let's give it the backdrop it deserves."

The camera operator retreated, and the sound man had

difficulty keeping his equipment above the constantly-moving reporter. Seeing other media crews approach, she didn't wait for her assistants to issue her the go-ahead.

"We're live at the scene at Taurus Studios." Kristina shouted to inject melodrama. "It was announced only moments ago that the games developer is to close its doors and lay off all staff. For these workers, this is certainly not a merry Christmas or a happy new year. Could it get any worse for the company, or Philadelphia's inept police department?"

She put brutal emphasis on the last sentence.

"Four victims have fallen prey to the Taurus Strangler — who detectives mistakenly assured us was James Fitzroy — and now it seems the empire Adrian Pryce built is well and truly crumbling. Details are sketchy, but speculation is rife that—"

Kristina cut her report short as the presidential SUV turned onto the approach road. It detoured around the news vans and parked on the roundabout lawn.

Adrian stepped down from the driver's seat, and every reporter on site fought to be first in line. Those that had arrived late were suddenly at the front. Dazzled by spotlights, the pressured CEO was surrounded in seconds.

Questions came from all directions, each person shouting over the last.

"Is it true that Taurus Studios—"

"—you planning to issue an apology to James Fitz—"

"Is there any connection between the two recent victims..."

"Will this affect the Christmas schedule? And is the company going to honor—"

Kristina was a frustrated onlooker, buffered from the besieged Adrian by the thick crowd. The interview degenerated into a hysterical shouting match as reporters jostled for position. The president forced his way through. It was a slow and difficult trek to the Taurus tower.

"You bastard!" a woman screamed over the noise.

The media backed off as the stiletto-heeled employee confronted her boss. Cameras rolled, and news crews held microphones over Adrian's head in anticipation.

"Please! This is all a misunderstanding. If you'd just calm down while I—"

The woman took a typed letter from her coat pocket and clutched it at the top. She waved it around, constantly turning. Spotlights failed to keep up, but the Taurus company logo was clearly visible.

"Seven years I spent working for him," she said. "And this is how he treats me. A termination notice. Are you planning to kill the rest of us now? You may as well. How am I supposed to feed my family, you money-grabbing leech?"

She screwed the paper up, threw it in Adrian's face, and slouched away in disgust. A few of the reporters chased the disgruntled ex-employee's story, but most stuck to the Taurus president. Kristina took advantage of the lull in questioning to get closer.

"Mister Pryce, does this closure have anything to do with the recent murders?"

She spoke quickly, getting her question out before anyone could interrupt. Everybody fell silent. Microphones dangled above Adrian, ready to record his answer. By some miracle — or expert handling — none of the rods collided.

Adrian turned to face Kristina. He gave the cameraman time to focus on him. "Whoever is doing this to me," he said. "To my company… I will find you. And then you will regret it. That's a God damn promise!"

"So you're saying it wasn't your decision to shut Taurus down?"

"I have nothing further to add."

He continued toward the office tower. The reporter's questions started again and quickly became an incoherent mess. Kristina signaled her assistants to stand back. She waited for the camera lens to focus on her.

"You heard it here first, folks," she said, unable to contain her delight. "Live comment from the prime suspect in the Taurus Strangler case. Reporting for Philly Today, this is Kristina Malloy."

The mass employee exit had slowed during her interview, and the black doors had closed. When Adrian finally reached the building, a cordon of police officers waited in the lobby. Burly men, and one short but strong female, kept reporters at bay.

Ron — the senior detective on site — was ready with a snarky greeting.

"You look stressed out, Mister President. What's the matter? Bad day at the office?"

CHAPTER TWENTY

Badge and Gun

Lucy pushed the redial button on her cellphone, standing firm in a gust of wind that blew many other pedestrians off course. She'd stepped out of her tenement without a coat on. As the breeze intensified, her shirt pressed against her body and formed a skin-tight sheet around her muscular figure.

Tania's eyes sparkled with admiration. One hand on her crash helmet, she snatched her long flowing black hair into a clump and fastened the ponytail with her jade clip.

"You were right about us being strong women," she said. "We don't need men in our lives. Especially not men like Adrian Pryce."

"He's still not picking up."

Lucy stabbed her thumb on the "End Call" button. She quickly scrolled through the phone's options menu and checked her mailbox. There were no new messages.

"I've tried him four times," she said. "And Ron hasn't got back to me. Do you think something's happened to Adrian? That the killer might have…"

She trailed off and looked worriedly at his name on the

cellphone screen.

Tania lowered her helmet onto her head, with the edges aligned carefully so she didn't nudge her spectacles. She mounted her motorcycle and lifted her reflective visor to expose the middle section of her face.

"He's alive!" She shouted to counter the muffling. "He just doesn't care. You mean nothing to him. Every project I've worked on has been exactly the same. The employees do all the hard work, and Pryce takes the credit. Do you think your police rules are bad? Outside Taurus Studios, I get to be myself. But at the company, we all have to follow *his* agenda. That man you shot… Fitzroy. He may have been crazy, but he was right about Pryce stifling creativity."

"That's very harsh, Tania. Adrian's different away from work, too. Flawed like the rest of us, but not a bad guy. If you knew him socially, you'd see another side."

The programmer revved her motorcycle engine. "I don't! And I don't want to."

"If you're not a fan, why did you help him?"

"I didn't. I helped you."

Tania lowered her visor. She let go of the brake. Her motorbike sped off, tires screeching against the tarmac.

* * *

A uniformed cop stood on Adrian's office desk. The removed ventilation grille rested against his knees. Black glass creaked as he reached into the recess. The policeman's face contorted as he grabbed onto something and pulled. Shifted off-balance, the cover tipped over and landed on its flat side with a resonant clang. There was a loud crack as it struck the floor, but no visible damage.

"Careful!" Adrian chastised him. "What are you guys

looking for, anyway?"

When the cop responded with a grunt, the president turned to Ron. The unconcerned detective kneeled by a display case and checked the paneling.

"We got a tip from your girlfriend. You're a popular man these days. It seems our strangler paid you a visit. Even left you a gift. Maybe more than one."

"What are you talking about?"

"Found it," the policeman said.

He jumped down from the desk. Adrian cringed as the glass wobbled in its chrome frame. His anguish turned to curiosity when he spotted the device in the policeman's hand. He grabbed it without asking permission, and ingested the key details: black box, lens, antenna.

"A camera." His grip tightened in rage. "Someone's been watching me!? Why the hell—"

Adrian glanced up at the open vent, then at his computer directly below.

"So that's how that bastard knew—"

He stopped, realizing the policemen were all staring at him.

"Finish the story, Mister Pryce," Ron said. "Some people are dying to know how it ends."

"Someone cleared out the company's primary bank account. They used my login details to make a transfer of thirty million dollars. All the currency we had in reserve."

"That's some reserve." Ron sounded more cynical than sympathetic. "Thought your company was struggling. You couldn't afford fifty grand for Norris, or to hire decent security. But the funds were there. Turns out you kept them all for yourself."

"For Taurus. Most of that money was left over from investment capital. We have to plan in case our titles don't do as well as we expect. We're not bedroom programmers anymore. Do you know how much it costs to make a video game?"

"Probably several hundred times my salary. What happened to the cash?"

"Numbered account, with no way to trace it. Dawson thought it was me. It wasn't, but it didn't stop him issuing a wrapping-up order."

"A lawyer concerned about money." Ron's tone was smarmy and confrontational. "Who could have predicted that? Guess that means Taurus Studios won't be on this year's top places to work list. So, does this setback mean I'm actually richer than you now?"

Adrian threw the wireless camera at the detective, who caught it without a blink.

"How about you stop gloating and do your job? Find out where that damn thing came from. Who put it up there, and how they got past our security so easily. And where..."

Bubbly saliva foamed through his teeth.

"Where your money is?" Ron said. "Thought that would be priority number one. You should watch that temper, Mister Pryce. With all the pressure to find this guy, cops are trigger-happy right now."

He turned over the camera and tapped the aerial.

"This seems to be a computer gadget. Like those in your display cases. And here was I thinking you were a whiz with technology. The great Adrian Pryce, asking me to solve a problem. Suppose I should feel honored."

The president let out an exhausted sigh, sat down in his chair, and looked despairingly up at the open ceiling panel.

"I design software, Detective. Not hardware. I do some coding, but my role at Taurus is mainly to manage things. I have the business acumen, but it's my staff who have the real expertise. Except they no longer work for me. I guess the company *is* finished."

His eyes dropped to the black glass. There was no reflection, only darkness.

"They probably all hate my guts. If I hadn't been such a bastard, one of them might have helped you."

"Someone like Tania Chin?" Ron asked.

"Tania?" Adrian sounded surprised. "She's just a programmer."

"You should give that programmer a little more credit. She's the one who found your hidden camera."

* * *

Tania typed furiously on the server room terminal, downloading software onto her computer. It was the only functional workstation. She'd cleared much of the debris, but there were a lot of empty slots where hard drives should be. Dozens of criss-crossed plastic cables linked power units and electrical systems.

Tania ducked under one and checked the wireless camera. The antenna was clipped with jump leads and connected to an exposed circuit board. Ron and the police officer remained by the sealed airlock, well out of the way.

Adrian watched Tania's every move, head hung in shame. "I didn't know you were so skilled with electronics."

"I helped install your home security system," she said. "Did you forget that? If you'd bothered to come down from your ivory tower, or talked to your employees, maybe you would have known what I could do."

She continued to type without a glance at Adrian. He moved a step closer.

"Why the hostility? I realize I've not been the best boss.

But I am trying to make it right."

"In case you missed the news, you're not my boss. I'm doing this as a favor for the police. And now, I'm free to tell you what I think."

Tania stabbed the enter key. The computer screen lit up blue and displayed a street map of Philadelphia. Bright green, triangular-tower icons were spread across the city, each labeled with an identification number.

A sonic ping played over the speaker, and a series of red circles emanated from two distinct points. The area they covered was several blocks in diameter. Every few seconds, the pattern repeated.

"The signal's very weak," Tania said. "And intermittent. It might take a few minutes to get a fix on the location. But I should be able to ping the wireless network cell towers to triangulate the camera transmission back to its source."

Ron came over, almost catching his foot on a dipped cable. "This is unbelievable. You can use a broken computer to..."

"I can find the killer. Or at least the receiver that camera's transmitting the signal to."

Ron whispered in Adrian's ear. "Miss Chin's a very talented girl. If you'd respected your staff, they wouldn't have left you to clean up the mess. Guess it's too late now, though."

The pings got closer together, and the red-circle zones smaller. The epicenters converged at a single point in downtown Philadelphia. Tania hovered the mouse pointer over the marked location. An information window appeared below, with the text difficult to read from a distance.

"That's two blocks west of here." Adrian turned pale. "I know that place. Let me see."

He attempted to look over Tania's shoulder. She stood tall and refused to budge. Unable to view the screen, he walked round the side. The caption was *Frank & Bennett - Law Firm Offices.*

"Dawson." Adrian thumped the desk in anger. "That greedy son of a bitch stole our money and had the audacity to accuse me? Can't believe it was him this whole time."

"Well, they say like attracts like," Ron said. "You'd better stay here where it's safe. Doesn't seem your attorney is that trustworthy."

He turned to the cop and shifted his mood to serious.

"Joking apart, these two are still in danger. Whatever happens, don't let them out of your sight. I'll call Blake, ask him to send some backup. You get the address from our girl wonder."

Ron exited through the sliding door. Adrian put both hands on the central console, wiped his brow, and looked pleadingly at Tania.

"I'm sorry I didn't value you." He struggled to find the words. "It's just... well, I screwed up. With you. Norris, Sophie. Everyone. Will you at least let me apologize?"

"Officer!" She beckoned the cop over. "You wanted the law firm's address."

The policeman negotiated the obstacle course of power lines and discarded hard drives. He barely made it to the screen safely.

As he bent forward to read the information window, Tania headed for the exit. She expertly ducked and weaved through the cables and never looked like tripping.

"I've had a lot of practice working with wires," she explained to the stunned Adrian. "And gymnastics. I did the motion capture before you decided I wasn't good enough and hired Jenna. You can apologize if you want, but don't expect me to listen."

"Where the hell are you going?" the policeman asked. "Detective Wallace told you—"

"He isn't my boss, and neither are you."

She left through the airlock. The cop chased her, but his attempt to leapfrog the cables was clumsy, and he soon tangled himself up.

He attempted to break free of the web, but the twisted wires were a mess, with little room for maneuvering, and the end connections secure.

"Some help? Please?"

Adrian ignored him and trod carefully to the exit.

"Sorry. I don't have time. I've got some important business to discuss with my attorney."

* * *

Lieutenant Blake slid Lucy's wallet across his desk, then an unloaded firearm and clip. No natural light came through the Venetian blinds. The sun had set on Philadelphia's skyscrapers, leaving isolated bright windows in rows and columns.

The boss lit up a cigarette, took a deep puff, and relaxed back in his chair. Lucy strapped a plain black Kevlar vest over her shirt and secured Velcro straps at the sides. She reached out to collect her badge, only for Blake to restrain her wrist.

"Your reinstatement's provisional," he said.

"I get it. You're doing this because you need me."

He waited a moment, then released her.

"Still got my doubts about this, but Wallace told me about the tip you gave him. Nice work. Really paid off."

"Thank Tania." Lucy collected her wallet. "She's the

programmer that helped us."

"I will. When we find her."

His response made her pause.

"What do you mean? Ron said she was at Taurus."

"She gave Capshaw the slip. So did your boyfriend. While our man was busy untangling himself. Don't ask."

"They're not safe."

Lucy buttoned her suit over her vest, obscuring it except for a bulky, V-shaped section below the neckline.

"Until we nail Dawson, those two are targets."

"We'll find them." Blake casually blew out a puff of smoke. "We got cops all over the city managing the panic. Do you know how many crank calls we've had about the Taurus Strangler? Confessions, stalkers. You name it. Point is, we're running low on manpower. So I need everyone that's available. And I need them focused."

Lucy rammed the clip into her pistol and flipped off the safety catch.

"I'm focused," she said.

"Then it's time to marshal the troops."

Blake stubbed out his cigarette, stood up, and strode past her to the door. She holstered her weapon and followed.

Every desk in the Homicide office was unmanned. The plain clothes personnel, without exception, wore bulletproof vests and shields on lanyards.

A police response unit kitted out in full riot gear and protective helmets had joined them. A tall African-American man stood at the back, the long barrel of his automatic rifle sticking above the heads of the assembled strike team.

The office had been converted into a war room, with building plans of *Frank & Bennett* taped over the Christmas tinsel and trophy cabinet. Photographs of Dawson and Lisa were pinned to a fold-out board. Real-time surveillance footage of the front entrance, lit up in night-vision green, was relayed via a TV screen.

"Boys and girls," Blake said. "The situation is this. The target — Miles Dawson — is believed to be at his downtown office. We can't risk a loud approach. If he sees us coming, who knows what he'll do?"

He let the overview settle in before continuing.

"This could turn into a bloodbath, and the press will have a field day. We've contacted as many offices in the building as we can, and had their staff discretely evacuate. We got eyes on the front entrance. As far as we know..." He looked at an officer watching the TV, who shook his head. "...Dawson's still inside."

Ron joined Lucy while the Lieutenant summarized the plan.

"I see the war dog has come out of his kennel. He must have smelled the glory. Of course, he's reinstated you in case things go sideways and he needs a fall girl."

"Enough with the humor. We have a job to do."

"Got something to add, Wallace?" Blake asked.

"Yes. I do, sir."

Ron pushed in front of the other detectives.

"Now that she's received your personal pardon for being treated like shit, let's welcome back our very own ice maiden. Detective Lucy Duvall."

Plain clothes and uniformed officers joined him in boisterous cheers and applause. Everyone except the livid, stone-faced Blake.

CHAPTER TWENTY-ONE

Legally Dead

The police van lurched as it drove over a bump, rolling back onto all four wheels after a brief sway on two. Lieutenant Blake clung to a perforated steel bench that resembled an enormous cheese grater. For him, it was literally a white-knuckle ride. Lucy and Ron — sat between him and three bulletproof-vested detectives — didn't seem as shaken, though neither were relaxed.

There were no spare seats in the vehicle's transport bay: a dull, gray metal box with riveted panels and tiny square windows. A policewoman outfitted in riot gear stared straight ahead, rifle-mounted flashlight illuminating her soldiery, tough-as-nails pose.

Ron watched Lucy check her weapon barrel, cringing as she angled its chamber toward him.

"Careful where you point that," he said. "That gun's got real bullets in it."

He looked round at the faces of his colleagues. Not a single person smiled at his reference to the Fitzroy incident, and the atmosphere in the van remained tense. A few seconds passed before Blake spoke.

"We all know what we have to do." His voice was burdened by apprehension. "Soon as we arrive, we seal off the building. Our surveillance man says nobody's gone in there except some rich asshole wearing a gray suit."

"Hope we got a pic of the guy's face. As wonderfully detailed as that description was, I wouldn't want to rely on it to ID a potential witness."

"Can it, Wallace. The only reason you're not on suspension is because I need you."

"And Duvall. Don't forget your scapegoat, boss."

Lucy, who'd shown no reaction through the heated exchange, put her weapon away and unbuttoned her suit to allow easy access to her holster. The passengers lurched forward as the van screeched to a sharp, sudden halt. Two metallic thumps came from the driver's cabin.

"We're here," Blake announced. "We got the killer trapped. This time, it's our turn to tighten the noose."

* * *

Dawson stuffed another wad of letter-sized paper into his brown leather satchel. Its folding base was extended flat, the lower section close to bursting. Sheets were densely packed into the bag, an entire ream's worth. He'd cleaned out the open desk drawers. Other than encyclopedia-like legal volumes on the bookshelves, there were no documents left in the office.

Dawson puffed with exhaustion, sweaty forehead glistening under the candle-lights of his chandelier. He glanced at his computer screen. Surveillance camera footage from the reception area showed his secretary at work. The dark glass sliding doors were closed. So he could see her, but not vice versa.

The attorney pressed the talk button on his desktop intercom to get Lisa's attention.

"Yes, Mister Dawson?" she responded through her headset phone.

"Book me on the first available flight to Rio de Janeiro. There are some investment opportunities I'd like to pursue. And call security. Have some men meet me in the lobby."

"There's a plane leaving in two hours. When are you planning to return?" Lisa stopped typing when he didn't answer. "Mister Dawson?"

The lawyer leafed through the papers in his satchel, squeezing them as narrowly as he could. The bag was so overstuffed he had to force the monogrammed locking pins in place.

"I'll come back after the police arrest Adrian Pryce," he said. "Until then, it's probably best I clear out of town. Consider yourself on paid leave until further notice."

"That's... most thoughtful."

His secretary was slow to acknowledge him. Her hesitation suggested the bonus was unusually generous.

"Make the arrangements. I've got some last-minute business to take care of."

He muted the intercom and walked to a watercolor portrait of the White House that decorated the wall between two bookcases. He slid his fingertips around the left of the gold frame and pulled. The painting swung out with a click, revealing a previously hidden safe.

It was a high security design with multiple layers of protection. The electronically locked door was smooth, silvery titanium with a hairline, force-proof gap between the casing. Dawson placed his right palm on a biometric sensor and waited for the indicator light to flash green. The attorney then typed a ten-digit combination on the touch-sensitive keypad.

The safe unlocked with an airy hiss, and its two-inch thick door swung upward. Three storage shelves were empty except for an American passport, a Harvard University law certificate, and high-denomination bearer bonds issued by the *Bank of America*.

The intercom crackled, giving Dawson a jolt of fright.

"What is it, Lisa?"

A strangled, drawn-out gasp came through the speaker, followed by sporadic choking noises. The attorney's face turned deathly white, his eyes shooting towards the office doors. He raced over to the desk and grabbed an infra-red remote control unit. Then he stopped, thumb over the untouched switch.

Dawson viewed his monitor. On the surveillance footage, the waiting room appeared empty. The secretary's chair was vacant. Uncollected paper spilled from the printer's output tray.

"Don't dare touch her, you bastard!" He yelled at the intercom. "I swear I'll..."

He paced back and forth in anguish. Heavy breathing filled gaps between scuffles and wheezy gasps. The puffs got louder as the chokes faded, until nothing could be heard except slow, steady panting. Then the connection went dead.

Dawson, shaking in fear, put down the remote control and grabbed a mobile phone off the desk. The attorney backed into the wall, watching the doors as his quivery finger tapped nine, then one. He was about to press the key again to complete the emergency number when he noticed a pulsing blue glow on his suit sleeve.

He turned to face the window, stretching on tiptoes to

view the street nineteen floors below. Five police vehicles — two patrol cars and three armor-plated vans — were parked outside the *Frank & Bennett* building.

"Pryce. The bastard set me up."

The cellphone slipped from his weakened grasp and landed with its screen face-up. Dialed digits disappeared as the device timed out.

* * *

"Why aren't the elevators moving?" Blake asked the duty clerk.

It wasn't the librarian lady who staffed the *Frank & Bennett* lobby, but a snow-bearded man who wouldn't need fake hair to portray Santa Claus. Other than that, he looked like the traditional doorman, dressed in a stiff-collared, royal blue blazer with shiny steel, scratch-free buttons.

"Don't ask me," he said. "I'm no maintenance guy. I only guard the doors."

The two security men in the corner seemed even more annoyed, but they kept quiet, wisely avoiding a confrontation with the heavily armed strike team.

"Blame those rich architects. They always try to outdo each other, build higher than the last. Police business or not, you'll just have to wait like everyone else."

Unlike Dawson's private detail, he didn't appear at all fazed by the double-filed queue of riot cops between the entrance and elevators.

"Thanks, pal," Ron said. "Really appreciate the help."

Blake pressed every call button in sequence, moving up the column, then back down. He tapped his foot as he watched the indicator needles. They all remained stuck on

XIX.

"This isn't a mechanical problem," Lucy said. "Dawson knows we're here. He's locked us out. We'll take the stairs."

She volunteered herself for point and opened the stairwell door without waiting for approval. Ron chased after her, followed by another plainclothes detective and the tough rifle-woman.

"You four!" Blake yelled at the two rearmost pairings. "You're on sentry duty. Watch the doors. Nobody comes in or out. I don't want this greasy bastard slipping through our net."

Once he'd finished issuing orders, he entered the stairwell and joined the strike team on the long, upward slog to the nineteenth floor. The police proceeded carefully, checking behind every door.

It was a professional search, but there were plenty of nerves on show. Nobody wanted a nasty surprise.

* * *

Dawson switched on the intercom and hunched forward to listen. Hearing only silence, he checked the security monitor, eyeballs rapidly oscillating as he scanned the image. There was no sign of anybody — Lisa or otherwise — in the outer office, and the printer had stopped spewing out paper.

The attorney reached for the remote control switch, held his breath, and pressed it. The doors slid apart with a beep. Lisa's body fell inward through the widening gap, head flopping back as she gathered speed. The corpse landed with a loud thump.

A computer mouse smashed onto the hardwood floor beside her neck, left button snapping off to expose internal wiring. Its white plastic cable was wrapped twice around the secretary's throat. Red scratches and peeled skin were visible between the taut wires, and fresh blood covered Lisa's outstretched fingernails. The victim's mouth was wide open, a dying gasp frozen on her lifeless face.

"Holy shit!" Dawson yelped. "Lisa!"

The killer stepped from behind the wall, having evaded the camera by hiding in a blind spot. They wore a graphite-gray suit, a marginally lighter shirt, and smart trousers. But the leather gloves and piercing eyes — visible through holes in a latex mask — belonged to the Taurus Strangler.

Under the blazing light of the chandelier, the fleshy-pink skin and blond hair were obviously plastic. With the clothes and black briefcase to complete the disguise, it would be easy to mistake the assassin for a harmless businessman. Especially at a distance.

"You sick mother —" Dawson lost the nerve to finish and retreated fearfully behind his desk. "Show me your face."

The impostor pulled off the mask to reveal another underneath. The lawyer shuddered upon seeing the identity-concealing balaclava and the murderous intent in the strangler's gaze. Sweat poured down his cheeks as the murderer discarded the false face and stepped casually around Lisa's body.

The attorney's eyes shifted to the briefcase. He watched with trepidation as the strangler put it down. The killer sprung the brass locking catches, and pulled out a tensile steel cable attached to a disc-shaped, rubber-and-plastic device. It was a modified motion capture harness. The wire had been coiled into a noose and fitted with a sliding clip. Its loop was just wide enough to slip over a human head.

"Stay the hell away from me!"

Dawson shifted round his desk, using it for protection. The predatory killer circled to his right and let the cable fall slack. Steel wires clinked together. The strangler waited for him to move, the mouthpiece veil fluttering in response to calm breaths.

The panicked attorney made a desperate dash for the exit. He hadn't gone ten feet before the murderer pressed the remote control button to block off his escape.

Dawson staggered to the closing doors — ignoring a squelch and hiss from somewhere behind — but arrived a split-second too late. He pounded the glass in frustration. Then he turned to see the Taurus Strangler stood before him.

A knee to the stomach left him out of breath and struggling to stand. The killer dropped the looped cable over his head, with the linking clip behind, and tightened the noose. Gasping for air, Dawson groped at the wire. Despite his best efforts to loosen the knot, the fastener wouldn't budge. The connector moved in only one direction.

Dawson gave up the hopeless struggle, realization dawning in his eyes. The strangler stepped aside, allowing the distraught man to see an elaborate, pulley-like setup. The cable looped over the chandelier branch, then down to the suction pad which had been fixed to the desk. A digital clock counted down seconds from three to zero, and a winch whirred into life.

The top section of the disc rotated, reeling in the hapless victim. The steel wire creaked with tension, and the light fixture shook under the extra weight. Dawson tried to hold his ground, but his shoes couldn't get enough traction on the wooden floor.

Dragged backward by the noose around his neck, the wriggling attorney slid past the watching killer. He grabbed the desktop and fought the pull of the winch. His grip weakened as his arm was forcibly stretched, and he could not prevent his feet from lifting off the ground.

The lawyer was hauled higher, to within inches of the screechy chandelier. The spool stopped turning, its preset program complete. Dawson, barely awake and choking constantly, reached up, nudging the gold-plated branch on which the cable hung.

He swung his body, attempting to dislodge himself. His flailing feet knocked the satchel over, but tight packing ensured the papers remained undisturbed.

The Taurus Strangler put the briefcase on the chair, removed a second, identical pulley system, and dropped the contraption by the window. As Dawson swayed, he looked down into the open case.

Inside were a mobile phone, torn scraps of paper in a plastic bag, and a company headed letter. From the attorney's near-unconscious perspective, the typed message was blurry and unreadable. Words came into focus as he concentrated.

I've just killed my secretary, Lisa. I didn't want to, but she saw me with the check. So I had no choice. The others I wanted to kill: Norris, Sophie, Jenna, and that useless idiot Gordon. They all misused the funds I provided. I was hoping to take that money from Adrian Pryce, but if I can't reclaim my investment, neither will he. The police are here. There's no way out. I hope that one day I am forgiven, and my actions understood. Consider my employment terminated. Miles Dawson, the Taurus Strangler.

The "suicide" victim looked dejectedly at the killer, seeing a sadistically gleeful smile impressed on the balaclava's veil. Then his body sagged, and he stopped breathing. With nothing to counteract the tension, his dipped shoes collided together.

* * *

The Taurus Strangler plummeted feet first, suit-tail and trousers flapping as they encountered air resistance. On the side street below, a dirty-skinned drunk cuddled up in a rubbish skip. If he'd been awake to see the blackish figure's rapid descent, he would likely be puzzled.

The steel line lined up perfectly with a building support strut, rendering it effectively invisible to the naked eye. The motion-blurred harness around the killer's waist was indistinguishable from an ordinary brown leather belt. Wire unwound from the suction disc attached to the office window, its rotation slowing as the killer neared the ground. With the briefcase held in one hand and the cable in the other, the masked assassin made a silent landing.

Everything about the Taurus Strangler's daring escape was precise and intricately planned. The near spot on wire length, the timer reaching zero at the exact moment of touchdown, and the detached suction pad dropping into their cupped hands.

Within a minute, the strangler had unfastened the harness, stored the equipment back in the briefcase, and replaced the rubber mask over the balaclava. The killer lined up the two sets of eye slits, flattened the creases from the suit, and left the scene.

Nineteen floors above, bright lights danced across Dawson's window, supplementing the steady glow from the chandelier. The beams converged, and a black-and-white image was projected on the glass.

A hung man twisted on a noose. His body, arms, and legs merged into one, and a vertical line appeared behind the forward-tilted head. The police had arrived too late to catch the killer. If any cops looked down at the street — and none did — they would have seen only a sleeping drunk.

Around the corner, out of potential eyesight, the Taurus Strangler removed a flat-screened tablet phone from their lapel pocket. Gloved fingers worked the controls, accessing a video file stored in memory. Footage recorded before the murder showed the attorney reveal and then open his safe. Gold sparkled to the upper right, giving away the hidden camera's location inside the chandelier.

The killer tapped an icon, and playback skipped into fast forward. A sequence of still images told the story. Dawson being attacked, the murderer planting items and replacing the picture frame, equipping the harness, an eye in close-up looking into the camera lens, a gloved hand closing around the device.

The strangler touched another button on the phone, and a message appeared on screen: *File Deleted.*

The disguised killer dropped a wireless video transmitter, indistinguishable from the gadget found in Adrian's office. A powerful toe jab, and the plastic box slid across the wet pavement into a drainage grating.

CHAPTER TWENTY-TWO

Rogue Cop

"Coward took the easy way out," Blake said. "Well, at least he saved us the expense of a trial. One killer less, and one lawyer less. All in the same night."

Vickers scanned the desk with a pencil flashlight and magnifying glass, careful not to miss anything — or bump Dawson's hanging feet — as she worked lengthwise.

"Little early to rule it a suicide. Usually, it's best to wait for an autopsy."

"I think we can safely call *that* a murder," Blake said, nodding toward the secretary. "Is there any evidence to suspect foul play in either case?"

Vickers shook her head. She was one of two forensics technicians present in the office. The other man dusted the suction disc for prints. So far, the crime scene had hardly been disturbed. The bodies were in the same positions the killer had left them, and no numbered evidence tags had been placed. Lucy kneeled down under the closed safe, gauging the distance from the glass doors to the desk.

"Good to see someone has doubts," Ron said.

He tested the window handle and found it to move easily.

"Does this all seem awfully convenient to anybody else? A device like that… weird noose thing, which this city worker just had around in case we called by his office. And let's not forget the unsigned suicide note."

"The strangler uses cables," Lucy said. "The setup is consistent with the equipment missing from Taurus. We're nineteen floors above ground. A fall from this height would be fatal. The elevator doors are jammed, so the only other way out is the stairwell, and we had that covered. Dawson was trapped, and he knew it. His options were to get arrested, die in a firefight, or kill himself."

A cellphone rang in Blake's jacket. He exited to the reception area to take the incoming call.

"You forgot to mention his computer," Ron said. "And the conveniently deleted security videos."

"Also consistent with the killer's MO."

Lucy stood up, slipping on a pair of surgical gloves. She walked over to the desk and touched the printed note.

"So is the letter. Dawson was intelligent and meticulous. He fits the profile."

"For such a smart guy, he let his secretary find out about him. Or so the bullshit story goes. Not to mention his suicide exonerates your boyfriend."

"Adrian has nothing to do with this," Lucy asserted. "Nor do my feelings for him. I'm simply looking at the evidence. The lawyer was getting ready to run. He must have known we'd discovered the camera at Taurus."

Blake returned with a newly found purpose in his stride.

"The law firm sent us the override code," he said, handing Vickers a tersely worded fax.

She put down her equipment and walked to the wall safe. Lucy stood aside to let her type on the keypad. The biometric sensor light flashed green, and the titanium door lifted.

Vickers handed over the contents. Ron and Blake crowded round as Lucy laid the items on the desk. Beside Dawson's possessions — his passport, bearer bonds, and certificate — there was a tablet device and nine rough-edged scraps of paper.

Lucy fitted the pieces together, starting with the corners and gradually matching up the torn edges.

The lieutenant impatiently grabbed the tablet and accessed its memory. He gave Ron a boastful smirk and pointed to a video file titled *Sophie-Pool*.

The boss tapped the relevant icon, and a recording of Sophie's murder played on the screen. Audio was crystal clear. Every choked cry and water splash could be clearly heard. The forensics technician winced as bubbly gargles drowned out her strangled gasps.

Blake stopped the playback and flashed the phone in Ron's face. The video had paused at a moment with Sophie's head dunked underwater. Still alive, she had one arm outstretched, reaching for the unseen killer.

"Remember her? And this clip? I think this settles it, don't you?"

Lucy nodded in agreement and completed the jigsaw puzzle. Now correctly assembled, the cashier's check and printed on the amount were legible.

"Thirty million," she said. "The money from the Taurus account."

Ron took the tablet from Blake and switched it off, blackening the image. "You should listen to Doctor Vickers. Don't trust modern technology. Or if that's too much, try listening to your gut. Why would this smart guy keep incriminating evidence around? He wiped the surveillance videos, but not his personal device?"

"It was in a locked safe." Lucy's patronizing tone suggested she was tired of arguing.

"We opened it. It's easy to find a combination or know someone who works at the security company. Forget who told me that. Think his name was Adrian something."

"Dawson is our guy!" snapped Blake.

"You said the same thing about Fitzroy. Better make certain you got it right before you call a press conference. One false accusation's bad enough. Two... Well, you might not get that lucrative promotion you're so busy chasing."

Ron stomped out of Dawson's office, ripped off his surgical gloves, and threw them in the secretary's trashcan. He entered the stairwell without looking back. Heavy footsteps echoed before the closing door silenced them.

"He'll come around." Lucy's voice was subdued by guilt. "He's just worried about me. Covering all the bases."

"Guy's a damn loose cannon," Blake said. "A cocky, hotheaded know it all. Should never have put him in charge."

"*I* shouldn't have been in charge. If I'd been honest with you from the start, maybe we'd have solved this case sooner. And that young girl..." She looked mournfully at Lisa. "...would still be alive."

The boss rested a comforting hand on Lucy's shoulder and placed a fresh cigarette in his mouth.

"We got him now. That's all that matters. But we made a mistake with Fitzroy. And five grieving families out there will want answers."

Lucy shifted uncomfortably under Blake's massaging grip, body stiffening as he continued.

"Three of the victims died when Wallace was in charge. And he doesn't have a personal connection to excuse his actions. Someone has to take the blame. We can pension him off. He's close to retirement, anyway. You've got a bright future ahead of you, Duvall. The woman who caught the Taurus Strangler, and proved the innocence of Adrian Pryce, a man who saved her life. It's a happy ending. People like happy endings."

Lucy gripped Blake's wrist and pulled his hand off her shoulder. The shock at her rejection was clear on his face.

"You should step outside," she said, "before you contaminate the crime scene with all that foul air you're breathing. Wallace is a damn good detective. He saved my life, too. You so much as whisper a bad word about him, and I'll mention this conversation to the press. Now, if you don't mind, sir, it's been a very busy week. And I'm tired of all the deceit."

Lucy marched off, leaving Blake alone with the forensics team.

"I'm really worried about her health," Vickers said, suppressing a smile. "Did that shoulder feel cold to you?"

The lieutenant hovered close by, blatantly unamused.

"This sarcasm seems to spreading through the ranks. So does insubordination. I don't like either."

He slapped his hand on her back, squeezing it with none of the comfort he'd shown Lucy.

"You feeling me? I'll be issuing a statement within the hour. This is an extremely high-profile case, so things need to progress quickly and smoothly. The evidence file you normally take a week to prepare... I expect it on my desk first thing tomorrow morning."

* * *

Rain drizzled down the *Frank & Bennett* tower, adding a watery sheen to the windows. No dry patches remained on the front-facing side. Droplets of water mixed in the wailing wind, the merged streams diverting diagonally across the glass doors. The breeze subsided, but the rainfall was constant and heavy.

The law office building was cordoned off with metal barriers that stretched the width of the main street. News vans blocked the closest intersections, creating a backlog of traffic. Headlamps pierced the drizzle for hundreds of yards in either direction, and the police on guard duty looked in no mood to deal with gatecrashers. Wrapped up in transparent raincoats, the assault team still had their automatic weapons to hand, tough lady included.

Only Kristina Malloy and a few other reporters had been allowed through. She waited with her rivals on the pavement outside the entrance doors. The umbrella-covered microphone arm hadn't shielded her from the rain. Damp hair stuck to her dripping-wet cheeks and her coat was waterlogged, but she wasn't budging from her prime broadcasting spot.

Excitement flared up, lights brightening Lucy's face as she exited the building. When she walked off without comment, the reporters returned to their patient waiting game.

The detective moved slowly past the police cars, seemingly not bothered by the soaking she received. Her bulletproof vest protected her shirt, but her suit and trousers were drenched when she reached Adrian's silver SUV.

The vehicle was parked down a side street, the passenger half covered by the awning of a corner grocery store. Wipers did a commendable job of clearing away raindrops from the windscreen, but condensation obscured the interior. It was only when Adrian opened the door that Lucy saw him.

"You're late," she said, taking shelter under the canopy. "Thought you'd come straight here."

"Got nervous about confronting a killer, so I decided I'd leave that to you."

She swung into the passenger seat and shut the door. Water dripped off her trousers onto the floor mat. She brushed damp hair from her eyes, her soaked suit squelching as she made herself comfortable.

"Armed and dangerous," Adrian said. "I always liked women of action."

"Especially when they're soaking wet, and you have to rescue them."

She returned his desiring stare, sucking water from her lips. He reached out toward her knee. Lucy did nothing to stop him from touching her.

"I know a place where you can relax. Get out of those soggy clothes. And I don't mean your place. I'd rather not die from food poisoning. One stale breakfast is quite enough."

Lucy chuckled as he moved his fingers up to her face. He gently stroked the hair behind her ear.

"Think I'll skip the meal and go straight to the interesting part," she said. "As you noted, I'm a woman of action."

Adrian grinned in anticipation. He started the SUV's engine and turned his attention to the road ahead.

* * *

Vickers' forensic laboratory matched her style. There were old-fashioned slide microscopes, storage trays, a well-organized file system with handwritten labels, and an adjoining dark room for film development.

The computers and analysis machines were in a separate section of the windowless, gray-tiled workspace, opposite the stainless steel dissection tables. White coats hung over modern, plastic-legged chairs, which suggested the hi-tech equipment was used only by assistants.

Vickers stood alone in the central, well-lit area. She looked up from her wooden, classroom-style bench as the hinged doors squeaked open. Ron entered the lab, passing underneath an octagonal-framed analogue clock. The time was two minutes past twelve.

"Visiting the morgue after midnight?" the doctor asked. "Not something I'd usually do, either."

"Has Blake got you working late?"

"Just about to start."

Already sounding exhausted, she gestured at the bags piled on the bench. Collected evidence was wrapped in plastic. Ron spied Dawson's satchel, assorted stationery, a disconnected intercom, smashed computer mouse, steel cable and harness, and all the incriminating items from the safe. The two bodies had yet to arrive, but morgue freezers were open in readiness.

"He read you the riot act, huh? Sorry if I got you in trouble."

"Whenever you sweet talk me, it means you need something."

Ron walked around the bench, paying particular attention to the tablet device. "Find anything out of the ordinary?"

"Ask me in the morning when I'm done."

Vickers noticed him smoothing the plastic over the screen.

"You still believe Dawson was framed? There's no evidence to suggest this was anything but a suicide. Go home and get some rest. I don't have that luxury."

"Were there any prints on this?" he asked, tapping the bagged computer mouse and cord. "Or the other cable?"

"No, we..." Vickers stopped to frown. "There were some smudge marks on the noose, but..."

"Nothing on the wires or the base. The suspect wasn't wearing gloves, yet no fingerprints on the equipment. I'm not a forensics expert, so I could be wrong. But I'd call that suspicious."

Vickers stood up straight. "If the real killer's still out there... Where's Lucy?"

Ron pulled a fresh set of surgical gloves from a supply box. "Not safe, and too smitten to listen to my concerns."

"You suspect Pryce is the strangler?"

The detective stretched the rubber over his hands, staring gloomily at the pile of items. Vickers leaned over the bags to offer cautionary advice.

"You don't have any hard evidence to support your theory. Only suspicion. Blake won't move on that."

"He's too busy basking in the applause. And looking for scapegoats. Which means it's up to us to find the proof. No matter how smart a killer thinks he is, he always leaves a clue."

Ron removed the tablet from its plastic bag.

"Figured I'd start with this, given your aversion to computers."

"What if you're wrong about this?"

He switched on the computer. The still video image from earlier reappeared, showing Sophie being held underwater.

"What if I'm not?" he asked. "Pryce doesn't know we suspect him. He thinks he got away clean, which buys us some time. But eventually, time runs out. He'll feel the urge to kill again, and then it'll be Lucy wearing a necktie."

213

CHAPTER TWENTY-THREE

Face of a Killer

Lieutenant Blake's face dominated the television screen, the summit of his bald head just below the top of the image. His cheeks were clean shaven, his tie straightened, and lips wiped free of tobacco stains. He'd smartened up his appearance for the *EXCLUSIVE WITH KRISTINA MALLOY,* a title prominently stated across the caption banner.

The news alert was being transmitted live from the lobby of *Frank & Bennett*. Except for Blake and Kristina's out-of-shot crew, the entrance hall was mostly empty. Only two police officers were on duty, posted by the elevators and stairwell.

"Anything further to add, Lieutenant?" Kristina asked.

She held her cordless microphone closer to his mouth, obscuring his stubble-free chin.

"Only that the people of this great city can rest easy tonight. Our citizens have lived in fear these past few weeks, but thanks to the tireless dedication shown by our detectives, we've brought this case to a swift resolution. Our thoughts and prayers are with the victim's families. We will look into our policies and procedures to ensure something on this scale doesn't happen again."

"Have you been in contact with Taurus Studios since tonight's events?"

Blake shook his head, frowning in frustration. "Their president is aware of the situation. I can't comment further until we've concluded our investigation."

Kristina pressed even closer, microphone base and smoothly curved fingernails coming into view.

"Is there any sign that Miles Dawson was influenced by the violence in Taurus' games? Everything suggests he was a model citizen. What led him to commit five brutal murders? Do you think Adrian Pryce should pull *Crimson Shadow* from the Christmas schedule as a mark of respect for the victims?"

"We're still looking into the motive, but I would like to emphasize that—"

The television screen went dark. Adrian was reflected on the gray plastic, aiming a remote control from behind his living room futon.

"Nothing interesting on TV. But I'm sure she'll keep pestering me."

He discarded the zapper on the cushion and turned to Lucy, who approached from the drinks cabinet carrying two glasses of wine. She passed the light stand, which doubled as a place to hang her wet suit and pistol holster. She had unfastened her top shirt button, revealing her lower neck between the open collar flaps.

"The hounding will stop soon enough," Lucy said. "Now there's only good news to report. All quiet out there. Just the two of us..." She offered Adrian a glass. "...alone in private."

"Thought you didn't drink on duty."

"The case is closed, and I'm not here on police business."

Adrian accepted her not-so-subtle proposal. They drank together, watching each other above the crystal rims. He downed his wine, supping away until only a red stain remained. She rose to his unspoken challenge and finished her own a second later.

Lucy took Adrian's glass and placed both on a table. There was an uneasy pause where neither spoke.

"You never really believed I was innocent, did you?" he asked. "Not completely."

The detective gave him a warm, disarming smile. "Of course I did. Not sure about my partner. Ron doesn't like to admit he's wrong."

"Forget about him. This is between me and you. In video games, the hero always gets the girl."

"What about heroines?" Lucy stepped closer, breast tips touching Adrian's chest. "Does it work in reverse? The tough girls such as *Crimson Shadow*. Do they get the guy?"

She groped around her host's back, moving her massaging hands down to his buttocks. Adrian jumped as she squeezed. Lucy's grip was firm, eyes sparkling with lust. Their lips touched briefly.

"These days, stories have multiple endings," he said. "It's usually left to the players to decide the outcome."

Lucy took the bait, pressing her breasts into him as she forced her mouth forward. The two lovers shared a water-testing kiss, then a long, passionate embrace. They fell together on the futon.

Lucy split her legs to allow Adrian's waist between. He unbuttoned her shirt and pulled it a to expose an army-fatigued sports bra. All the prior confrontation, mistrust, and awkwardness melted in an instant. They wanted each other. His trousers stiffened around the groin area. She unbuckled his belt and twisted the leather ends.

"Don't get any ideas," Lucy said.

Her lover looked into her mischievous eyes. "I've got plenty."

"So long as none of them involve choking, we're good."

She pulled out the strap, held it over the sofa's backrest, and let it drop. Adrian pressed her wrist into the sofa cushion and kissed it softly. He did the same with her forearm, then the inside of her elbow, and repeated the action until he reached her neck.

"I just realized," Lucy said teasingly. "You never showed me your bedroom. Shall we finish this upstairs?"

* * *

Ron rewound the video of Sophie's murder and watched it over from the start. Screams and gurgles came through the tablet's speaker, then the rustling of cloth as the victim ripped off her unseen attacker's balaclava. A giant air bubble rose from her mouth and popped on the pool's surface.

"Do I have to listen to that again?"

Vickers inserted a blank report form into her typewriter. She sat on the other side of the laboratory with her back to him.

"Even a technophobe like me knows computers have mute buttons."

Ron gripped the device tighter as he watched the gloved killer force Sophie underwater. He rewound three seconds to review the footage. And then viewed it a third time.

He stopped playback and advanced the images frame-by-frame. Ron tilted the phone to its side, shifting the reflection of an overhead neon light off the screen.

"Look at this," he said.

Vickers walked across to the desk.

"Look at what? It confirms what we already know. The killer drowned Sophie Gallier."

"Not before she pulled off his mask."

Ron pointed to a spot below her head. The pool appeared darker between the strangler's arms, with a curved upper outline bordering a brighter section.

"There's a face in the water. I can't make it out. It's definitely there, though."

"You've got a blurry shadow, at best."

"It's Pryce," Ron said with utter conviction. "I know it. Can you enhance the image?"

"Can *I* enhance it? That's not my area of expertise. I don't touch computers, and for good reason. The outline's vague, not to mention the water distortion. I'm sure you could change the black spot into Pryce. Or Elvis Presley. Or even the President of the United States if you really wanted to." She sighed in surrender. "But you're determined to prove your case. Come back tomorrow and talk to my assistant. Maybe he can help you."

"It might be too late by then."

* * *

Adrian Pryce's bedroom was a gamer's paradise. There were multiple televisions, surround sound systems, and hardware hubs. Unlike his office, no old computers were on display. Only the latest consoles were wired up, all well-maintained and looking brand new.

Recessed, multi-leveled shelves lined every wall. Games, not literature, occupied the storage space. The inverted-pyramid light stands were the same design as those downstairs, forming the four corner posts of a chrome-framed, king-size bed.

"Just how many computers do you own?" Lucy asked.

"Enough. Why the precaution?"

Adrian nodded at the pistol holster balanced on the wet clothes bundled in Lucy's arms.

"A paranoid habit." She dropped them on an empty chair. "I always sleep with my gun close."

Home-owner and guest were both naked except for underwear. Lucy paused by the balcony window and looked through the brass rails at the dark-surfaced swimming pool in the garden. The drizzle had stopped, but traces of water remained on the glass.

Adrian sprawled on his bed. "Come away from there," he said invitingly. "I find the view inside much more exciting."

Lucy walked barefoot across the fluffy black carpet. She pounced on the mattress and crawled cat-like over the duvet cover.

She held the tantalizing position above him for a few seconds, then lowered herself gently onto his body. The two lovers interlocked their fingers.

Lucy stretched Adrian's hands up and back, holding them against the rear corner lampshades. Beads of perspiration trickled down the glass pyramids, soon evaporating in the heat.

Her elbow caught a game controller on the bed. She snagged its cable between her toes and yanked the wire from the console port. Its unconnected end bobbed across the carpet as she shifted forward into a lovemaking position.

"How about you forget your games? And let someone else take control tonight?"

Adrian kicked the gamepad away, and the loose cord trailed after it. He wrapped his ankles around Lucy's and sunk his head into the pillowcase.

"I'm all yours," he said.

* * *

Ron glanced at his wristwatch, then at the Taurus Studios roundabout. Philadelphia had shut down for the night. An occasional vehicle drove through the nearby intersection, but none turned toward the black tower. Some office buildings were still occupied, illuminated windows shining through gaps between dark skyscrapers. Clouds had cleared after the earlier rainstorm, but treacherous-looking frost had formed on the roads and pavement.

The detective had parked his Chevrolet on the kerb, a few yards from the entrance doors. He leaned against the vehicle's hood, watching the approach road. Ron's eyes brightened with hope as a throbbing engine broke the silence. Then the noise got louder, becoming the distinctive, constant buzz of a speeding motorcycle.

A solitary headlamp shone on the detective as the motorbike turned a corner. Ron stood up sharply and shielded his face, unable to see past the blinding glare. He hurried behind the car, took cover, and drew his weapon. The helmeted rider circled the bull statue, giving him some temporary respite from the light. He aimed over the hood, sights lined up with the leather-clad motorcyclist.

"Don't shoot!" the biker shouted over the engine.

The vaguely feminine voice gave Ron pause. He kept his firearm trained on the woman in black as she decelerated to a stop, lowered the support stand, and removed her visored helmet. It wasn't until Tania stepped in front of her headlamp — and showed her face — that he relaxed.

"Didn't expect you to show up on a motorcycle," Ron said, putting away his handgun.

She switched off the lamp and engine, and brought her computer laptop and Taurus ID card across to the meeting point.

"You said something about enhancing a video image. Don't the police have people who do that?"

"None who'd volunteer for night duty at such short notice."

He followed Tania to the doors, where she slid her identity badge through a scanner and input a keypad code.

"I thought they'd closed the building," Ron said.

"They did. But I helped design the security system."

She held back and let him take the lead. Their overlapping footsteps echoed round the empty lobby. Lights turned on automatically as they passed underneath, but the deactivated surveillance cameras remained stationary.

"Where to?" Ron asked.

"From what you told me, the picture is very blurry. We'll need a lot of processing power and graphic enhancement software to clean it up. So we should use the computers in the main project room. They can handle the latest graphics packages, so I doubt one image will be a problem."

Tania pressed the elevator call button.

"So, what does this footage show?"

Ron stalled while the disc platform descended, as if deciding how much information to share.

"A murder," he said, breaking it gently. "Sophie's murder. We think there may be a reflection of the killer's face in the pool."

"But I thought Dawson was the strangler. We traced the

signal to…" Tania's knees shook under her leggings. "Are you saying he's not?"

"We don't know. That's why this is so important."

The elevator arrived with a ping. Tania lurched back from the opening door, one hand on her heart. It took her a few seconds to recover.

"My god. If the killer's still out there…"

She looked fearfully round the deserted lobby, scanning the many shadows.

"Don't worry. Nobody else knows we're here. I only contacted you. And you've got me around for protection."

Tania quivered as she stepped into the elevator. Ron held his hand over the selection keypad.

"Floor eleven," she said, her voice still a little shaky.

"I knew that." He waited for the door to close. "Most girls wouldn't have done this. Come out here all alone at one AM. This is the second time you've helped me today."

"I guess I'm not like most girls, then."

Tania unzipped her leather jacket and parted the flaps to allow fresh air to her sweaty skin. Her form-fitting cream vest was damp around the breast area, nipple points showing through.

Ron couldn't take his eyes off her athletic figure. She slipped her coat off her shoulders, pulled the sleeves across her waist, and tied them in front. The detective blinked on seeing Tania's bare, muscular arms for the first time. She took off her leather gloves and stuffed them into her pant pockets.

"No," Ron said. "You're just a little tougher than most."

The elevator pinged, and the door swiveled open. Tania walked past him into a black-tiled corridor. Ceiling lights flickered on as she came within sensor range.

"It's all the overtime I put in doing the motion capture.

Before Adrian decided I wasn't slim enough and hired Jenna. And he planned to use me for the *Crimson Shadow* posters until…"

She slumped against the wall and sniffled, abandoning the harsh commentary in favor of fond reminiscence.

"They used sexy Sophie."

"Well, sexy Sophie can't help me crack this case. But tough Tania might. The room we want is through there?"

The technician straightened her spectacles and opened the double doors to the Taurus project area. Automatic lights flickered on above the hive of computer workstations. Tania quickened her pace, heading straight for the big screen at the center.

Ron gazed up at the bare ceiling. It seemed much emptier now that the suction discs and harness cables had been removed.

"So that's where the killer got the equipment from. And how he escaped the murder scene. We missed that bastard by minutes. Maybe seconds."

Tania booted up a computer terminal and opened a command prompt window.

"Do you have the image?" she asked, typing a series of commands.

Ron pulled out the tablet, hesitant to show her the still of Sophie drowning.

"It's on here."

The programmer frowned as he handed it over. "Can't do much with that. Good thing I came prepared."

She reached into her jacket pocket and removed a strong, flexible USB cable.

Tania plugged one end into the device and the other into a computer socket. After a few seconds, an enlarged high-definition image appeared on the big screen.

Sophie's dying scream was captured in minute detail, down to individual air bubbles, wavy hair, and lines on her open lips. In this blown-up picture, the reflection of the killer was less contentious, distorted outlines of their facial features visible in the water.

Tania looked away. "I can't do this. I never liked the woman, but watching her drown. It's... sick."

"What did tough Tania go?"

Ron came over to comfort her. The hug appeared to stiffen her resolve a little, but she refused to view the image.

"She works out on weight machines and codes computer games for a living. *Crimson Shadow* is just make believe. This is real life. I'm not sure I can do this."

"I'm afraid we have to."

Tania glanced briefly at the screen, then averted her gaze again. "The software's set up to run automatically. You should get a result in a few minutes."

A green outline had appeared around the killer's reflection. Within that border was a square grid. Colors changed block by block. Black became dark gray, white turned to pink. Then the next cycle started.

The computer program drew a second lattice over the original, its squares half as long. Parts of a human face emerged in the enhancement area: irises, hairline, the bridge of a nose. The image was still too fuzzy to identify the person.

"That's absolutely fan—"

Ron turned to see Tania already halfway to the exit.

"Where the hell are you going? I don't want you out of my sight."

"The building's locked down! Nobody else can get in here. Please, just do your detective work and go."

She was through the door before he could argue further.

He snarled in frustration and looked back at the image. Ron stared straight into the unmasked Taurus Strangler's jumbled up, multicolored eyes. The second iteration finished, and a third began.

"Come on, you bastard," he vented at the screen. "Show me your face. I know it's you."

Ron accessed his phone's address book and selected *Duvall* from the menu. He waited with his thumb on the dial button, ready to make the all-important call.

* * *

The lovers rolled over, their stretched hands locked together. Bed springs creaked as Adrian flattened his chest against Lucy's, transferring weight to her. She wrestled back, grunting as she forced a gap between them. It was a physical contest to assert control, with neither party willing to yield.

"What happened to letting go?" she panted.

Adrian released her and rose into a sitting position. His briefs rubbed against his lover's own masculine-style shorts. White flakes fell off a sticky patch around his groin, floating down onto the bed sheet between her thighs. He exhaled, breaths growing quieter as the peaky bulge above his crotch flattened out. The end of a sex session with all the excitement, but no risk.

"This reminds me of a scene from *Crimson Shadow*."

Adrian scrunched up the pillowcase in his sweaty hand. Repeated buzzing came from Lucy's discarded clothes. Her shirt pocket vibrated as a green light shone through the white cotton, vaguely in the shape of a telephone receiver.

The detective ignored the incoming call. She was on guard, suspiciously eyeing her host.

"Thought we were done playing games."

Adrian rolled off her and onto his side. He brushed loose hair off her neck, exposing the strangulation bruises left by the killer.

"What can I say? I'm addicted to them."

He reached out behind his back and patted the carpet. Finding the controller, he roped in the plastic cable and clenched the connector in his fist.

"What happens in this scene?" Lucy asked.

"It's a classic. With a twist."

Adrian looped the cord around his wrist and lifted up the attached gamepad. The corner lamp between his legs shone on the taut wire.

Lucy noticed its shadow pass across the shelves. She recoiled back, hands moving to a defensive position below her chin.

"You bastard. Ron was right. He tried to warn me, but I didn't listen. Dawson was never the strangler. It's you. It was you all along."

CHAPTER TWENTY-FOUR

The Taurus Strangler

"You've reached Detective Duvall. I'm not available to take
—"

Ron ended the call, cutting the recorded message short.
He turned his attention back to the computer screen.

The enhancement grid was a lot finer than earlier
iterations, the square edges now only a few pixels wide. The
distorted image had been cleaned up considerably. What
had been a shadowy reflection was clearly a human face,
chin arc and reddish lips visible above a smooth, hairless
neck.

Ron squinted. "Wait a second. That's not Pryce. It's…"

He ran his finger across the killer's sharply outlined
features. Long, loose hair now appeared shiny black. Two
darkened, but soft-skinned cheeks, thin eyelashes, and a
glossy mouth.

"The strangler's a girl?"

He gasped in disbelief at his own conclusion.

"It can't be. To do those murders, she'd have to be super-
strong. Like…" His limp hand dropped. "Like Tania."

The detective spun round, drawing his weapon in mid turn. There was nobody else in the project room, but he didn't lower his gun. Ron pushed back into the screen, cutting off a potential rear attack, and steadied his aim at the door. He half-squeezed the trigger.

He had shaken off his initial surprise. Should Tania return, there would be a psyched up cop waiting to shoot her dead.

* * *

Lucy watched Adrian, eyes following the straight-lined cable. She kept her hands before her neck, ready to block an incoming swipe. He lunged forward, then stopped in mid-thrust, laughing as she rolled off the bed.

"Fooled you."

The detective sprung into a standing position. She edged warily toward her pistol holster.

"Real funny. But I don't buy it. Maybe I should shoot you, just to be sure."

Adrian dropped the controller on his bed and raised his hands to protest his innocence.

"I could never hurt you, Lucy. I was only playing."

"You're a jerk. Pulling a shitty stunt like that after what we've been through. Are you crazy?" She stepped back toward the bed, sticking to the middle ground. "What if I'd shot you?"

Lucy's phone vibrated in her shirt pocket. A name shone through below the green incoming-call logo: *Wallace*. She made no attempt to answer it.

"Who's that?" Adrian asked.

"Ron and his wild goose chase. Another stupid asshole who doesn't know when to quit. I seem to collect them."

Her lover wrapped the cable around his wrists and bound them together. Lucy watched the half-naked man tie himself to the corner post lamp. Behind her, the phone stopped vibrating.

"As I was saying. Just another asshole."

"Come on," Adrian enticed her. "This is the scene where the heroine saves her true love. Usually it's a guy who rescues the girl. That's the twist I was talking about. Well, are you going to untie me?"

Lucy mounted the bed and dropped her crotch hard on Adrian's, doing nothing to shield him from the brute force impact. He grunted, trying to keep a brave face. A moderately successful effort, but he obviously felt the blow.

She rubbed his groin, scraping away the last remaining white flakes. "I'll think about it. First, it's my turn to play."

Lucy's phone vibrated again, but she stayed with Adrian.

"You should get that," he said. "What if it's something important?"

"I wouldn't worry about it." She dismissed his concerns with a passionate, forgiving kiss. "The only thing important to me is right here."

Adrian grabbed the rear strap of her sports bra and pulled it over her head. Tossed blonde hair settled over her bare upper body, loose strands tickling his skin.

He squashed the sweat-stained garment into a ball of fabric and threw it away. It unwrapped in flight, landing on top of Lucy's clothes. The dangling, lowermost cup covered the shirt pocket, obscuring the projected green receiver icon.

* * *

Tania operated the server room computer with cool

professionalism. There was no triumphal smirk, no gloating, and no lapse in concentration. The cold, calculating killer typed a series of instructions on the keyboard, pausing after each entry to verify the on screen messages.

Camera Tracking On. Front Door Locks Engaged. Emergency Exits Sealed. Communication Links Inactive. Wireless Network Jammed.

It took Tania less than thirty seconds to secure the Taurus Studios tower and convert it into an isolated hunting ground. She stepped back from the monitors, eyes shifting between two active workstations. One showed a three-dimensional blueprint of the building, the other a security feed from the project room. The camera was opposite the entrance, above and behind the watchful Ron.

Tania removed her spectacles and carefully folded the ear rests. Her nose and lips appeared distorted through the convex lenses, but magnification was minimal. The glasses were little more than a cosmetic fashion accessory, a "Clark Kent" style disguise to bolster the appearance of a shy computer technician. Without them, and with her hair tied in a ponytail, the muscular Asian looked far more dangerous. Tania Chin was the Taurus Strangler.

The murderess stepped out of her leather boots and untied the knotted sleeves of her jacket, letting it drop off her waist. She unzipped the fly of her men's trousers, and wriggled her body so they slid effortlessly off her smooth, agile legs.

Wearing nothing except underwear, Tania walked backward to the storage lockers. She ducked, turned, and stepped past the webbed cables, bending her twisty, athletic limbs through the narrowest of gaps. She kept her head upright and never took her eyes off the computer screens.

Tania sidestepped to the locker she'd "hidden" in after

the attempt on Lucy's life. She entered a code on the keypad without turning around, using a different finger for each digit to shorten the input time. She reached for the handle, but froze in mid-action when Ron moved.

With his weapon aimed at the project room door, the policeman turned to view the large imaging screen. From the camera's angle, the cleaned-up video image wasn't visible, but a brief muttered curse told the story. He had just seen the incriminating reflection.

"You conniving bitch."

His voice was amplified with no background noise. Tania's multi-speaker setup made it sound as if he was actually in the server room.

"You were setting us up the whole time. First Pryce, then Dawson. Well, it's game over now, Miss Strangler."

Ron disconnected his mobile phone from the USB cable, held the receiver to his ear, and pressed the call button. He looked at the screen in bewilderment, tapped it, and tried again. An angry shake and frantic keypad taps suggested he hadn't gotten through.

"Damn it!"

Tania's iron concentration broke as her lips curved into a familiar, sadistic smile. She turned round and opened the locker with a powerful tug.

The killer lifted out a scratched toolbox and a plastic bag, and reached into the now-empty storage unit to unscrew four loose rivets on the rear panel. A black metal sheet came free, scraping aside to reveal a hiding space in the ventilation duct.

Tucked inside the hole were two neatly folded outfits: the Taurus Strangler's all-leather gear and balaclava, and Jenna's motion capture suit.

Tania reached for the mask then stopped, her smile

broadening as she decided on the catsuit. Electrical transmitters clinked together as she took it from the locker. Light shone on a harness, coiled steel cables, and suction-pad discs.

The murderess forced her powerful arms through the black Lycra sleeves and extended her feet into the stockings. She reached behind to seal the well-concealed zip up her spine. The sensor-fitted, elasticated material had reshaped around her: bulgy biceps, sturdy thighs, rounded buttocks.

Tania pushed her hair inside the ninja hood and lifted it over her face. It snapped against her neck when she released, elongated slit lining up perfectly with her eyes. Other than her joined-up breasts that replicated the shape of her sports bra, the assassin resembled a naked woman with black Lycra skin. She twisted the mouthpiece vent, and tiny red sensor-dots lit up across her entire body.

"Detective Wallace."

The taunt echoed back through the speaker system. On screen, Ron remained still, but a quick glance up revealed he'd heard the broadcast.

"It's time you met *Crimson Shadow*."

* * *

Ron looked round the project room, pistol unsteady in his hands. He swept the hexagonal desks and separating aisles and kneeled to check under the terminals. That's when he spotted a green glow coming from somewhere behind.

He did a sharp U-turn and raised his gun at a wireframe woman's head. The enhanced camera image had disappeared from the monitor. The motion capture avatar now occupied the screen, showing its wearer's every move. Tania moved her thick-muscled arms and legs skillfully and precisely, navigating an unseen obstacle course.

"Do you want to know why I killed them?"

The avatar's mouth synchronized perfectly with the voice.

"Not really," Ron shouted up at the PA speakers. "Just feel like returning the favor."

"I'm the one that created *Crimson Shadow*. I designed her code. Without me, she would never have existed. I have so much talent, and what did they do with it? They left me to rot in the basement. Adrian didn't think I was athletic enough to do the motion capture."

The wireframe woman somersaulted and landed perfectly in a half-crouch. There were no stumbles or awkward movements. If Tania was still in the server room, she hadn't touched a single wire.

"So he hired *Jenna*," she said. "I wasn't sexy enough to appear on the poster." She arched her back so her breasts thrust up. "So he used *Sophie*. After Norris left, reviewers claimed his *music* was the best thing about the trailer. They never mentioned the game engine that I spent six months programming."

"And Lucy? What the hell did she do?"

"Do you want to see what she's doing right now?"

The wireframe Tania leaped to her feet, walked two paces, and held her palm out. Her fingers closed round the edges of an unseen, four inch wide object. She reached with her other hand and pressed the invisible screen with her index finger.

There was a beep, and Ron's mobile phone lit up. He moved cautiously across to the desk where he'd left it, covering the aisle with his pistol. He glanced down to see a mailed digital image sent by *Crimson Shadow*.

It was a top-down photograph of Adrian's bedroom.

Lucy straddled her tied-up host. Blonde hair streamed down her naked back. Her firm nipples pointed forward, his head between her bare breasts.

"You sick psycho bitch," Ron said. "You've been watching her?"

"Watching *him*. She's at his house."

The avatar walked on, an unseen object held up with her palm facing inward. Her pace was steady with the motion capture tracking. The animation was akin to a person walking on a slow-moving treadmill.

"I left a camera behind on my last visit. I can design electronic systems. They didn't need Levitt to handle security at Taurus. But the money they wasted on him is nothing compared to what Dawson kept in reserve. He got rich off my work. I wanted to ruin Adrian and let him take the fall. I gave him to you, but then you got nosy."

Tania walked on, maintaining her pace. Ron deleted the image from his phone and tried to call Lucy again. *No signal*.

"You won't get through. I've blocked all external communications. It's just you and me."

Ron put the cellphone in his pocket, eyes moving between the wireframe video and the door.

"So, you're still in the building," he shouted.

"Almost at the exit."

Tania stopped to reach out for something, possibly a handle, and continued on.

"And then you'll be trapped inside. Nobody works at Taurus Studios any more. I can come back for you later, but a dead cop needs a killer to pin the blame on. With Dawson unavailable, I'm thinking Adrian will do. And since Lucy doesn't want to leave him alone, she'll have to be a victim."

"You're bluffing. You're still here."

"So stop me. You have a gun, don't you?"

Tania pushed forward, her palm encountering resistance. There was a squeak in the background as an unseen door opened, followed by more footsteps, then a click.

"I've only got this computer cable."

The avatar reached toward her waist, pulled her hand away, and clenched her fist. If the actual killer held a cord, it was half an inch thick.

The wireframe image flickered. Vertices scattered. Green lines fuzzed into smudge-like blurs, bent at strange angles. The figure vanished, leaving only a black screen.

"If you hurt her…" Ron said.

"You're too… ate…" Tania's reply was badly distorted, with a lot of static mixed in. "Det… ec… ive."

The intermittent chug of a motorcycle engine came over the loudspeakers. The screech of rubber on tarmac. Then nothing.

* * *

Ron rode the elevator platform down. He stood opposite the passing doors, back pressed against the glass tube. His suit squeaked, its flap folding up above his waist. As the tension mounted, the pressure from the bulletproof vest dragged his shirt out of his trousers.

He maintained position, making frequent, wide-arced sweeps with his pistol. The cop aimed just about everywhere: tinted office windows, dark corridors, emergency gantries. As the lobby's balcony came into view, he did a full one-hundred-and-eighty degree turn from left to right. Then the elevator arrived at ground level, and the door swiveled open.

There was no sign of the Taurus Strangler. If Tania was

somewhere in the lobby, she'd hidden herself well. Ron edged forward. With the wall behind him, he sidestepped toward the entrance side. Pyramid lights switched on under the balcony, tracking his cautious progress.

Ron looked up frequently, guarding himself against a potential attack from above. He made his way past dark television screens and unoccupied advertising stands, taking extra care as he passed the reception desk. He turned at the corner and followed the same tactical approach to the exit.

With his gun aimed inward, Ron groped for the door release button. He pressed it twice, but the entrance remained sealed. A sheet of white paper flapped against the glass, disturbed by his shoulder.

The detective jerked back and gave the two taped notes a quick, fearful glance. The adjacently posted letters were almost identical. Both had a Philadelphia Police Department logo printed in color at the top, and the same typed memo beneath.

Your job was to capture the Taurus Strangler, but you have repeatedly identified the wrong suspect. Your performance has been unsatisfactory. Consider your employment terminated.

The only difference was the addressee's name: *Lucy Duvall* on the first sheet, *Ron Wallace* on the second.

The cop wiped his brow, clearly unnerved. He stood still and watched the lobby. It was deathly quiet. The balcony lights switched off one by one, retracing his path from the elevator tube around the side wall. Only two above the entrance remained lit.

"I'm here."

The killer's voice came from behind the reception desk. Ron aimed his gun in that direction without straying from his vantage point. From there, he couldn't see the elaborate setup under the receptionist's chair. "Tania" spoke through an MP3 player connected to two external speakers.

"I'm the huntress," the prerecorded voice said. "And you're my prey."

The phantom killer breathed. Softly to begin with, then more savagely. The right speaker volume got progressively louder and the left quieter, creating the illusion of movement.

Ron pivoted his pistol clockwise, deceived by the ruse. Above him — unnoticed — a female figure vaulted over the balcony rail. Light briefly illuminated Tania's hooded face as she climbed down to the edge. The sensor lights on her motion capture suit were dark and inactive.

The killer reached out and placed a suction pad disc on the underside of the platform. She swung across on the attached harness cable, spinning around in mid-leap. The agile assassin thrust her chest forward and elevated her knees, making only minimal contact with the glass window.

Tania was a master at remaining undetected. Ron saw and heard nothing.

"In the early build of *Crimson Shadow*, the main character strangled her targets with a garotte."

Tania's recorded voice moved to the center of the speakers.

"I did the motion capture and coding, but Adrian never used it."

The steel cable unwound from its winch, lowering the Taurus Strangler toward her unaware target. Against the solid-black background, the Lycra suit was well-camouflaged, and she was practically invisible except for the glinting wire.

Tania placed her stockinged feet on the ledge-like door frame, allowing the cable to slacken behind her belt. The winch stopped unwinding as the timer reached zero. Ron was still hunting the phantom killer, unaware the actual murderer was perched a few yards above.

"He thought it was unrealistic that a woman could strangle so many men. So he planned to use my animation for a male character in the sequel."

Tania pulled back her ninja hood and tossed her hair. She unfastened the Lycra suit's zip, timing her actions precisely. The recorded words masked any noise.

The killer reached into her loosened outfit and pulled out a gray-insulated ethernet cable. She gripped the two wire ends just inside the connectors, breathing softly through her narrow lips.

The Taurus Strangler extended her arms and pushed off the glass. The steel line clinked as she fell, her shadow falling across Ron's face. He saw the danger too late.

Tania's stockinged feet slammed into his wrists, knocking away the pistol. The weapon collided with the marble floor, discharging a bullet which chipped the reception desk.

Tania split her legs, lifting them into an inverted-T. The winch cable snapped taut, with her waist-line three feet above ground. Gravity shifted the murderess toward Ron.

Dazed from the initial strike, he was still recovering when the strangler swung into his stomach and trapped his body between her closed thighs. Facing her victim head-on, she wrapped the ethernet cable around his neck, crossed the wires behind, and pulled the ends apart.

"He didn't believe she'd be strong enough to do it," said Tania. The real one.

Ron's eyes bulged in their sockets. To save his energy, he silently endured the assassin's asphyxiating grip. He reached his foot toward his pistol. His shoe heel scraped the handle, drawing the gun a half-inch closer.

Tania kicked the entrance doors, spinning herself and her trapped victim. Stamping in desperation, he inadvertently knocked the weapon away. The murderess smiled as it slid across the floor.

Ron reached behind his head, grabbed her wrists, and attempted to force them together to give himself some breathing room. Lycra tore around the strangler's throbbing forearm, but she was more than equal to the challenge. The detective's throat compressed as Tania pulled her garrotte even tighter.

"Do you think it's unrealistic?" she asked between two sharp breaths.

Forced to open his mouth, Ron let out a strangled gasp. His fingers slipped off Tania's wrists. He twisted hard, slamming her into the door.

It was a final, desperate act to shake the killer off. She grunted as the cable swung back, holding her victim's tiring body tight between her thighs.

Ron expired with a defiant stare into his assailant's eyes. The termination notice, ripped during the impact, came unstuck. When the letter floated between the Taurus Strangler's legs, she was still throttling his limp corpse.

CHAPTER TWENTY-FIVE

Final Notice

Fallen raindrops had frozen solid on Christmas decorations, forming snaky trails on the baubles and miniature plastic sleighs. Only the lights were completely free of ice, their glass covers heated by bright burning electric bulbs. Snowflakes precipitated, sleet building up on hedges, car windscreens, and lampposts. Every patio door, window, and garden gate — including Adrian's — was closed. No residents ventured into the chilly December night.

The motorcyclist didn't encounter a soul as she weaved her slow-moving vehicle between the parked cars and SUVs. The engine's throb was subdued, almost inaudible against the wailing breeze, colliding tree branches, and clinking baubles. There was a short, powerful roar as the leather-clad rider mounted the kerb. The wheels left a straight, flattened path through the white bladed grass.

The biker's silvery visor reflected the planks of a familiar wooden picket fence. Now at her destination, she switched off the engine, removed her helmet, and placed it on the handlebar.

Tania's hair was tucked inside her rolled up balaclava. The Taurus Strangler had ditched the motion capture suit and replaced it with her all-leather outfit. Snowflakes blew into her smooth oriental skin, melting upon contact. Her face and neck were exposed to the freezing cold, but there were no shivers.

Tania reached into her jacket pocket and removed her tablet phone. She activated it, and live camera footage of Adrian's bedroom appeared on the screen. Erotic grunts and groans were muted, but the two lovers were engaged in passionate sex. She was on top, bouncing so hard the bed frame shook. Light reflected off her bare, sweat-drenched back as she leaned forward to kiss the tied-up man.

Tania pressed her thumb down on Adrian's head, turning a patch of the screen black. Warm air condensed to steam on the transparent plastic as she exhaled. She traced her gloved finger across Lucy's neck, her lips curving into a scheming smile.

The murderess turned to inspect the camera above the gate and typed on the phone's virtual keypad. Computer code replaced the video, and a preset program entered commands with no further input. After several automated tasks had completed, a message appeared between two asterisks: *Security Offline*. The recording light blinked out, and the device stopped in mid-rotation.

Tania stepped off her motorcycle and wheeled it around the picket fence. She rested the seat backrest and handlebar against the white wood, put the phone away, and pulled the balaclava down. The mouthpiece veil fitted over her lips, and the tiny circular eye slits over her irises. Her feminine features were obscured by the leather jacket. No potential witness could identify the masked intruder as a woman.

Tania leaped into the fence and kicked the planks to

extend her jump by a good few inches. She grabbed the top, heaved her body up, and swung her legs over the pickets.

The killer dropped into Adrian's rear garden. She circled around the dark pool and approached the house. The Taurus Strangler was a natural at finding shadows to conceal her approach, and keeping her balance on the iced-over paving stones.

When Tania reached the patio, she took out her phone and re-established her connection to the hidden camera. Lucy held Adrian in a tight, chest-crushing embrace. Her attention was fully on him, and his on her. With the alarms deactivated, they'd receive no warning of any intrusion.

Tania looked up at the bedroom balcony, dropped the switched-off phone in her pocket, and climbed the wall. As at Norris' warehouse, where she'd claimed her first victim, there was no drainpipe, ladder or rope to assist her.

The Taurus Strangler slotted her fingertips and boot soles into the smallest of gaps, and closed in on her unsuspecting prey.

* * *

Adrian exhaled and rested his head against the bed frame. Lucy recuperated from her exertion, then released her grip on his waist. The naked blonde dismounted, sat up, and reached over the bedside, her shadow obscuring his privates as she reclaimed her underwear.

"Aren't you going to untie me?" he asked.

Lucy slipped on her shorts, fastened her bra strap, and shook her clammy hair until it dropped behind her ears. She leaned over in a cross-legged, seductive pose, and tickled her lover's chin.

"No sleeping around this time. Promise?"

"I was stupid back then," said Adrian. "Now I'm older and wiser."

Lucy unfastened the cord. The depressions it left behind on his wrists were deep red.

"A lot older." She wrapped the wire around the controller. "And a little wiser. At least you haven't run off yet. I'd better get myself cleaned up."

She placed the gamepad beside the console and made for the upstairs landing.

"What are you saying?" Adrian called out after her. "That I'm a dirty man?"

Lucy replied with a joyful smile. After she'd left the bedroom, he rolled onto his side, put his shorts back on, and moved his damp-haired legs into a more comfortable position.

A leather-gloved hand extended above the exterior balcony and closed round the lower rail. Tania lifted her head and shoulders up to peek through the window. Her eyes quickly surveyed the room: exhausted man, body-shaped trough in the sheets behind him, unlocked bolts on the sliding frame, discarded controller.

The killer reached for the middle railing.

"You lousy bastard!" Lucy yelled.

Tania ducked just before the furious woman stormed in and threw a soaked facecloth at Adrian. The missile flew across the bed, shedding soapy water. It squelched as it struck the window and dropped less than three feet from Tania's exposed hand. But the detective's full, undivided attention was on her lover, and the killer remained unseen.

The mattress creaked as Adrian sat up. "What did I do?" he asked, looking completely bewildered.

"Quit playing games. I know she's here. Where is she?"

"Who?"

Lucy sighed in resignation. "Fine. If you want her. You two are a perfect match for each other. Can't believe I trusted either of you. So much for the new Adrian Pryce. You haven't changed at all."

She marched over to her clothes, grabbed her trousers, and put them on. She pulled her buttoned shirt over her head, letting it hang loose.

"Who the hell are you talking about?"

Lucy tied up her shoelaces. "Your Chinese girlfriend. It's no use pretending, so drop the act. What was the plan? Do her after you'd finished with me?"

"Tania? You think I'm screwing Tania?"

Instead of answering, she tucked her shirt into her pants, pushing it down with quick, firm prods.

"Wait a minute," Adrian said.

He climbed off the bed, outrage turning to concern.

"Why would you suspect Tania's here?"

"Game over. And there's no point in continuing. I saw her motorbike parked outside."

Adrian stiffened. Lucy's eyes narrowed a little, as if she wasn't sure whether to believe him. Neither of them looked at the window, or saw the masked killer step over the balcony rails.

"Your partner called earlier," Adrian said. "What did he want?"

"He thought you—"

She lifted the mobile phone from her shirt pocket. She scrolled through the list of missed calls and selected the most recent.

"Lucy, where are you? Pick up, God damn it," Ron's recorded voice said.

Tania slowly opened the balcony window, squeezed through the narrow gap, and closed the panel to block the draught. The strangler crept across the carpet and stooped low to collect the controller. Her fingers deftly unwound the plastic cable, not making a sound.

"Dawson's not our guy," Ron said. "I found something on the recording of the Gallier murder. A reflection in the water. The killer's face. Vickers couldn't enhance it, so I've gone to Taurus to see Tania. Maybe she can—"

"Lucy!"

Before she could react to the warning, the masked killer garroted her from behind. Taken by complete surprise, she accidentally knocked the chair over. Her weapon slid from its holster. Adrian wasted no time grabbing it.

Lucy writhed about in the strangler's grip. She attempted to stomp on Tania's foot, but the killer expected the attack and skipped expertly aside.

The murderess pressed one knee into Lucy's back and pulled. Her leather sleeve caught the cable and slipped down, exposing light brown skin. The struggling detective elbowed her attacker in the chest, but the hold didn't weaken.

Adrian fumbled with the gun. His hands shook uncontrollably.

"Don't move," he said, even though there was no clear shot.

Lucy let her body relax. Her limp legs swung like a toy doll's and bumped weakly into Tania's. The detective gasped, her face contorted in agony as she forced her head to tilt sideways. The strangler's right eye slit came into view. She stared at Adrian with pure hate.

"Tania?" he said, sounding only half convinced it was her behind the balaclava. "Why are you doing this?"

The only response was a heavy, drawn-out breath. Lucy, choking badly, mouthed a voiceless instruction. *Shoot her. Shoot her!*

"He can't hear you."

The veil distorted the Taurus Strangler's whispered voice, but her lip movements showed through.

"Or shoot you. I think he genuinely cares."

"What do you want!?"

Lucy, gasping continuously, struggled to free herself again. Tania dragged her victim's slipping feet back, giving Adrian even less of a target to aim at. He remained rooted to the spot, unwilling to squeeze the trigger.

"To watch you suffer," Tania said.

"Do it!" mouthed Lucy. "Do it!"

Adrian still wouldn't take the shot. She concentrated, exercising her arms as she prepared to try something.

Lucy grabbed Tania's balaclava, one hand over each ear, and twisted. The leathery mask turned. Eye slits moved away from the killer's irises onto her hair and nose bridge.

Blinded, the murderess stumbled back. Lucy stamped on her foot, her blow connecting this time, grabbed the controller cable, and pulled. It loosened a touch, then Tania's glove came off.

Free of the strangler's deadly hold, the cop pushed herself away and lashed out at her assailant's face. The attack caught the killer on the chin.

Weakened from her long, near-fatal struggle, Lucy spluttered and coughed.

"Shoot her!" she said. "What are you waiting for?"

Tania ripped off her balaclava and threw it on the floor. Her jade ponytail clip came loose and bounced off the window with a clink. Messy hair dropped on her shoulders. Her eyes were wild with lunacy.

"He can't do it." She stared straight down the gun's barrel. "Adrian's a bastard. But he's no killer."

Her taunt only hardened his conviction, and he took aim. All hesitation was gone, replaced by cold-eyed ruthlessness. The Taurus Strangler's smile faded.

"Didn't you get Dawson's memo, Miss Chin?" Adrian asked. "You're fired."

He was still closing his mouth when he squeezed the trigger. There was a loud bang, and a bullet hole appeared below Tania's left breast. Fluff fell from her ripped-open leather jacket. She stumbled, barely able to stand. Adrian shot her again. And a third time.

The Taurus Strangler toppled backward, eyes rolling up into her sockets. Her body slammed onto the carpet, foot landing hard on the controller pad. It flipped up and dropped next to the killer's twitchy fingers.

Adrian discharged three more shots into her. After a brief spasm, the killer lay still. Hair dropped into her open mouth.

He let go of the gun, hand shaking, as he ran to Lucy's side. "I couldn't... I didn't want to hurt..."

"It's all right," she comforted him, groaning as she stood up. "You did great."

"That's twice I've saved you."

She stumbled into his waiting arms. "This is becoming a good habit. Make sure you keep it up."

Adrian kissed her, came up briefly for air, then did so again. Lucy rubbed his naked back. His hands went to her shoulders.

A gloved fist pummeled his cheek. He fell face-forward, knocked unconscious with a single blow.

The cop instinctively dived for her weapon. Tania — very much alive — got there first and kicked it under the bed. Another kick, this one to her victim's stomach.

The murderess opened her leather jacket and

unstrapped a bulletproof vest. It was Philadelphia Police Department equipment.

"I took this from your partner." She tossed it by Lucy's side. "Ron doesn't need it any longer. Did I not tell you? I served him a notice, too."

Lucy clenched her fist, fingernails ripping bristles from the carpet. Shaking with anger, she forced herself into a sitting position. Tania reached under the bed and grabbed the pistol. The killer was three feet away and had a point black shot.

"As an experienced gamer, Adrian should have known to go for the head," she gloated, aiming between Lucy's eyes. "But I'm smarter than him. And you."

Tania stepped on the controller cable, pressing it beneath her boot. Lucy shifted the weight to her buttocks to free her hands. She reached discreetly for the bulletproof vest, talking to distract the murderess.

"What does the Taurus Strangler need a gun for? Aren't you strong enough?"

The psycho grinned, relishing her moment of victory.

"I don't have to prove it. Only a weak cop would get shot with her own weapon. What? You thought this was some dumb movie, and I'd throw away my advantage?"

The killer lined up the sight, her finger squeezing the trigger halfway. Lucy grabbed the vest and flung it before her face. The bullet hit the Kevlar, and the squashed round fell off the fibers.

Undeterred, the assassin kicked Lucy's lifesaver away, spread her legs, and retook aim. Adrian stirred from his slumber. Quickly assessing the situation, he grabbed Tania's ankle and pulled it to unbalance her. The off-target bullet shattered a lampshade, showering the bed sheets with glass fragments.

Balancing expertly on one leg, Tania wrestled loose from Adrian's tired grip and kicked him squarely in the face. The force of the blow knocked him unconscious. Blood trickled from a nasty cut on his cheek.

Lucy staggered to her feet, but the killer had already regained her posture. She had the detective at her mercy once more. This time there was no escape, and she didn't hesitate to pull the trigger.

The gun clicked. Its magazine was empty.

The murderess hissed in fury and threw the weapon at Lucy. The pistol handle whipped her chest, but that didn't slow the detective's forward lunge. She thumped the killer in the stomach. A powerful strike that made her step back.

More attacks followed, but Tania shook them off and grabbed Lucy's throat with both hands. The strangler's fingers pressed deep into her victim's neck, the remaining glove creaking under mounting pressure.

Lucy chopped repeatedly at Tania's arms to break the choke-hold, but the blows simply bounced off. The strangler used her superior muscle strength to force her victim back against the balcony window. Unable to stop — or even slow — the momentum, the detective found herself trapped, with her cheek pressed against the glass.

The Taurus Strangler slammed Lucy's head into the window, causing the pane to split down the middle. Tania panted as she continued her relentless squeeze. More cracks appeared, branching out from the first. A few tiny slivers fell off.

Lucy held the balcony door handle for support and lifted her knees up. She kicked out, launching both her feet at Tania's chest. Strained wrinkles appeared on the cop's face as she pressed. It was a contest of strength. The strangler had more muscle power, but her prey had greater leverage.

The killer's iron grip loosened, thumbs snapping together. A final, assertive push, and Lucy was free.

She landed awkwardly on one leg, spraining her ankle. Seeing her quarry was wounded, Tania kicked high. Her boot found the gap under Lucy's chin. The resulting impact was enough to shatter the window pane and send the cop reeling back.

Her head banged on the frosty upper balcony rail. Wind blew through the dazed woman's hair, snowflakes landing on her bruised neck. In the garden below, glass shards fell on paving stones. Most smashed into gravel-sized little pieces, but a few remained intact.

Tania grabbed Lucy's legs and tipped her over the safety bar. There was a heavy thump below, then nothing but whistling wind. The killer leaned over the balcony to look.

Lucy was sprawled by the pool, three feet from the black water. Weak, condensed breaths revealed she'd survived the fall. But one leg was twisted back on itself, and her hair stained with sludgy, purple-red blood. The crippled woman was an easy target.

Tania took her time. She removed her leather jacket to expose her cream vest, dumped her trousers, and shook off her boots. The killer vaulted over the balcony and leaped down to the garden.

She threw the power lever under the patio roof, switching on the swimming pool's underwater lights but leaving the mist generator inactive. Thin, smooth-edged ice sheets bobbed on the water's surface.

Surrounded by precipitating snow, Tania had the stamina to stand in the open and not be affected. Without help, Lucy could well freeze to death, but the killer was determined to finish the job herself. It was obvious what fate she had planned: a watery grave.

She kneeled down and grabbed her victim's shirt. The barely conscious detective could just about move, but she snagged a long, dagger-like glass shard with a lethally sharp edge.

"For such a cold-hearted bitch," Tania said, not noticing the fragment, "this seems a fitting end."

The killer showed no sign of fatigue. Before the cop could lift her arm to attack, Tania heaved, slid her body across the ice-coated stones, and released.

Lucy splashed into the pool. Water closed over her hand, and the shard slipped from her numb fingers. It sank through a light beam and disappeared into the black depths.

Lucy coughed up a mouthful of fluid and grabbed a floating ice sheet. It cracked and split in two. The detective's clothes rapidly took on water and dragged her under.

Tania lowered herself into the pool, arms pivoting to grab the edge. She endured the cold with a triumphant smile. The Taurus Strangler scissored Lucy's neck between her thighs and squeezed from both sides.

The killer fished her prey up, watched her weak struggles, and dunked her victim's head back underwater. Buoyant blonde hair floated on the surface, air pockets popping amid the strands.

Lucy grabbed Tania's legs, but against a much stronger opponent, she did nothing but waste vital energy. Bubbles got bigger as her mouth filled with water.

The killer's grip on the poolside slipped as the conditions sapped her strength. She released Lucy's neck and pushed down on her shoulders, submerging her completely. The drowning woman had seemingly given up. Her prone body spun around, passed through a light beam, and floated into the darkness.

Tania exhaled, letting her legs swing back against the

pool wall. She licked the moisture from her lips and stroked her damp hair.

Lucy surfaced right in front of her, bloody hands clutching the glass dagger she'd retrieved from the pool. She caught the Taurus Strangler completely off guard. The murderess could do nothing to prevent the razor-sharp shard from being plunged into her heart.

Blood diffused across Tania's wet vest. She gulped, kicking as she made a desperate grab for the paving stones. The icy water slowed her movement and softened her blows, and the detective kept her grip on the fragment. The wounded killer struggled to hold on. Now it was the intended victim who was confident.

"Miss Chin," Lucy said. "Consider your employment…"

She pushed the glass harder. Its bloody tip went all the way through, piercing Tania's vest at the back. The killer's arms flopped into the pool, and her kicking ceased.

"Terminated."

Lucy released the Taurus Strangler, allowing the icy water to claim her lifeless body.

Teeth chattering, the detective swam to the poolside. She reached out and slapped her white fingers on the paving stones. Paralyzing numbness set in, and she slipped back. One hand fell in, and the second was about to when Adrian grabbed her wrist.

He dragged Lucy from the pool, lay her down, and pumped her chest. She opened her eyes and coughed. He placed Tania's leather jacket over her body as a blanket to shield her from the falling snow.

"I'm losing count," he said. "Is this the third time I've saved you?"

"I think we can call it even now."

Lucy forced herself up. Adrian moved to intercept her,

but she shook her head. She fell into his arms, standing on her good leg. Her other limped badly, but didn't seem broken.

Emergency sirens wailed in the distance.

"Thought we'd let your police friends clean up," Adrian said. "Soon as we sort the money out, Taurus Studios can reopen for business."

Lucy looked at the pool. At the bottom, lit from below, Tania's dark face-down corpse was surrounded by chlorinated blood. The Taurus Strangler — and self-appointed *Crimson Shadow* — had taken her last breath.

"Sure about that? Looks like you…" Lucy grunted. "… will need a new programmer."

"And a head of security. You fancy working for me?"

"Why not? Think I'm done with the cops." She winced, fighting back pain as they walked toward the house. "One condition, though."

Adrian opened the rear patio door and assisted her inside.

"Name it."

"No mention of *Crimson Shadow*," she said, giving him a gentle kiss.

"I think that's dead in the water. But I've got a different project to work on. Something from my college days. Not sure it will be a success, but I'm hopeful."

Adrian kissed Lucy full-on, hands brushing melting snowflakes from her hair. The embracing lovers smiled at one another. He reached out and slid his patio door closed.

ABOUT THE AUTHOR AND PUBLISHER

Andy Phillips was born in Oldham, England. He holds a PhD in Applied Mathematics and a BSc Joint Honours Maths/Physics degree. In a varied career, he has worked as a scientific researcher in the USA, a police intelligence analyst, a data analyst, and a higher education teacher.

From a very young age, he became fascinated with strong female characters — whether good, evil, or somewhere in between — that appeared in action, science fiction, and thriller movies. His favourite era is 1990s direct-to-video, back when VHS tapes and rental stores were still a thing. Determined to tell stories of his own, he wrote five freeware interactive fiction games, and later founded the publishing imprint *Action Girl Books*.

His novels deliver fast-paced tales of action, suspense, and danger, including multi-faceted plots, high-intensity scenes, and cinematic storytelling. He thrives on creating strong heroines and complex villainesses, often pitted against each other. Drawing inspiration from books, TV, and film, he hopes to inspire others to be creative, too.